SUDDEN DEATH
RITA MAE BROWN

"LOVE, SEX AND LUST FOR FAME AND MONEY compete in this humane, seriocomic romp through the world of women's professional tennis."
—*The Detroit News*

"If you thought Nora Ephron's *Heartburn* has cornered the market on true heartbreak, thinly veiled, make room for *Sudden Death* . . . It not only chops the stars of women's professional tennis down to size; it tackles the whole pro tennis establishment."
—*The Washington Post*

"AN ENERGETIC ACCOUNT."
—*The New York Times Book Review*

"ROMANTIC FICTION WITH A VENGEANCE."
—*The Denver Post*

"A SCATHING NOVEL."
—*The Seattle Times*

"AT ONCE [A] POLITICAL MANIFESTO AND A COMIC NOVEL OF MANNERS."
—*Philadelphia Inquirer*

"A SHARP, INSIDER'S VIEW of the pressures and pleasures of the women's professional tennis circuit."
—*The San Francisco Chronicle*

"DESCRIBES MATCHES AS GRIPPINGLY AS ANY SPORTSWRITER . . . Very good on the commercial huckstering and hustling that plague professional tennis."
—*The Chicago Tribune*

"LOVE, CORRUPTION, BETRAYAL AND AMBITION INTERTWINE to create a real life panorama of personal and professional relationships . . . Outrageously interesting characters that transcend the page . . . Razor-sharp."
—*The Toronto Sun*

"HER BOOKS ARE FUNNY, OUTRAGEOUS, BAWDY, TENDER AND FILLED WITH LOVE. *Sudden Death* is no exception . . . Through it all, Brown writes so beautifully of that special and mysterious feeling we call love."
—*The Cleveland Plain-Dealer*

SUDDEN DEATH

... ...

RITA MAE BROWN

BANTAM BOOKS
TORONTO · NEW YORK · LONDON · SYDNEY

SUDDEN DEATH
Bantam Hardcover edition/May 1983
2nd printing . . . . May 1983
3rd printing . . . . May 1983
4th printing . . . . June 1983
Bantam Paperback edition/April 1984
Bantam Export edition/April 1984

Library of Congress Cataloging in Publication Data

Brown, Rita Mae.
Sudden death.
I.   Title.
PS3552.R698S9   1983   813'.54   82-45948

ISBN 0-553-24030-7

Published simultaneously in the United States and Canada

Bantam Books are published by Bantam Books, Inc. Its trademark, consisting
of the words "Bantam Books" and the portrayal of a rooster, is Registered in
U.S. Patent and Trademark Office and in other countries.
Marca Registrada. Bantam Books, Inc.,
666 Fifth Avenue, New York, New York 10103.

PRINTED IN THE UNITED STATES OF AMERICA

O   0 9 8 7 6 5 4 3 2 1

Dedicated to

JUDY COOK LACY

She had no intention of leaving this earth;
Death kidnapped her.

GENESIS

Judy Lacy was constantly on my case to write a book about the tennis circuit. I scoffed at this idea since I considered it the material for her first novel. She was a sports columnist for the *Boston Herald American*. She was a lot else as well—a good athlete, a woman of solid integrity, and a buoyant friend. A few days before she died, she asked me to write a book using tennis as a theme. I didn't know how sick she really was, so I declined. She insisted I write this book. I finally said yes. *Sudden Death* is the result. It began as a book about women's tennis today, but as the work took shape, I realized there was far more I wanted to portray than could be done by basing it on my own experiences and relationships. And so, the story evolved in an entirely different direction.

Although this novel uses as its theme the world of women's tennis, the problems and pressures the characters confront are faced by lesbians in all sectors of our society. The characters and incidents of this book are, then, merely illustrative and entirely imaginary. None of these events actually occurred and any resemblance to individuals of the circuit is purely coincidental.

This is really Judy's book. Whatever virtues the novel possesses are more Judy Lacy's than my own. The faults, however, are mine alone and no reflection upon my inspiration.

Ten percent of the author's royalties derived from the sale of this novel go to:

The Judy Lacy Memorial Fund
Massachusetts General Hospital
Oncology Department, Cox Building
100 Blossom Street
Boston, Massachusetts 02114

Should any reader wish to contribute to this fund, the author would be grateful.

· · · ACKNOWLEDGMENTS · · ·

The following people contributed to this book and I thank them: Susie Baker Adams, Donald Alex, Jerry Astrove, Julia Ellen Brown, Rebecca Brown, Betty Burns, Elaine and Don Candy, Doodles, Linda Damico, Trish Faulkner, Joan and Jim Freeman, Lee Jackson, Baylor Johnson, Larry King, Bill Leach, John Lowe, Regina McCormack, Colleen Moreland, Martina Navratilova, Tove, Troost, Elizabeth and Karin Parker, Rachel and Phil Rogers, Marion Roth, Clare Schaefer, Susan Scott, Elaine Spaulding, Rita Speicher, Alice and Jimmy Turner, Mona Vold, Ruth Weeks, Martin Weiss, Cazenovia and Baby Jesus, the only real character in my novel.

Louise, one of the cats, went into heat for one month. This may or may not be reflected in *Sudden Death*.

Bud Collins, by his example of courage, kept me going.

I am especially grateful to Deborah Mogelberg for not giving up on me while this book took shape.

And thank you, reader, you contribute to my book because I imagine you as I write. I imagine you looking like a latter-day Carole Lombard, Vivien Leigh, or even a Latter-Day Saint and falling in love with me, overcome by my talent. Or I imagine you as a born-again Ronald Colman or Douglas Fairbanks, falling in love with me, overcome by my talent just like your female counterpart. If not overcome by my talent, then how about overcome by my ego?

Are writers really that egotistical? No, but if I don't believe in myself, it's a sure bet you won't believe in me at all. Unfortunately, a lot of people confuse that with conceit. I'm not conceited, but I am vain. I expect you to frame the photo on the back of this book and swoon at regular intervals. Go on, a little worship is good for the soul—mine.

ONE

Miguel Semana lifted a cut crystal glass full of golden brandy to his moustachioed lips. He had been in America for two weeks in order to celebrate Christmas with his famous sister, Carmen. For the last six years, Carmen hovered somewhere among the top three players of women's professional tennis. Miguel, a gifted athlete himself, hated the discipline of sport. He hated discipline, period. Carmen hated it, too, but she put in just enough practice time to keep her extraordinary natural skills sharp. Miguel loved his sister as much as he loved anybody. When they were children, he coached her, played with her, and made her game what it was today because he never gave her a break. When she was good enough to compete on the pro circuit, it was Miguel who pleaded with his father to let her leave Argentina. He accompanied her during her first year on the road; she was fifteen. After that he attended college, as was planned, and emerged a lawyer. While he was pondering torts, wills, and other subjects of ultimate boredom, Carmen was rising steadily in the tennis firmament to become a great star.

Now twenty-four and at the peak of her physical powers, Carmen again had Miguel by her side. She wanted to win the Grand Slam of tennis, a nearly impossible feat, but one which would guarantee her athletic immortality as well as gorge an already fat purse.

To win the Grand Slam a player must win in the same year the French Open, Wimbledon, the U.S. Open, and the Australian Open. In the history of tennis only four players ever achieved this feat: Don Budge in 1938, Maureen Connolly in 1953, Rod Laver in 1962 and 1969, and Margaret Court in 1970.

Miguel knew that this year would be Carmen's chance. She was a serve and volley player, and they take longer to mature on the court than do backcourt players. They need to be quite strong, so their bodies must reach full development. They also need to settle down emotionally. Carmen was at the top and free of injury. This would be her year, and both she and Miguel knew it. Now or never. Just as timing was critical to her serve, so was it critical to her whole career. She was in the right place at the right time.

Miguel looked over Cazenovia Lake, a beautiful four-mile stretch of fresh water in upstate New York. The smooth waters glistened in the pale afternoon light. Miguel, raised in luxury, was not especially impressed by the beautiful mansion that commanded a view of the lake and hills beyond. The Semanas enjoyed the privileges of an upper-middle-class family in Buenos Aires, so Carmen's surroundings left him cold, literally. Winters in Cazenovia were fierce and sometimes lasted eight months. Four feet of snow covered the ground. When the whole continent of the United States was at your disposal, why sit in snow? Miguel frowned as the warm brandy glowed inside his stomach.

Carmen's roommate, Harriet Rawls, was a professor at the little college in Cazenovia. When Carmen moved here, they bought the house together. That was three years ago. Within the first year of their living together, Carmen talked Harriet into resigning her post and traveling full time with her. Miguel thought they might be lovers. If Carmen chased girls as well as forehands, he didn't want to know about it. The possibility that a feminine woman might want a woman lover escaped him. Miguel was, after all, a very Latin, very handsome man. He flirted outrageously with Harriet, since she was the only woman in sight and she wasn't bad to look at, but he never got very far. He was anxious to get on the road with his sister. There had to be more receptive game out there.

Miguel also needed to make money. He gambled. He could control it, but he had a worse vice—he loved power and beautiful things. Being a lawyer in Buenos Aires wasn't enough for him. For twenty-eight years he had been a dutiful son; now he wanted to do things his own way. His sister would win that Grand Slam if it killed both of them in the process. Miguel wanted the win. As her new business manager, he would have success at last. The fact that Carmen did not know her brother was to be her business manager didn't bother him. He'd get to that in good time.

Side by side, viewed from the rear, Miguel and Carmen looked like brothers, so closely did their bodies resemble each other's. Only when they turned around, could one see that the taller was male, the shorter, female. Curly black hair, aquiline nose, and dove-gray eyes were their common heritage. Broad white teeth set off a charming, slightly crooked mouth. Like all the Semanas, they had beautiful, beautiful hands. These traits made Miguel the very image of what a man should be. Carmen, however, was left midway between male and female. A generous soul would call her androgynous. As a child, Carmen was subject to ridicule. Tennis saved her. She might not be gorgeous or sweetly subservient, but, by God, she was the best at what she did. Her entire adult identity was bounded by the perimeters of a tennis court. At this point in Carmen's life, if people found her masculine, they said it behind their hands. To her face, people shouted only praises. She loved the praise, and she earned it. If she ever wondered what people really thought of her or what she thought of herself, she locked it deep inside.

Her tennis glory would make up for whatever wounds she suffered in her childhood.

Dr. Arturo Semana never intended to wound his children. They were glutted with material possessions at home and whacked into severe piety at the most aristocratic Catholic school in Buenos Aires. Miguel, the elder child and only son, felt daily pressure from his father to be a man in all things. Carmen received an equal pressure from her mother, one of Buenos Aires's leading hostesses. When Carmen became the athlete instead of Miguel, Theresa Semana took to her bed for a week. Arturo resigned himself to Carmen's career and eventually took pride in it. Theresa reached the point where she didn't blanch at the mention of her daughter's accomplishments but she still found the tennis life unacceptable for any woman, her only daughter included. Small wonder that Carmen confined her visits home to once a year. No matter how many trophies or how much money she won, when she saw her reflection in her mother's clear eyes, she saw a failure.

Miguel didn't understand the peculiar pressures of being female, but Carmen was his sister, and he loved her. Besides, he had his hands full with his own pressures. The two of them formed their own bond against their loving but demanding parents. It was as though brother and sister lived in a very elegant war zone, two soldiers from different backgrounds on the same front. In their case instead of class or geography being the difference, it was sex. And though neither sibling could look into the heart and mind of the other, they depended upon one another and loved one another. It was their strength, and also, their undoing.

◆ ◆ ◆

The telephone pierced dinner. Harriet got up from her spaghetti with pesto sauce to answer it.

"Merry Christmas, Harriet." Jane Fulton's throaty voice echoed on the line.

"Merry Christmas to you, too, and to Ricky."

"How's the visitation program going?"

"It'll take time."

"That's what Mother said about my breast development when I was thirteen. Look at me now."

Jane's voice was overshadowed by Ricky in the background, saying, "Anything more than a handful is a waste. Merry Christmas to everyone and to everyone a good night."

Harriet smiled. "Ricky sounds full of spirit."

Carmen called from the table, "Merry Christmas!"

Miguel joined in. "Happy New Year!" He spoke with an English accent as did his sister.

Carmen explained to him Ricky's love of eggnog. Miguel had not yet met Ricky Cooper but anyone who liked a good belt now and then sounded like his kind of man.

"Are you two covering the Tomahawk Championships?" Harriet asked. Tomahawk, the cosmetics division of Clark & Clark, a huge pharmaceuticals company, sponsored women's indoor tennis. Their theme was "Slay Your Man." Ball girls wore feathers and war paint and this theme was beaten to death with banners, advertising copy, and the packaging itself.

"We'll be there. Staying at the same place?"

"Yes, all three of us."

"Okay, we'll take you to dinner. We want to meet Miguel. Is he as handsome as his photo?"

"He's pretty handsome." Harriet laughed as Miguel preened his moustache for effect. "They invited us all to dinner in Washington, D.C."

"Perfect." Miguel beamed.

"Can't wait, Jane. Kisses to Ricky. Merry, merry Christmas."

Ricky Cooper and Jane Fulton were a well-matched cou
ple. She was a reporter for the *Philadelphia Inquirer* and Rick
covered sports for *The New York Times*. He also did the or
camera coverage for the new sports cable network. Whe
they married, instead of sacrificing one career to the othe
they very sensibly settled in Princeton, New Jersey, which
midway between both cities. Ricky was in his forties and Jar
was in her late thirties. Closer to Harriet in age, they were al:
closer to her as friends, but they adored Carmen who live
for the day and never gave tomorrow a thought. To Prote
tants drenched in the work ethic, that was an incredib
thought.

◆ ◆ ◆

"You hit forehand crosscourt, and I'll return crosscourt."

"Okay." Carmen trotted back to the baseline.

Miguel, right-handed, drove deep into his sister's fo
hand side. Since she was left-handed, he did this off his o
backhand.

"Too shallow. Come on, lazy, drive me way back."

"It's Christmas Eve. Give me a break."

He cracked the ball harder, singing a Christmas caro
he did so. Soon she joined him in song, and the two poun
the ball to lyrics in English and Spanish.

"You know what you'll get under your tree, Miguelet
He called her by her old nickname.

"Don't tell. It's supposed to be a surprise. Hey, no fa
slowed down to talk."

"That's your problem. If you don't keep your eye on
ball, what am I supposed to do about it?"

For spite, she clobbered the ball. He returned it witl
full weight behind it. They went on like that for an hour
Miguel called it quits.

"I'm not playing on Christmas Day."

"How tragic." He wiped the sweat from his forearms.

"You're worse now than when we were kids."

"You're still a kid."

"Just keep it up and you won't get anything under your tree."

"I'd like Margot Kidder adorned in a red ribbon."

Carmen thought that wouldn't be so bad for herself but kept her mouth shut. "You'll have to wait and see."

"After Christmas, we've got to work out longer."

"What for?"

"Your backhand has zero topspin, that's what for."

"So what woman has a topspin backhand?"

"You're strong enough and so is that new German kid."

Carmen ignored his remark. Christmas took precedence over work. She'd bought Harriet a set of Erté prints, and she hoped her lover would like them. For Miguel she purchased a gold Rolex watch. It was hideously expensive, but she knew it would please him enormously. "Longer workouts." She patted him on the back.

"And weight workouts."

"Miguel."

"Yes. This is your year. Everything's got to be perfect." He walked over to the soda machine and bought a Coke for himself and a sparkling water for Carmen. "Do you mind if I read over your contracts—the product endorsements and all that stuff?"

"No. Why would I mind? I never read them. Seth Quintard does all that. I just sign on the line."

"I'm sure he gets the best deal he can; that's an agent's job. But I'm a lawyer, and I'd like to carefully go over everything. I might see something he missed."

"Fine. Is it snowing again?"

He walked over to the clubhouse window. "Yes. At any moment Santa Claus will appear."

"Bet it's hot at home."

"Guess we should call them tomorrow."

Miguel put on his parka. "You know, it's the damnedest thing. Telephones link up everyone in the world. It's one world technologically but no one can get along with anyone else. I still can't get over the fact that we went to war with England."

Carmen wrinkled her nose. She hated politics. Even more she hated war. It made not one bit of sense to her even though she was very patriotic. As far as she was concerned, the Malvinas belonged to Argentina, but war? Why didn't the leaders of bickering countries pick up tennis racquets and go settle it on the court? Or they could play golf if they were too old for tennis. Winner takes all. There'd be nothing to argue about.

◆ ◆ ◆

With two days to go before they departed for Washington, D.C., and the Tomahawk Championships, Carmen practiced double time. Miguel, resplendent in new sportswear, accompanied her in the mornings and sometimes the afternoons.

Cursing, Harriet leaned over the ironing board to attack one more recalcitrant box pleat. She liked ironing, but today, ironing didn't like her. She ironed the wrinkles in as opposed to out. As she smacked the steaming instrument down one more time, she heard the car roll into the driveway. Only one door slammed. Carmen, flushed, danced through the kitchen door.

"Joe is taking Miguel to Syracuse." Joe was one of Carmen's practice partners.

"That's nice." Harriet missed the import of the news since the shirt demanded her attention.

"They'll be there at least an hour and a half. Maybe we'll be alone for two hours."

"Did you say alone?"

"I did." She tossed her racquets on the kitchen table.

"Mirabile dictu."

"Are you going to stand there and iron that shirt?"

"No." Harriet yanked the plug out of the wall. The two chased one another up the stairway to the bedroom.

Lovemaking suffered under the continued presence of Miguel. By the time Miguel was asleep, Harriet and Carmen were usually exhausted. Harriet never was the greatest fuck-of-the-night to begin with. Her true abilities displayed themselves in the afternoon.

"Will you get in the bed?" Harriet shivered under the covers.

"I better take a shower first."

"We haven't time."

"I'm sweaty from practice."

"I'll suffer." Harriet reached out, grabbed her sweat pants by the waistband, and flopped Carmen on the bed.

"Wait a minute. Let me get out of these goddamned pants."

"One, two, three, four, five, six, seven, eight—"

"What are you doing?"

"Counting up to a minute." Harriet pulled a now naked Carmen under the covers. "Warm me up. Consider it a charitable act."

Carmen kissed Harriet's neck, her forehead, and her lips. Tennis was what Carmen did second best. Her greatest achievement was kissing. Her mouth must have been like Ganymede's, cupbearer to Zeus, so perfectly formed were her lips. She could take up to an hour simply kissing. Today, they didn't have that kind of luxury. She slid her body over Harriet's small frame and worked her way down.

"Undercover work," Carmen whispered.

Harriet smiled and ran her fingers through Carmen's silky black hair.

Carmen kissed and licked Harriet's groin. Suddenly she stiffened. "Ouch!"

"What's the matter?" Harriet lifted the blankets and discovered two glowing eyes at the bottom of the bed. "Baby Jesus, get out of there."

Baby, Harriet's eighteen-year-old cat, burrowed under blankets, then lay flat on her side so she couldn't be seen under the bedspread. She resented this disturbance of her slumber. Biting Carmen's heel was the result.

"Come on, Beejee Weejee," coaxed Carmen.

This syrupy comment met with a snarl of disgust. It was bad enough Carmen stuck her foot in Baby's face. Having to endure the Beejee Weejee routine heightened the ancient's foul temper.

"Your mother is speaking," Harriet commanded. "Out of the bed."

A suspicious silence followed.

"Shit!" Carmen howled. "She bit my other foot."

"That does it." Harriet threw off the covers, picked up the beast and lovingly placed her in her fur-lined sleeping box, replete with catnip toys, scratching post, and stuffed bird. Baby sat in this splendor for less than one minute and then grandly vacated the bedroom.

"I'll kill that cat someday." Carmen nursed her heel.

"She has an artistic temperament."

"Will you look at my foot?"

Harriet noted the small indentation made by two fangs. No blood rose to the surface, but Baby didn't strain herself overmuch. "Here, I'll kiss it and make it well."

"That feels better. Could you move up a little higher?"

Harriet laughed and began to work her way up Carmen's muscled leg.

• • •

Lavinia Sibley Archer, breasts heaving like a flight deck, navigated her way through the sponsor's opening night cocktail party. Lavinia won Wimbledon in the late forties as well as the U.S. Open the following year. After her illustrious career, she settled down with a man too dull to be born and became both a housewife and the terror of her country club. Wendell, her husband, passed on to his reward in the mid-sixties. She'd forgotten the exact date, but he was convincingly dead.

By this time, women's tennis, struggling for professional status and recognition, found its young lion in Billie Jean King and now had its business bear in Lavinia. Lavinia did a great deal for the game. For one thing, she gallantly faced the horror of working for a living. Using different titles in different years, Lavinia was really the tennis version of the head of the Joint Chiefs of Staff. She wasn't God, but she came damn close. You didn't cross Lavinia Sibley Archer.

Lavinia didn't like Harriet Rawls and Jane Fulton because they didn't take tennis as seriously as she thought they should. This kind of intellectual treason tried Lavinia's famed nerves of ice. She was billed as "nerves of ice" in her heyday. She was also billed as carrying around the biggest tits in tennis, but that was whispered as opposed to set down in type.

Worse, Harriet and Jane once did something both unpatriotic and in bad taste. Tiring of endless renditions of the national anthem—Jane called it our national anathema—they committed their dastardly sin during a tournament in Seattle. The semifinals and finals of every tournament are the nights on which promoters make money. Over eighty-five percent of the gate comes in at that time. Lavinia found a charming mariachi band, which is hard to find in Seattle, to play the national anthem for the semifinals. Lavinia thought it would be good for relationships with third world groups. Where she expected this roaring host of Mexicans to come from in the Pacific Northwest, only she knew, but the mariachi band was a significant cultural event in her mind. The glittering group of men, waddling under their giant sombreros, stood in the center of the tennis court and sang "The Star-Spangled Banner." The crowd, as usual, turned to face the flag. As Old Glory was hoisted up the pole and unfurled, a cascade of brassieres and jockstraps delicately floated to the earth below.

Lavinia vowed to find the perpetrators of this horrendous and sophomoric deed. No one would have known a thing except that Jane had tossed in a bra of Carmen's. This evidence in hand, Lavinia cornered Carmen and ripped her three ways from Sunday. Truthfully, Carmen protested her innocence.

Harriet, of course, neglected to tell Carmen of her plans. How was she to know Jane would grab bras from the dryer down at the locker room? Unfortunately, Carmen's name was neatly sewn on the strap. Harriet hit the locker room just in time to gleefully confess.

By the time news of this scene reached the press booth, Ricky Cooper was laughing so hard he didn't know if he could pull himself together in time to broadcast. It reminded him of summer camp. Jane, in a fit of WASPish responsibility, confessed her participation to her husband. Ricky's initial response was, "Did you use my jockstraps?" Since the answer was yes, Ricky marched her off to Lavinia. Jane's confession really was too much to bear, a member of the press mocking our national anthem.

Over the last year, Lavinia finally reached the point of cold cordiality with Harriet and Jane. She could bring herself to do no more, but she could bring herself to do no less because for the last six months, Carmen Semana was ranked number one by the computer. Every time Lavinia had to nod her head to Harriet at a tournament, she thought, "Lesbian flag desecrator."

The cocktail party was obligatory. In the tennis world it ranked on a par with death and taxes. Players showed up when the main sponsor wanted their asses there. Since each tournament usually had local sponsors as well to chip in on prize money, players shook the hands of bank presidents, furriers, car dealers, and other businessmen too exciting to mention.

In tennis, sponsors are courted. It costs between $100,000 and $150,000 to promote a major tennis tournament. That's only promotion, not players' winnings. If a sponsor doesn't pick up at least seventy-five percent of the prize money, the promoter loses his shirt. Therefore, sponsors, not the Women's Tennis Guild, really determine the game.

To Lavinia's credit, she realized this before anyone else. She was the person who cajoled Tomahawk cosmetics into sponsoring the women's indoor tennis circuit from January to the end of March: The Tomahawk Circuit. Tomahawk needed an image, and Howard Dominick, the new man in charge of Tomahawk, was an old personal friend of Lavinia's. She convinced him that tying Tomahawk to the women's indoor tennis circuit would make American women forget Revlon, Clairol, and Max Factor. While women's tennis didn't make the buyers forget those companies, they did remember Tomahawk. The girls walked on the court reeking of Tomahawk's latest perfume. They wore Tomahawk nail polish in an array of blood-curdling colors. Their hair was caked with Tomahawk hair spray until enough of them rebelled for that tactic to pass. Wags had it the ladies even flushed out with Tomahawk's super douche, TeePee. Howard Dominick and Lavinia Sibley Archer gave women the means to earn a living at their sport. The stars that developed proved the wisdom of their foresight.

TWO

The sports arena off the Capi-
tol Beltway was a hymn to
the fact that urban planners don't know shit from shinola.
Equally inconvenient to dwellers of Washington, D.C., and
Baltimore, Maryland, the sports arena squatted on the land
with little to soften its blunt features.

Each January Tomahawk sponsored a championship. The
top eight players from the indoor circuit competed in a round
robin. The beauty of the round robin format was that no one
understood it. Despite numerous diagrams and explanations
from Lavinia at the microphone down on the court, the structure remained unintelligible. The fans didn't care since the
finals cleaned up the mess. The prize money was a whopping
$250,000 compared to the normal $150,000 for a regular tournament in a city such as Minneapolis.

Miguel marveled at the miniature tepees crammed with
Tomahawk products. It had been ten years since he accompanied his sister and in those ten years an explosion of commer-
cialization had taken place. He wandered through practice
sessions and watched the players. The excitement of the game
captured him once again. He loved tennis although he wasn't
really sorry he went to law school. He knew he didn't want to
be a washed-up jock at thirty-five, but he also wasn't too keen
about being a lawyer either. Hearing the reassuring sound of

the ball against tight gut strings lifted his spirits. The Cazenovia winter had already dampened them.

◆ ◆ ◆

Carmen polished off the first set of her first match. She drew Michele Kittredge, an Australian with a deadly forehand, serviceable backhand, solid first serve, and pea brain. Michele played; she didn't think. She was the same off the court, which gave her a consistency people found reassuring. Despite not being overly intelligent, Michele had a good heart and a strong sense of fair play. Her pals called her Beanie because of her beanballs; she would usually hit her opponent at least once in a match because her powerful forehand had erratic moments. Tonight she played well, but Carmen knocked off the first set six-four.

In the second set, two-all, Beanie began picking the corners. The surface was carpet laid over boards; under the boards rested the ice hockey rink. Because the surface was fast, it was to Beanie's advantage as well as Carmen's, since they played the "big game," serve and volley.

Beanie got hot. Her serve twisted into Carmen's body, causing weak returns. Beanie rushed the net, putting the ball away. As the match became more interesting to the fans, Harriet moved from interest to anxiety. Placid though her exterior was, every time the ball hit the center of Carmen's racquet with a twang, Harriet could feel the vibrations up her own arm. Beanie was putting up one hell of a fight.

Howard Dominick, watching from the control booth, was anxious, too. He wanted a good match, but since Carmen was seeded number one, she'd better get in those finals. Carmen fattened the gate. When she was in the draw, a promoter rarely lost money, and that many more fans would be assaulted with a barrage of Tomahawk products. If that didn't give them the hint, the banners plastered all over the arena would.

Carmen sliced her backhand returns. She wanted to keep the ball low. Her backhand was strong, but not overpowering. Every now and then she'd give it a rip, but right now, her full concentration was on breaking Beanie's hot streak. Beanie usually couldn't sustain this level of play more than a set, but Carmen didn't want to split sets.

At six-all, Miranda Mexata, the best umpire in the business, informed the audience a twelve-point tie breaker was now in effect to determine the outcome of the set. Up until 1971, tennis sets had to be won by a margin of two games. If you couldn't break your opponent's serve, and she could not break yours, the two of you could conceivably be there on the court until the Second Coming. In 1963, it took Billie Jean King thirty-six games to defeat Christine Truman during the Wightman Cup Competition: six-four, nineteen-seventeen. In 1968, John Brown of Australia defeated Bill Brown of Omaha after seventy games. The first set went thirty-six–thirty-four. Obviously, something had to give. Maybe the players could stand it, but the spectators couldn't. It was rumored that several actually perished of fanny fatigue during the Brown versus Brown match. After much argument between the Old Guard, old and guarded, and the young professionals, the tie breaker was established.

The twelve-point tie breaker was used: sudden death. Carmen served first. She would get one serve, Beanie would get two serves, Carmen would get another two serves; the two-service pattern would continue, but the two opponents would change sides after six points. Even in indoor tennis, changing sides is fair and upheld. Sun and wind are obvious enough reasons for changing outdoors, but in an indoor arena, the lights are often better on one spot of the court than another. The tie breaker was a simple solution to a complicated problem. Whoever reached seven points first would

win the set. Whoever won two out of three sets would win
the match. Should the competition be so equal that even in
the tie breaker the score reached six points all, then they
would continue the two-service pattern until one player won
by a margin of two points.

Tie breakers speeded up the sport and excited the fans.
They were excited now because Beanie shot ahead five-four.
She broke Carmen's serve.

Miguel put a cigarette in his mouth but didn't light it.
Jane and Ricky held their breath up in the press booth. Too
much chat during a tie breaker didn't go down with a tv
audience. Harriet calmly stared straight ahead.

Carmen, champion that she was, got tougher as the situation worsened. She focused all her energy on one single task
and tore through the next three points before Beanie or the
crowd knew what hit them. She nailed down the match.

Back in the locker room, icing her knee after interviews
and a massage, she said to Harriet, "No way was I going to
three sets with Beanie."

Lavinia breezed by the locker room door on her way to
the hospitality bar. "Good work, Carmen." Lavinia Sibley
Archer could gulp a lake of vodka and remain coherent. Her
Wimbledon victory diminished next to this display of bodily
power, especially at her age. Harriet said there was nothing to
it. Lavinia was already pickled.

◆ ◆ ◆

Hurtling down the corridors, Harriet and Miguel almost col-
lided with Susan Reilly as they all turned a corner at top
speed. Susan carried her equipment bag over her shoulder.
Harriet looked at Susan, Susan looked at Harriet. Each moved
out of the other's way.

"Buenas noches, Susan." Miguel had known her for
years.

After Billie Jean King and the original crew of professionals founded the circuit along with Lavinia, Susan came along to reap the benefits. She was six feet tall which gave her incredible reach at the net, and surprisingly, she was fast for a tall woman. Her court presence was electrifying. She possessed the charisma of leadership and discipline, but had no organizational skills. Luckily for her, there were plenty of people around to pick up the pieces. Susan at thirty remained a formidable foe.

Trailing behind Susan was Happy Straker, her current doubles partner and past bed partner. Happy flashed a smile at Miguel. "Haven't seen you since Wimbledon. You look great."

Lisa, Susan's seven-year-old daughter, caught up with her mother as did Craig Reilly, Susan's husband. Craig was a doctor and rarely joined his wife on the road. That was just as well.

"Still great," Miguel said as Susan's entourage moved down the hallway. Susan was one of the greatest. She was also one of the greatest liars, but why spoil the illusion? Harriet once described her as exhaustingly dishonest, which covered it.

"Why don't you two play doubles anymore?" Miguel asked.

Carmen shrugged her shoulders. "Susan likes to change partners. Keeps her fresh."

Miguel eyed his sister. Carmen and Susan had won every doubles championship there was to win. Changing for the sake of change sounded odd.

Carmen returned his gaze. "That's the way she is. Fickle."

"Doubles partnerships may be like marriage, but you don't need the pope to break up." Miguel touched a nerve without realizing it.

What he didn't know was that Susan Reilly was the first woman to sleep with his sister. Carmen was sixteen and highly impressionable. At twenty-four, she was still plenty impressionable, but at sixteen she was so emotional as to be helpless. Susan bedded down what was then an ambitious Argentine kid on her way up, if she could ever control her temper. Susan told Carmen that she loved Craig but they had an understanding. He went his way and she went hers. She neglected to tell Carmen that she also serviced an expensive, beautiful matron high on Nob Hill. Whatever else she said, it was enough to convince a kid in the throes of first love, not to mention first lesbian affair, that she had to live with Susan. Indeed, Carmen felt she couldn't live without Susan. So Carmen packed her bags and left for the U.S.

Carmen didn't discuss this with Susan. She assumed Mrs. Reilly would be thrilled to see her and live with her. She'd have to make periodic visits to Argentina to keep her citizenship intact and to satisfy U.S. bureaucratic standards, notoriously hard on resident aliens. When she arrived unannounced at Susan's house, Susan looked right beyond her, told her she was crazy, and slammed the door. She ignored Carmen's phone calls and entreaties. Carmen, stranded, lived with a tennis player and her family in Palo Alto until she could pull herself together.

Harriet wondered if Carmen ever settled the issue, if not the score. Carmen preferred to avoid conflict. If something was rotten, ignore it. If it got worse, take a drink, smoke a cigarette, or puff on the magic weed, but under no circumstances face the pain.

Carmen eventually signed on as Susan's doubles partner. This lasted for three years and then Susan dumped her without warning for Happy Straker, another fleeting fancy but a terrific doubles partner. At no time did Susan ever sleep with Carmen again or mention the affair which had preceded Carmen's arrival on her doorstep. Susan had moral amnesia. Why Carmen remained friendly to Susan mystified Harriet, for she felt, like a deep undertone beneath human hearing, that the other shoe had yet to drop.

Miguel ordered cherries jubilee for dessert. All that blue flame at the table gave dinner a slightly exterminatory air. Miguel and Ricky talked about the expansion of cable television. The women talked among themselves.

"I haven't had cherries jubilee since baked Alaska and I haven't had baked Alaska since my senior year at Smith College." Jane shoved the dripping concoction into her mouth.

"Did you bring your Smithie T-shirt?" Carmen had already finished her dessert. "The one that says Smith College, A Century of Women on Top." Carmen coveted that T-shirt.

Miguel turned to his sister. "Did someone say 'women on top'?"

"Forget it, Miguel, you're a chauvinist. You'd never get it." Carmen turned back to Jane.

"They're talking about Jane's college," Ricky explained.

"Oh, for a moment there I thought we'd be embarrassed by the ladies." Miguel's teeth looked almost silver in the light.

"We'd be embarrassed all right, but not tonight." The two of them returned to their discussion.

"Jane, what do I have to do to get one of those T-shirts?" Carmen inquired.

"You can't climb Mount Everest, that's been done to death. Let's see, you could bring me a good photograph of the Loch Ness monster or you could win the Grand Slam—or you could simply ask me."

"Please get me one of those T-shirts, and get one for my brother, too."

"I'll write to my alma mater and see what I can do."

Harriet surveyed the room. "Full of Republicans."

"How can you tell?" Jane scanned the room.

"Thin lips."

"Aren't you nasty?" Jane toyed with her dessert.

"Jane, I'll finish that for you." Carmen reached over and grabbed the plate. Jane looked perplexed. "Oh, come on, I know you'd kill for chocolate. Waiter, chocolate mousse."

"Am I that transparent?"

"Carmen, I've got some contracts to discuss with you."

"What?" Surprised, Carmen twirled around to discover Seth Quintard standing behind her. Either he dug his way up from the potted palm or he walked in on moccasins because no one heard him coming.

"Oh, yeah. Well, can't we do it later?"

Miguel perked up. "If you don't mind, I'd like to be there. My sister has asked me to review her business affairs."

Seth quickly said, "Sure."

"I'll call your room in about an hour," Carmen told him.

Athletes Unlimited crept over the sports world like a wild vine. From a tiny seed, the corporation threatened to take over the whole forest. Football, tennis, baseball, basketball, soccer, track and field, you name it, Athletes Unlimited represented the best in each sport. Their only competitor was a small firm headed by a former basketball star who couldn't delegate authority. That wasn't real competition. Seth headed the tennis division. He proved endlessly fertile in his ability to arrange deals. He had in his briefcase a contract for Carmen to sign endorsing socks in Japan and a teaching pro offer in darkest New Mexico. For one week out of the year, she'd get paid $140,000 plus a condominium thrown in for good measure.

All of these contracts had sweeteners. If she won Wimbledon, she'd get a bonus. If she won the Grand Slam, she'd get immortality as well as elephantine bonuses. Carmen, thanks to her phenomenal athletic ability and good court sense, could never be counted out of winning the Slam, but the odds were against any player, no matter how remarkable.

Seth left the table and hovered over Rainey Rogers, another of his clients. Rainey's mother acted as flak catcher. He asked her to listen to the deal he had for Rainey. If Rainey, and Mom, naturally, would just consent to play in a midsize tournament in West Germany, the promoter would slip in— under the table, you understand—the prettiest BMW ever seen. Mom was sharp and ruthless in her dedication to her offspring's success, and she played it cool.

"I've never been to Germany, Mother." Rainey worked a one-two act with Mom. They both knew Seth would report back to the promoter there was active interest.

Carmen watched Rainey as Seth spoke with Mrs. Rogers. Rainey was okay away from her mother, but with her mother, watch out. Rainey's grim determination wore down opponents. Her mother's grim determination wore down everyone else. Rainey and Carmen were about even in win-loss records. It hadn't occurred to Carmen to try to like Rainey because Carmen never got emotionally close to her competition. Susan had taught her that.

"What do you think of Seth and his firm?" Miguel asked Ricky.

"Oh, I don't know, Miguel." Ricky paused. "The money pouring into tennis has been good in many ways, but I have a few reservations. I think that's because I grew up with tennis as a country club game, so even though I think the expansion has been healthy, I sometimes get a little nervous with all the hucksterism."

"I grew up that way, too. Father Perez, my boyhood coach, used to say that sport was a test of man against man. Father Perez also implied that games should be dedicated to the glory of God. That's all very well, Rick, but you have to be able to afford his view."

"Sure. That was always the problem with tennis."

◆ ◆ ◆

"Your racquet contract expires on January first." Seth's papers neatly filled up the coffee table. Miguel sat catty-cornered to his sister and listened, his face turned toward Seth.

"That's a year away."

"We should start thinking about it now. I think they'll come up with two hundred thousand dollars for a three-year contract plus huge bonuses if you win any of the Grand Slam events. Of course, if you win the Grand Slam, it would come to about seven hundred and fifty thousand."

"Sounds good." Carmen liked hearing about the money.

"However, there is a West German sporting goods firm, Mach, that is trying to crack open the American market. I think we might even get more from them if you'll play some European exhibitions."

"Really?"

"I'm working on it." Seth smiled the smile only a crocodile can approximate. Since Athletes Unlimited took a twenty-five-percent commission on all contracts and exhibition fees, it was in his self-interest to get the most money he could. Whether or not the products were good mattered very little. Often a manufacturer would provide custom-built racquets or shoes for their hired help, the stars, and then sell an inferior product bearing the star's name. The product on the marketplace looked exactly the same but it wasn't. The trick worked many times over. Duffers wouldn't know the difference between a first-class racquet and one made from cheap alloys anyway. Seth never explained this to Carmen. He assumed she understood the game, his game. Miguel grasped the concept instantly.

"How about the condominium in Savannah, Georgia? They really want you for the new club there."

"I don't know." Carmen pushed down, then retracted the ballpoint of her Gucci pen. "Two weeks out of a year doesn't seem like much, but I don't get enough time to spend at home now."

"Carmen, think it over. What's two weeks for this deal? One hundred and fifty thousand dollars a year plus the condominium free and clear if you fulfill your contract of five years."

"I don't know."

"You've got the rest of your life to sit in Cazenovia. Strike while the iron is hot."

"I hate giving clinics." Carmen, like most talented people, enjoyed teaching other talented people. She hated the clinics filled with middle-aged ladies vainly trying to find the service line.

"A little sacrifice." Seth began packing up. "You think it over."

What Seth didn't say was that these deals were only for the top three or four players in the world. And the top three or four male players in the world got much more than the women. The less the girls knew about the financial transactions of the men players, the better. Let sleeping dogs lie. Given people's reluctance to talk about money, Seth figured the women wouldn't find out. Besides, tennis players didn't think about long-range plans, that was his job. As long as the players walked out on the court and won matches, that was what counted. And Athletes Unlimited rolled over the money. Who didn't? Everyone got the contracted sum. What's three months waiting time?

Seth kept a lot to himself. He never discussed kickbacks, especially with Athletes Unlimited. Incentive was what it was all about. A player like Carmen would never suspect Seth was lining his own pocket off the manufacturer. So he got a little extra for signing her up. Who was the wiser and who did it hurt? Besides, Carmen should know this, Seth thought to himself. Americans were nothing compared to South Americans. Now they were really dishonest.

If Carmen's head were to go through the window of her sports car, all Seth's plans would fall apart, and hers, too.

There were no clauses in the contracts to protect the player should she receive an injury that would end her career. There were also hidden clauses that could dump a player quickly should a scandal erupt. Usually he could contain scandals, but sometimes the firm would balk, and he'd have to let the contract go.

"Keep your nose clean, Number One." Seth smiled and exited. That was his usual exit line to all his players.

Miguel closed the door to the bedroom where Harriet was reading. He wanted to talk to Carmen alone. "Carmen, have you audited Athletes Unlimited's books?"

"No."

"How do you know they aren't cheating you?"

"They wouldn't."

"You should audit the books."

"Miguel, I haven't the time. Besides, it would cost thousands of dollars."

"You trust strangers with these decisions? You pay them a fortune in commissions, little dove. Don't you know you're such a big star the manufacturers would come to you with or without Athletes Unlimited?"

"I play tennis. I pay people to take care of business for me. I can't do everything."

"I'm a lawyer. I know about these things."

"I need someone in America. The money is here except for a few major tournaments. I need Americans to do business with Americans."

"I don't think so, Migueletta. You must not entrust such things to outsiders. They get rich off your work."

"Miguel, I don't like to talk about these things when I have to play."

He shrugged his broad shoulders. "Later then."

♦ ♦ ♦

After Miguel left, Carmen came in and sat on the edge of the bed.

"Seth said something about my playing a week of exhibitions in Europe."

"When would it be?"

"Sometime between Wimbledon and the U.S. Open. August, probably."

"Oh."

"Will you go with me?"

"I'm supposed to teach that three-week summer session."

"That's zip money."

"I know, but I like to teach and it's only a seminar."

"You can teach when I retire. I've got, what, five years left?"

"Your point being?" Harriet shifted on the bed.

"You resigned from your job at Cazenovia College. Why take these little things?"

"Honey, I love my work and teaching requires skills like anything else. I'm getting rusty."

"Yes," Carmen's voice raised up a tone, "but you can do it when I retire, and then you can teach forever."

Harriet said nothing. She walked into the bathroom and washed.

Carmen followed behind her and wrapped her arms around Harriet's waist. "I hate to be without you. Please come with me. I promise you when I retire at thirty that I'll attend all your classes, Professor Rawls."

"I hate being away from you, too, sweetheart. I do. I—"

"Please."

"You talk about five or six years as though it's nothing."

"I love you."

"I know." She toweled off. Carmen made perfect sense if money were the only issue. Harriet felt uneasy each time the topic came up. She coveted those few weeks out of the year when she was teaching. She wanted the contact with her peers and her students. The intensive three-week summer course in Occidental religion—Harriet's speciality was ancient Greek religion—kept her on her toes. It wasn't as though Carmen were saying, "Walk ten paces behind me," but she never seemed to understand that Harriet really liked her work, that the salary didn't matter.

"Why can't you just give yourself to me?" Carmen demanded.

"Come on, honey, I only want a little time to myself."

"I never feel that you need me."

"We've been over this before. I don't think need and love are necessarily the same thing. I like my work. I slogged through years of college like you slogged through years of practice sessions. I want to use my stuff a little bit."

"Use it later. I can't stand being away from you. I hate looking up in the stands and not seeing your face. I play for you."

This argument never failed to dump a load of guilt on Harriet's head. Here was this young woman, locked into a very short career, jerked all over the world. All she wanted was one true fan. When they were apart, Carmen would call Harriet as often as eight times a day, no matter where she was in the world. And she'd cry. Carmen was glad-handed, back-slapped, and star-fucked since she was fifteen. She had no sense of proportion and no sense of a world outside athletics. She could understand a baseball player's life, but not a professor's.

Carmen had also learned to weigh things by their monetary value. If she made millions, she had to be worth more than someone who made less. She didn't really think she was better than Harriet, but the idea that Harriet would want to earn a small salary when she could be with Carmen seemed ridiculous and offensive. Carmen didn't mind paying the bills. She paid for all her other lovers, although she didn't think of that. Each lover for Carmen was the lover that would last unto eternity.

"I love it when you look at me. You know I want you to be happy, and when you win, that makes you happy." Harriet was very careful never to overemphasize winning. Carmen used to complain about an earlier lover who would get so completely wrapped up in Carmen's game that she would sulk when Carmen lost. Harriet didn't really care about tennis. If winning made Carmen happy, then she wanted Carmen to win. If Carmen had been a stockbroker or a supermarket clerk, Harriet would have loved her just the same.

"How can I win if you aren't there?"

"Oh, Carmen, you can win anywhere and anytime. You're the best."

"I want to be the best with you, not without you. Please come with me on that exhibition tour. You'll get to see Europe."

"Honey, that won't work." Harriet laughed. "We only see hotel rooms and stadiums."

Carmen sighed. "Please, please. I don't want to be alone. I really need you. I love you. I'll never love anybody but you."

Harriet turned around and ran her fingers through Carmen's hair. "Yes," she said. "I'll come with you." Carmen felt for the first time that Harriet was hers, one hundred percent hers. The emotional and sexual connection was the deepest either of them felt. Carmen dropped off to sleep afterwards, happier than she'd ever been in her life.

A decision was made. A peacefulness follows any decision, even the wrong one. Harriet nestled up behind Carmen, slid her arm under the long and graceful neck, and drifted off into a glittering nebula of love. She slept, as do all lovers, with one synchronized heartbeat, for she was one with another human being and the universe as well.

◆ ◆ ◆

"Crosscourt, crosscourt, crosscourt!" Miguel shouted from the sidelines.

Beanie, practicing with Carmen, stifled an urge to blast an optic yellow ball right down his throat. What prevented her was that she found him terribly attractive. Carmen was irritated, but she didn't openly flare up at Miguel. When she did flare, it was at linesmen, waiters, or cab drivers. Anger was directed downward, not upward or in lateral motion. She gritted her teeth, thumped to the baseline, and hit deep into Beanie's forehand court.

"What angle? Where's the angle?" Miguel kept it up.

"I need to hit a couple more shots."

"You don't get a couple more shots in a match." As he drummed on her, Beanie slashed a backhand down the line.

The down-the-line, crosscourt drills were tedious to Carmen. Some players enjoyed practice. Carmen endured it. She came to life under the pressure of competition. Practice was like a dry hump. Beanie would hit a backhand down the line and Carmen, being left-handed, would blast it crosscourt with a backhand. Then they reversed the procedure, Carmen's forehand down the line, Beanie's forehand crosscourt. There were countless drills, all of them useful, and as far as Carmen was concerned, all of them boring.

Miguel reached inside his jacket, extracted a handkerchief, and strode onto the court in the middle of a rally. Beanie put her hands on her hips.

"Here!" He put the handkerchief at the baseline corner, backhand court for Carmen. "Hit this."

The veins on her neck stood out. Carmen picked up three balls, stuffed two in her shorts, and started again.

"Hit it."

She concentrated, and with a powerful stroke, she caught it. She missed the second time but came close the third.

"You call that control?"

Furious, she twisted her entire torso into the shot and

pinpointed the handkerchief, knocking it behind the base-line. Miguel cheered, and their practice continued for another forty-five minutes.

Beanie and Carmen dragged into the locker room which was painted a ghastly orange.

Beanie said, "Christ, he's bloody tough. Was he like that when you were a kid?"

"Pretty much." Carmen slowly sat down on a bench.

"I'd 'uv taken his head off. My Dad and I used to go at it, hammer and tongs. You'd 'uv thought it was his match, not mine."

"He only wants the best for me."

The sound of the pinball machine in the players' lounge punctuated their remarks.

"You going to Kansas City?"

"We'll be there. I take off the week of Cincinnati. How about you?"

"Playing both this year." Beanie pulled out a bottle of non-Tomahawk shampoo, hid it under her arm, and streaked for the showers. Beanie had her favorite shampoo and no corporate sponsor was going to keep her from those penetrating bubbles.

◆ ◆ ◆

The crowd filled up the arena early. Today was the final match. No surprises. Rainey Rogers versus Carmen Semana. So far, the tennis had been good, but nothing electrifying. Lavinia, encased in an eggplant-colored jacket and lemon pants, gave orders. Harriet and Miguel occupied the complimentary seats grudgingly given by Tomahawk to friends and family. The sponsors liked Miguel in the audience. His presence could be milked for a bucket of publicity—beloved brother puts aside legal career to coach beloved sister.

Lavinia took the mike and walked out onto the center of the court after a traditional version of the national anthem. Linespeople filed in wearing forest green jackets, Tomahawk's color. Next came a battalion of ball boys and ball girls, wearing forest green T-shirts and feathers in their hair, all of whom were thanked for a week's service. Lavinia at the mike created terror in Tomahawk's hearts. She liked to talk. After ten minutes of explaining the inception and development of women's indoor tennis sponsored by Tomahawk, the audience was thoroughly bored. Had she said anything more complimentary about Howard Dominick, he would be expected to walk on water.

"And now, ladies and gentlemen, it gives me great pleasure to introduce Carmen Semana's first coach, her older brother Miguel."

A spotlight zeroed in on Miguel, now standing. The crowd applauded.

Lavinia launched into an explanation of the nature of the two finalists' games—the attacking player, Carmen, versus the backcourt artist, Rainey. Rainey Rogers seethed in the walkway, waiting to come on. Cheap publicity, this brother crap.

Mrs. Rogers was in a holding pattern nearby, also seething. Miguel Semana couldn't have sacrificed more than she and Bill, Rainey's father. Why didn't the press pay more attention to Americans? Rainey was a homegrown product. She made the cover of *Seventeen*. What are a couple of Argentines with their flashing smiles to being on the cover of *Seventeen*? Oh well, she thought, soon Miguel will be as ignored as everyone else in this world who isn't actually swinging the racquet on the court. Mrs. Rogers' shoes were tight. She wiggled a toe in vain hope of stretching them just a bit. She tried to keep her mind busy until the match actually started. Then her adrenaline would pump up the same as Rainey's.

Lavinia relinquished the microphone with reluctance. Miranda Mexata took the chair, and to everyone's relief, the match began.

To everyone's surprise, it was a close match, though not exciting. The carpet was Carmen's surface. Rainey almost took her to three sets, but Carmen closed it out in a lopsided tie breaker. It was sudden death for Rainey.

The postmatch ceremonies exceeded the prematch ceremonies in orchestrated tedium. Every sponsor came forward with a necklace or check or lifetime supply of aspirin. Everyone praised the victor and patted the vanquished, telling her she put up a great fight, better luck next time. When the microphone was passed to Rainey, she also praised her opponent in a jesting manner. The crowd always loved that act. As this was the major Tomahawk event, the culmination of the prior year's indoor season, Howard Dominick presented the winner's check.

Mike in hand, Carmen trotted through the well-rehearsed plaudits to ball girls, ball boys, and sponsors—especially Tomahawk. "And thank you to all you fans who came out here this week. You are what makes women's tennis what it is today. Thank you." The fans cheered. In Carmen's case, routine though the acceptance speeches were, she really did like the fans. She was a creature of performance. An audience could affect her far more than a player like Rainey who locked in on a single wavelength and blotted out the rest of the world, including the fans.

Ricky was at courtside and interviewed Carmen. "What a way to start the New Year."

"Right." Carmen smiled.

"Rainey chipped away with short backhand crosscourts. You didn't have much trouble with that shot today."

"Rainey pulls you wide with that and then threads the needle off your weak return. Today the surface favored me a bit, and I was moving well."

"Do you have any New Year's resolutions?" Ricky paced technical data with personal.

"Well, I've got to give up hot fudge sundaes."

"Anything else?"

Carmen paused a moment, then said, "Yes, I'm going for the Grand Slam this year."

"Good luck to you."

"Thanks, Ricky, I'll need it."

◆ ◆ ◆

Watching Carmen on television was Susan Reilly, bounced out in the round robin semifinals by Rainey Rogers. Susan's bags were packed for a flight to Kansas City in another three hours. There was nothing to do but watch the tube. Craig and Lisa left for San Francisco last night. Seated next to Susan in the king-sized bed was Alicia Brinker, her latest. Happy Straker once tried to warn Alicia about Susan's love'em and leave'em pattern, but Alicia was sure she could change all that; love was the answer. Love might be the answer but it had better be well hidden. Alicia was so far in the closet, she was in danger of becoming a garment bag. Her ranking was high enough so she didn't have to play too many qualifying tournaments to get on the "A" circuit, tennis's version of the major leagues. But when they were playing in the same tournament, Alicia and Susan checked into different rooms on different floors, and the players joked about Alicia sliding down hallways so that no one would see her go into Susan's room. Other than laughing about Alicia's paranoia, the players ignored the affair. The beaches of every continent were strewn with the corpses of Susan's discarded lovers.

As of this moment, however, Alicia was in no danger of being dumped. She and Susan were watching the tv screen intently as Carmen told Ricky she was going for the Slam this year. "Like hell she will!" Susan said, flicking to another channel.

Susan had done everything there was to do in tennis. She won every title in singles and doubles, but she never put together the French Open, Wimbledon, the U.S. Open, and the Australian Open in the same year. She never got that Grand Slam. Now thirty, she should have known better. The years of repetitive competition had taken their toll on her body, but she possessed a fanatical determination regarding the one goal that eluded her—the Grand Slam. She wanted to win it, but if she couldn't win it, she'd make sure no one else did. Not while she was alive.

THREE

Kansas City rose out of the plains like an act of human imagination. The tournament was on the Missouri side of town. Straight as the crow flies, 277 miles to the east lay St. Louis, perched on the banks of the Mississippi. No two cities could be more different and yet belong to the same state. A remembrance of the East Coast still lingered in St. Louis. Kansas City belonged to the West, to the legend of cattle drives and cowboys and perhaps to the future. No one would accuse K.C. of being a beautiful city, but it possessed an energy which was infectious.

This was Harriet's third go-round on the Tomahawk Circuit, so she could untangle the labyrinth under the downtown arena with ease. Just knowing one's way around made any tournament that much more pleasant. She looked forward to visiting the small but excellent art museum. If Carmen had a full day off, they'd go together. If not, Harriet would hop a cab and go by herself. The travel of tennis is dislocating enough, but often players didn't know their schedules until the day they arrived or the morning of the first day of play. Dinner plans, movies, and a quiet walk were all subject to the tyranny of scheduling. Scheduling was done with an eye to the gate, so Carmen was pressed hard by promoters and Lavinia to do this little appearance and that little clinic, just this once. Just this once stretched into eternity. If she said no, she was called an ungrateful bitch. If she said yes, she exhausted herself, to say nothing of Harriet, and risked blowing a win as well. Carmen's compromise was to let Harriet deliver the no's. In exchange she did the cooking whenever they landed in efficiency rooms, plus she did most of the cooking at home. On the road, however, the scheduling and lack of time made any kind of equality wishful thinking. If one went into tennis as a player's lover, any illusions on the subject of equality would be quickly dispelled.

Miguel rose early every morning. Carmen slept late. After a few bickering scenes with a sleepy Carmen at the door of her room, he let her sleep in peace. The minute she was awake, however, he crowded into the room. Miguel would review Carmen's game and wink at Harriet.

This late morning, it was too much. Harriet excused herself to Carmen's dismay. She put on her fur coat and headed for the art gallery. Harriet bumped into Jane Fulton at the front desk.

"Jane, I didn't think you were coming in until later in the week."

"Me neither, but the paper wants a story on the Infant Prodigy. So I get to tail Trixie Wescott for the rest of the week."

"These kids are on the assembly line. Backcourt stance, two-fisted backhand, and appalling patience. Ribbons in the hair helps."

"Where are you off to?" Jane asked.

"The art museum. Come along."

Jane readily agreed.

Walking through the museum halls, they admired the sculpture and painting.

"What's up?"

Harriet sat on a little bench in the middle of a brightly lit room. The floor was highly polished and the paintings well mounted. No one was around this morning hour except a guard.

"Jane, I miss teaching."

"Thought you might."

"I try to go out on the road with Carmen as much as possible. The only teaching I do anymore is a short summer seminar. She wants me to go with her on a European exhibition tour which conflicts with my seminar. Her career is short and I can always teach when she retires."

"The tennis circuit is a short circuit." Jane rolled her eyes at her obvious humor.

"The times we're apart are wrenching."

Jane said, "What happens to Carmen when the cheers are over, I mean, when real life sets in with a vengeance and all of its aches and pains. Christ, Lavinia Sibley Archer is two years older than God, and she still can't give it up. Think about it."

"I do, a lot. I feel disloyal bringing it up with Carmen."

"I hope she can back you up when you need her. Right now, Harriet, she needs you."

"What the hell. Love is a risk. I've loved her for three years. She's grown so much in that time. So have I. I know I have to take the chance and hope she's as good as her word."

"Susan's going strong. Maybe Carmen won't retire."

"I hope she will. Carmen greatly admires Greta Garbo who knew when to exit."

"You're putting all your eggs in one basket."

"What do you mean?" Harriet looked at her sideways.

"You have nothing for yourself. You're cut off from your work and old friends. I doubt if Carmen ever thinks of it. She doesn't have the time to think about anything but tennis. It's all she knows."

"Yeah."

"And did you ever think that you're an invisible wife?"

"Come on."

"Really. If Ricky does a good job, I get spillover credit. Who will ever give you credit for backing up Carmen?"

"I'm not with her for credit."

"No, of course not, but social and emotional support

helps us all in hard times, and you're not going to get either."

"You sound downright antilesbian."

"No, I'm just reporting what I observe. No one, including other lesbians, is rushing forward to help two women love one another."

Harriet fidgeted. "Since when is life fair?" She paused, then looked thoughtfully at Jane. "Where were you in the sixties?"

"What brought that on?"

"I don't know. Feeling old, maybe, or feeling very different from the people around me right now."

"I organized busloads of concerned Smithies bound for Washington and the peace marches."

"No shit."

"Where were you?"

"William and Mary. It wasn't a very radical school, but I was. I trekked to the marches, too. Funny, the other night I thought of the candlelight vigil in New York City. Remember that?"

"Sure."

"We must have stretched for miles and miles. I still remember my soldier's name—Vincent Masconi. There I stood with his placard around my neck, my candle burning in the night."

"My soldier's name was Roosevelt Cogger."

"Odd what we remember. I wish I'd known you then." Harriet picked up Jane's hand.

"You know me now. Haven't you suffered enough?"

Harriet laughed. "Let's eat. I'm starved."

As they retraced their steps to the hotel, Jane said, "Back in the sixties, I don't remember anyone being paid for their work. We were all volunteers. How did we expect to pay for the revolution?"

"MasterCard," Harriet said matter-of-factly.

• • •

The week progressed like most weeks on the Tomahawk Circuit with Carmen dispatching her opponents. Page Bartlett didn't play the Tomahawk Circuit. She saved herself for the major tournaments plus a few other tournaments important to her or important for the money. She also saved herself for her husband.

Page Bartlett, a lovely woman, danced into America's heart at age fifteen when she made the quarterfinals of the U.S. Open. That was twelve years ago. She stayed in people's hearts ever since. She was feminine, well-spoken, bright, and well-mannered. Mothers thought Page was the perfect idol for their little girls, and in that, they weren't far wrong. Of course, no one bothered to ask Page Bartlett what price she paid, and Page Bartlett knew better than to offer any glimpses into her soul.

Jeffrey Campbell was a handsome, virile quarterback for the San Francisco Forty-Niners. They met, fell in love, treated the country to a storybook wedding two years ago, and rode into the sunset. Page played about half the year; the other half was devoted to Jeffrey's football schedule.

She was an opponent any player feared because she rarely suffered a bad day. Her patience and razor-sharp skills usually overcame her more dazzling foes.

Page was living proof that one could be married and maintain an athletic career. However, as she was one of the few married players, she was the exception that proved the rule. For most women, marriage and sports don't mix.

Most of the players were too young for permanent attachments. If they weren't too young, where could they find a date brave enough to ask them out? After one week in Kansas City, the tour moved to Cincinnati, then on to Chicago and on and on. Even airline pilots had more stability than tennis players. So for the most part, the women had fantasy lovers back home. There was often an actual person there, but the intimacy of the relationship was manufactured to fend off loneliness.

The lesbian threat cowed the women. Each player over the age of twenty knew what it was like to be regarded as a freak because she liked sports. Lesbianism insinuated itself into the consciousness of women and frightened them. It frightened the lesbians most of all. It was an open secret that Carmen was gay, but as long as she didn't say so, everyone pretended not to know. She lived in a zone, a DMZ between lies and truth. They didn't want to lose their lucrative product endorsements.

Women would be a long time in overcoming their sexual conditioning, but it took them no time at all to overcome their noncompetitive conditioning. On the courts, they fought like tigers. It was good for the gate and good for Tomahawk. Whether it was good for the players wouldn't be clear for some years. The first generation of true professionals was entering their late thirties. Attrition was setting in, and so far it looked as though it would be similar to the attrition pattern for male athletes—a slow slide from glory, the death of a dream, a retreat either into the past, the bottle, cocaine, or Valium. But then many a secretary beat the same retreat around age forty. Who was better off than whom seemed a profitless discussion. In pro tennis, there are no profitless discussions. There are no discussions at all. There's just the game. Age, injury, the grief that accompanies this life, and inevitably death are unknown on this side of the service court. That's another world.

In this land of health, prizes, and simplicity, one wins or one loses. Carmen Semana was a winner, a queen. Queen for a day, a month, a year, maybe a few years, but she was queen and she liked it. She also discovered winning was one thing; defending, another.

With Page out of the Tomahawk Circuit, the real threat was the ever-present Rainey Rogers. Rainey and Carmen divided the Tomahawk Circuit between them and only played head to head at two of the season's tournaments. This suited everyone fine. Each promoter got at least one highly publicized player plus enough other players to make it a contest, and the people paid their money to see it all. When Carmen was on a hot streak, they watched her with the same fascination that draws people to hurricanes, earthquakes, and car accidents. At her peak, she was so awesome as to be slightly terrifying.

◆ ◆ ◆

Amalgamated Interstate Banks kicked in $50,000 toward the prize money for the tournament, although Tomahawk, as parent sponsor, got the lion's share of the publicity. In each city local sponsors would contribute to the pot. Tomahawk would supply a base for each city, usually $25,000. The local promoter had to come up with the remaining money, usually between $75,000 and $125,000.

Amalgamated joined in because they wished to attract female customers. Women were doing their own banking these days so Amalgamated wanted a young, modern image. Short of film stars, there were few women with visibility. Dennis Parry, a vice-president of Amalgamated, figured the $50,000 was worth a new level of visibility. Within Amalgamated, the Tomahawk Circuit afforded Dennis a new visibility. Dennis harbored ambitions.

When Miguel Semana walked into Amalgamated's courtside box, he and Dennis struck up a casual conversation. Since the matches hadn't begun, the two were alone. They bantered pleasantries, talking of rampant inflation and Carmen's serve.

"Don't you ever want to compete yourself?" Dennis wondered.

"Sometimes, but I'm glad I became a lawyer. After all, what would happen to our investments if both Semanas were playing? Someone needs to concentrate on business."

"Carmen's lucky to have you."

Miguel chuckled. "I'd say I was lucky to have her." He paused. "Speaking of business, we're currently developing a line of clothing for Southeast Asia. The clothing she now endorses covers the U.S., Europe, and South America. You know, quite a market is developing in Japan, Hong Kong, the Philippines, and India. We're hoping to take advantage of her reputation. After all, she's world famous."

"Would you mind telling me what you're doing?"

"Not at all." Miguel beamed. "We're creating shirts and blouses with her personal logo and selling them overseas. Of course, the prices will be lower abroad, except in Japan. That way Carmen doesn't have to divide the profits with a middleman. The line will be manufactured in Hong Kong."

"Zip labor costs." Dennis's slender hand convulsively clutched and released his keys inside his jacket pocket.

"Shipping is low, too. And who knows, we can always swim the line across to mainland China. That market is bigger than India."

"Are you looking for investors?" the banker asked.

"Only one. We're using about three hundred thousand dollars of our own money. Too many cooks spoil the stew."

"Yes, yes." Dennis squeezed his keys. "Why don't you stop by my office Monday? I'd like to discuss this further."

Not wanting to appear too eager, Miguel hesitated. "We'll be off for Chicago."

"Perhaps you could follow a day later. I think I could find you that investor."

"Since you put it that way . . ." Miguel's moustache twitched upwards.

"Here, let me give you my card." Dennis rummaged in his pocket. "I know I've got one somewhere." He pulled out a hunk of brown fur. "My lucky rabbit's foot."

"Carmen's got a pair of lucky socks."

"Is that right? Oh, here it is." Dennis handed over the card.

Miguel shook his hand and excused himself from the box. The only one who should put faith in the rabbit's foot, he thought, is the rabbit.

◆ ◆ ◆

Susan Reilly plopped on the trainer's table to get her left ankle taped. There wasn't anything wrong with it or the rest of her body except that she pounded it every day for the last twenty years. The constant slamming of feet on clay and grass and carpet, the quick stops, turns, and leaps for overheads begin to take their toll.

In tennis players, the knees are most vulnerable. Then comes the elbow. Shoulders don't dislocate, but the muscles rip apart. Bone spurs congregate on joints. Ligaments pop. Piece by piece, under repeated stress, the body unravels itself.

Susan was crossing over the line and she knew it. Injuries didn't heal as fast. Ice packs helped out but not for long. She took better care of herself at thirty than she did at twenty. Superb conditioning and a sixth sense on the court kept her formidable. She turned her ankle in practice this morning. It didn't hurt, but she was taking no chances. The trainer, a cheerful woman, expertly wrapped the famous ankle. Susan brooded while Alicia Brinker sat nearby, reading the Bible.

Alicia, a far better tennis wife than Harriet, found comfort in religion. Susan tolerated it because Alicia was so pliable in other ways. Away from Susan, a rare occurrence, Alicia would quietly discuss her religious beliefs. She earnestly wanted to reconcile her homosexuality with St. Paul. As St. Paul expressed nothing but contempt for women, her hopes of winning some approval for lesbians was futile. Still, she read on.

Lavinia stuck her head in the trainer's room. "Everything all right in here?"

Alicia glanced up from her book.

Susan answered, "Fine. What's the score out there?"

"Five-four in the first. Carmen's serve."

"Thanks." Susan lay back on the table. Another half hour, forty minutes at most, and she'd be out there unless Hilda Stambach could turn back the tide. Hilda would harden eventually. Now, she could still be undermined by an older player. Carmen was the better player, but Hilda was seventeen with forearms like Virginia hams. Susan would keep her eye on Hilda.

Miranda Mexata passed the trainer's room and waved. Lavinia, further down the hall, caught sight of the umpire and flagged her down.

"Miranda, I want to talk to you."

Miranda, acquainted with Lavinia's vocabulary of self-regard, sighed.

Lavinia spoke in a significant whisper. "She's been more high-strung of late." She nodded her head in the direction of the trainer's room. "That's why I put you on the second singles. Carmen and Hilda won't get out of line. Beanie and Susan though, well, the fur may fly. You've got to be firm, Miranda, be firm."

Appearing to absorb this oft-repeated advice, Miranda replied, "Alicia's had a calming effect, I think."

Lavinia quickly checked out the area to see if anyone could hear what Miranda said. "We don't speak of that."

"M-m-m." Miranda wondered if Ricky had a player up in the press booth. Occasionally he'd take up a player and give them a chance to provide color commentary. It was great for the players and great for the viewers. Ricky was generous that way. He made everyone look good. Miranda was dying to be asked into the press booth for her version of events. Perched high in the umpire's chair, she saw the game the way no one else saw it, even the players.

"Miranda, are you listening?"

"What do you want me to say? I've handled Susan before, and I don't think she'll be troublesome tonight."

"I've been in this business a long, long time and I can tell you, she's tense. She's working herself up. How I remember that myself. She still thinks she can win the Slam, you know. She's already starting to turn the screws tighter. Oh, yes." Lavinia inhaled.

Siggy Wayne, fat as a toad and on a search-and-annoy mission, sauntered over to the women. "Anyone seen Chuck?" Chuck Lowry was the Tomahawk representative in Kansas City.

Lavinia supplied the obvious information. "He's probably watching the match or hanging around the hospitality lounge."

Miranda escaped. "I'll see you later. I want to observe how Danielle's doing in the chair." Miranda supervised the local umpires. Locals could be intimidated by the players.

Lavinia yearned for a vodka gimlet, and she knew it wouldn't take much coaxing to steer Siggy Wayne to the bar. Siggy wooed sponsors to women's tennis. Originally, Lavinia performed that function, but as the sport mushroomed, her job had to be broken into component parts. Siggy turned out to be perfect, so on the payroll he went. He flew from city to city, a pied piper of women's tennis. No one was sure if the rats were driven out or in, but at any rate, he did bring in the loot and that made him indispensable. He and Seth Quintard of Athletes Unlimited were kindred spirits. Seth grabbed goodies for his players; Siggy grabbed it for the entire sport. He thought of women's tennis as his burlesque show with clothes. As far as Siggy was concerned, women's tennis couldn't compete with men's tennis. The men's game was faster, stronger, and longer. All the women had to sell was tits and ass. Plenty of them had neither, but the few that did, the Page Bartlett Campbells, the Rainey Rogerses, they were his aces. Since Navratilova was out because of an on-court accident and Austin still had back trouble, Sissy shepherded his healthy stars . . . especially his healthy heterosexual stars. The president of a local bank would love to rub shoulders with Terry Bradshaw, but Susan Reilly? Possibly not. It would take the men running corporations a long time to appreciate women as athletes.

Siggy gave Lavinia his arm, for she lapped up courtliness, and they strolled toward the bar. Lavinia thought Siggy's methods were questionable, but he did bring in the money. All the girls had to do was stand around at a few parties and try to look attractive on the court. She had a great passion for women's tennis, but that passion didn't blind her to the fact that for today, Siggy Wayne was right. The next generation would have to find their own way to sell themselves and tennis. For now, it was selling women as women. Nothing wrong with that.

Lavinia was often angry about the regard in which women tennis players were held. Their scores were reported after the men's scores. At the giant tournaments like the U.S. Open, there wasn't even an attempt at equal television coverage. Every year that was supposed to be changed. Promises, promises. She knew the game wasn't behind the eight ball, but it wasn't in the pocket either. Why would a corporation pour money into women's tennis if that money could more profitably be spent elsewhere? The image of women's tennis had to lure them. As for emphasizing sexuality—in a subtle way, of course—she thought that was fine. Vive la différence. Except the difference for most women meant a difference in salary. The women were catching up until one looked under the table and at endorsements. Tennis remained a man's world, subject to change and changing, but a man's world nonetheless. Since Lavinia prided herself on her looks and her femininity, it didn't seem all that bad . . . until she thought of a lesbian scandal and her blood ran cold.

She was once told she resembled Marlene Dietrich and

she never fully recovered from the compliment. Each morning she religiously painted on her eyebrows. The arch depended on how much she'd drunk the night before. From the look of it as she chatted with Siggy, those eyebrows would be inverted V's for tomorrow's finals.

◆ ◆ ◆

The morning of the Kansas City final, Carmen ordered her usual breakfast of steak, pasta, and coffee. She ordered a cold Coca-Cola for Harriet.

"Where's the goddamned food? I ordered half an hour ago!" She tossed the Sunday paper across the room.

In the beginning of their relationship, Carmen's irritability upset Harriet. Now she knew that before a final, Carmen would either sizzle like a firecracker or withdraw into the remoter recesses of her being. At least with a sizzle there was contact. Harriet also learned never to criticize Carmen about anything, even the color of her shoelaces, before a final.

Harriet picked up the phone.

"Are you dialing Room Service?"

"No," Harriet answered.

Carmen grabbed the phone out of her lover's hand, stabbed the number, and let fly. "Room Service, this is Semana in three-two-six. Semana!"

The voice on the other end of the line displayed the famous inability to understand or pronounce non-English names. "S-E-M-A—goddammit, forget my name. The room number is three-two-six, and where's the food?" She slammed the receiver on the hook where it rocked in its cradle.

Harriet again picked up the telephone and dialed. After a suitable interval, she spoke with cheerfulness. "Baby Jesus, how are you? This is Mother. Yes, Carmen is here, too. What

kind of tub do we have? A pink one with wallpaper to match."
Harriet listened intently.

At first Carmen paid no attention as she retrieved the
sports page from the other side of the room.

"I don't care if you don't like Friskies tuna; eat it anyway."
Pause. "We'll be home tonight. Carmen has a week off before
Chicago. You want to come to Chicago?" Pause. "What do you
mean you need a new coat? Your gray tabby will do just fine.
You want to wish her luck?" Harriet cupped her hand over the
receiver. "Honey, Baby Jesus wants to wish you luck."

Carmen looked up from the paper. "Loco."

"She says, 'Thank you.' You're writing a new novel?
Catalogue, a book about feline lumberjacks. Well, good luck
with it. Bye, bye. We love you."

The bell rang. Food, at last. Carmen sat down and started
eating while Harriet signed for it. She sat down and picked up
her Coke.

"What book did you say Baby Jesus was writing?" Carmen asked.

"*Catalogue*."

"Hmm." She attacked her steak and then brightened. "I
think she'd make more money if she wrote one called *Cate-
gory*."

"Oh, why is that?"

"Kitty murders. Couldn't miss."

◆ ◆ ◆

Miranda Mexata, poised in the chair, began the day's
matches. Susan Reilly versus Carmen Semana. Susan won the
toss and elected to serve.

Up in the stands in the sponsor's box, Alicia Brinker and
Harriet Rawls sat next to one another, a small breach in tennis
etiquette, but Chuck, Kansas City's Tomahawk representa-

tive, could be forgiven. He'd never watched a tennis match in his life. The husbands, wives, lovers, and relatives of opponents are usually kept apart. They can't help knowing where the other party is, but to smack them next to one another was insensitive. If either cheering section had any manners at all, it couldn't rejoice when its woman hit a good shot or hiss when the opponent whacked a winner. Alicia, never comfortable around Harriet to begin with, hid her slender New Testament in the folds of her sweater, which she placed on her lap. Miguel and Dennis Parry sat in an adjoining box festooned with Amalgamated Banks' pale blue banners.

Up in the press box, Ricky Cooper, his headphone in place, waited for his cue. Jane sat off-camera with special diagrams to enable her to chart the match. She usually left that chore to statisticians, but today she felt like charting. Susan walked to the baseline. Jane muttered, "Lucretia Borgia of Sunnybrook Farm."

Ricky, smiling, received his cue. "You're right on time, ladies and gentlemen. Susan Reilly won the service toss, and we're ready to go."

Lavinia made a nest in the Tomahawk box. The wife of a local sponsor quickly sat beside her as Susan's familiar, high service toss climbed upwards. The famous deep swinging serve was in action. Whenever the players switched sides, Lavinia would warble in conversations with sponsors. She could hit high C for cash.

Alicia didn't beam. Carmen won the first set six-four. Three sets was what was going through Susan's mind. She dug in harder. If Page Bartlett Campbell had the best balance and Carmen had the greatest athletic ability, Susan possessed a degree of drive and guile that never ceased to astonish her opponents.

On her serve, she drove deep into Carmen's forehand. Carmen hit the ball solid and hard. Good. Susan liked pace and she knew Carmen would never stoop to garbage shots to

win any match. The harder Carmen hit the ball, the better
Susan liked it. As the ball zoomed for the backhand corner,
Susan met it with every fiber in her body and fired the next
shot down the line. Her backhand was deadly, powerful, and
never to be trifled with. It brought the crowd to its feet. There
was life in the old dog yet—and bite. For the next point, she
bore down harder. The first serve caught the corner, but
Carmen's lightning reflexes and strong wrist slapped the ball
midcourt but deep. From the stands, Susan's return looked
like a weak shot. But from Miranda Mexata's viewpoint, the
ball crossed the net, fell midway in the service court, and then
spun backwards. Carmen got to the shot in plenty of time, but
she didn't calculate the spin. It might have been the angle at
which she was running or any number of causes, but she
overran the ball slightly. Her return wasn't deep enough, and
it was to Susan's backhand, the only shot she could make. She
had to commit herself to the net. On a weak return to a player
like Susan, Carmen might as well be charging a machine gun
nest with a rubber knife. Susan ripped a backhand down the
line again. On the next point she drove a backhand crosscourt
off the return of serve. She closed out the game with an ace.

Carmen hated playing Susan. When Carmen was out-
smarted with a shot like the retrograde dink, she could feel
Susan gloat, "Sucker." Susan sharpened with each point. If
Carmen were the tiniest bit mentally shaky, Susan could pick
her apart, even though Carmen was physically her superior.
Playing against Susan was like toying with a cobra. However,
Carmen was certain that today she would be the snake
charmer.

On the first serve of the second set, Carmen laid down an
ace with the precision of a bombardier. The next point was
long, and Susan finally grabbed it. Carmen's serve held up,
however, and she won the game. The rest of the set went like
that, back and forth, back and forth. It was the tense kind of
tennis that brought people out on cold January days: The Old

Master versus the Young Master. At twenty-four, Carmen couldn't be considered young in her profession, but against Susan, she could still look callow.

Susan's tactic now as they wrestled at four-all was to go all out on the serve and use the follow-through motion to propel herself to the net. Her sheer aggression excited the fans. She hit a forehand volley for a winner that brought them to their feet. Susan glowed. She had an infinite capacity for absorbing adulation. She not only held her serve, but she also towered over that game. Carmen was just as fierce as she held on to her serve. They went to five-all. In no time, they were at six-all. Another tie breaker. The fans went wild, for tennis fans. They wanted the match to go three sets.

Harriet wiggled in her seat. Alicia gripped her New Testament.

The tie breaker was electrifying. There wasn't a sloppy point in it. Each woman called upon herself to perform the heroic and did so. Susan lunged for a forehand volley that looked like a winner since Carmen hit the shot at an easy ninety miles an hour. Susan stretched out parallel to the floor as she leapt for the shot, and by God, she made it. She hit the floor, rolled and got up in case Carmen made the return. Pandemonium broke loose. The next serve was Carmen's. The score was five-five. Carmen took a chance and served to Susan's strong side hoping to catch her off guard. She did. Susan's return had authority, but not enough power. Carmen coasted across the court—she seemed always to glide—and unleashed a shattering forehand cross-court, perhaps her best shot. Susan, her uncanny sixth sense at full operating capacity, was there. She got her racquet on the shot, and the ball sailed over the net. The linesman called, "Out." The shot was dangerously close to the back-court line. Carmen moved behind the line, took a ball from the ball girl and turned around to see Susan at the net, hands on hips.

"Out! What do you mean, out? That ball was in by a yard!"

The fans on the unhappy linesman's side agreed. To most of them the ball looked good. The linesman said nothing.

Carmen waited. Miranda said something to Susan, but no one could hear it.

Susan, livid, continued, "That ball was good. Miranda, you know that ball was in."

"I saw the ball out," Miranda coolly said. She always supported her linespeople unless the mistake was glaring. In this case, the linesman hadn't fluffed any calls so far. Miranda knew it was a close call, but she had to maintain rule or Susan would tear apart every linesman on the court.

"No way." Susan threw her racquet to the ground. She leaned over the net and yelled at Carmen, "Did you see the ball?"

In truth, Carmen was running so fast, she had her eye on the ball, not the line. "No."

"Carmen, you know that ball was good."

This pissed off Carmen. She had a reputation for being fair on calls. Susan was making her out to be a thief.

"I didn't see the ball, Susan."

"Goddammit, I'm playing my heart out, and the linesman wins the match."

"Settle yourself, Susan." Miranda was firm. Right now, she had to be.

The fans were now screaming both for and against the call. Susan thundered to the backcourt and took up position to receive serve. She returned the serve with a high, arching lob, an act of total contempt. The ball hit inside the baseline. For an entire point, Susan gave Carmen nothing but garbage shots.

Clenching her teeth, Carmen ran down each rotten shot until she finally blew one by Susan, winning the match. The crowd bellowed. Harriet stood up. Alicia unclasped her New

Testament. Ricky tried not to let an edge of disgust creep into his patter. Jane knocked off the last point card. They looked down at the figure of Susan Reilly moving toward the net like a panzer.

Carmen was angry, but she pulled herself together and extended her hand. Tennis matches have been ending with cordial handshakes for over a century. Susan walked up to the net and put her racquet head on Carmen's outstretched hand. With her other hand, she hit Carmen squarely on the mouth. Carmen's head snapped back, her lip split. She stood there stunned. The crowd switched off its volume. Miranda climbed out of her umpire's chair faster than a squirrel goes down a tree. Carmen, still stunned, wiped the back of her hand across her mouth. It was covered with blood.

"Take care of her!" Miranda commanded the trainer. The trainer positioned herself in front of Carmen and began ministering to her. What she was really doing was trying to keep Susan out of Carmen's sight lest Carmen's famed Latin temper should explode.

Miranda grasped Susan by the arm, none too gently, and forced her behind the umpire's chair. Flashbulbs crackled. The crowd began talking again, first in a low buzz, then louder, until finally a roar of disapproval hit the rafters in Kansas City. Alicia hurried up on the other side of Susan. Miranda, without saying a word, indicated they were to get Susan back to the locker room immediately. As Alicia touched Susan's arm, Susan spat, "Don't touch me. Not in public."

◆ ◆ ◆

The next morning, the story not only filled up the Kansas City papers, but it also screamed out over the AP and UPI wires. Carmen was okay. Lavinia Sibley Archer couldn't make a silk purse out of a sow's ear, so she spoke instead on the pressures

55

of competition and travel. The other players couldn't believe it. Nothing like that had ever happened, no matter how angry anyone was, and there had been plenty of angry moments over the years.

The fans, for the most part, reviled the act. But the promoters were in hog heaven. A little drama would bring in the people. Susan had just lined their pockets. Naturally, promoters would never publicly encourage such outbursts. Even though the public disapproved of the act, the fact that there might be more explosions attracted them. After all, it wasn't just a sport anymore, it was entertainment. Susan publicly apologized. In her heart, she felt she had done no wrong. Carmen robbed her. Since Susan couldn't admit she had any faults, she was in no danger of correcting herself. Carmen understood. Between her first lover and herself, it was no longer tennis; it was war.

◆ ◆ ◆

"That's an interesting offer." Miguel sat across from Dennis Parry in the bank office. "I think we can do business."

"I'm always looking for new ideas." An unctuous smile crossed Parry's lips.

Riding in the taxi to the Kansas City airport, Miguel glowed. The meeting with Parry was better than he'd hoped.

Amalgamated would loan Carmen $600,000 at an interest rate of 21%. The term of the loan was one year. $300,000 was to be paid in equal, quarterly installments, a balloon payment of $300,000 was due at the end of the year. But it could be renegotiated at the end of that year. Parry congratulated himself on being a genius because Carmen would pay him $50,000 under the table. Obviously no record of that exchange would be on paper. Carmen only had to sign the loan agreement, and Miguel would have $550,000.

Miguel glanced at his gold Rolex. He'd be in plenty of time. Some of what Miguel told Dennis Parry was true. Much was not. He did have a friend who would manufacture the clothing line in Hong Kong. And he would sell the product in Southeast Asia. He also had every intention of peddling the goods in the United States through the outlets his Hong Kong friend used for designer rip-off clothing. Miguel had found a distribution network and all the retail outlets without spending a penny of his own cash. The shirts would be sold for 20% less than the legitimate item. Even at that discount, the profit was enormous.

Of course, Sunny Days, the company that manufactured Carmen's endorsed clothing line, would eventually discover that a bogus line was being sold at discount stores. But by the time they would find the parasite company—not an easy task—and then try to prosecute, huge profits would have been made and Miguel and his Hong Kong buddy would have discontinued the line. Sunny Days would be furious but the American legal system being what it is, it would probably cost Sunny Days so many hundreds of thousands of dollars in legal fees that they'd settle out of court if the false line was removed. Of course, if Sunny Days did prosecute, the entire garment industry would benefit. However, it was unlikely that Sunny Days would set a legal precedent so that their competitors could profit from it. It was still every man for himself in the garment business.

Miguel was sure that there was no way he could lose. Carmen didn't need to know any of this. Why should she? Her attention span was short; business would only distract her. She needed to concentrate solely on tennis. The more she won, the more clothes Miguel would sell.

As for her signature on the loan agreement, Miguel would merely forge her name.

FOUR

$\bullet \bullet \bullet$ $\bullet \bullet \bullet$

Chicago hung on Lake Michigan like a glittering choker. The snow reflected off the buildings and lights gave the city an extra dimension.

Harriet, Carmen, Miguel, Jane, and Ricky were staying at The Tremont, an elegant, small hotel off Michigan Avenue.

Ricky held a light lavender tie next to a pink Oxford-cloth shirt. He was a man unafraid to look dashing. Mustard pants and a navy blazer would complete the outfit. As he stood there in his Jockey shorts, Jane admired his legs. True, she'd seen those legs for years, but she still found them appealing. Ricky Cooper, short of stature, was a man who attracted women. His sophistication, tempered with a genuine affection for people, made him a popular television commentator. Offscreen, he had his moments of irritation and worry, but such moments were few.

Jane frightened many men because she was so strong. In Ricky, she met her match. It didn't hurt their relationship that she was a knockout. If Ricky was jaded by the availability of his female followers, he had only to look at the constant trail of men hunting down Jane to keep on his toes. By now, both knew they could have just about anybody they wanted. They wanted one another.

The first day Jane met Ricky, six years ago, he swaggered over and whispered, "You have beautiful eyes."

"Can't you think of anything more original?" came the tart reply.

No woman talked to Ricky that way. Jane Fulton could care less that he was a man about town, a world traveler, and a television personality. He was a dude on the make and she was bored. Stung, he wanted to win her affections simply to prove he could. All the old ploys were used. Flowers were sent first. They were sent right back to him. He tried phone calls, notes, and candy. He went so far as to hire a high school band from Philadelphia to file into the *Inquirer* and play John Philip Sousa marches. Jane hated John Philip Sousa. This dragged on for months. Finally, getting nowhere, Ricky hopped the Metroliner to Philadelphia and waited for her to leave work. She was leaving with a date. Undaunted, Ricky walked up to her and said, "I've tried everything. Nothing works. Okay, so maybe I do lack imagination. I'm worth knowing anyway."

On the spot, Jane disengaged from her date. She and Ricky ate in a tiny Italian restaurant that was her favorite. They closed the place down. It had taken Ricky many flowers, candies, and one high school band to learn to deal with Jane as a person, but once he learned it, he never regretted it. They were lovers from that night on. In a year they married.

Once Harriet asked Jane if she ever thought she could divorce Ricky. The question came after one of their fights. Jane fired back, "Divorce, never. Murder, yes."

"What time is it?" asked Jane.

"Time for both of us to get to work."

Jane, forlorn, waved good-bye to his Jockey shorts and the riches therein. "Damn."

Ricky zipped his trousers. "If all the girls would finish their matches in forty-five minutes, we might not be too tired."

"Wouldn't Siggy Wayne shit a brick?" Jane relished the thought of Siggy, sticking to a sponsor like a leech, feverishly explaining that most opening rounds were interesting. Most opening rounds were boring as bat shit, and the public knew it. That's why they didn't show up until the semifinals and the finals. As good as women's tennis was, it still did not have the depth the men's game possessed.

"Siggy Wayne has the personality of a gargoyle." Rick knotted his tie. He decided against a tie tack.

"If I had to sit around with local sponsors, I think I'd get weird myself."

"Are you ready?"

"Yes, I'm ready for another week on the Tomahawk Circuit, a small pool filled with man-eating sharks." Jane grabbed her full-length silver fox and sailed out the door on Ricky's arm.

◆ ◆ ◆

"Hey, creep," Jane saucily called to Harriet, who was picking her way around the empty seats, moving down toward the practice court.

"Creepette. I'm too little to be a creep." The two embraced. "Where's the best-looking man on the women's circuit?"

"Who could you mean? Let me guess. Seth Quintard just flew in from New York City. No? It must be Siggy Wayne, world's perfect ectomorph. I'm running out of men."

Harriet linked her arm through Jane's. "How's our last choice?"

"Fussing. You know how he is the first day of a tournament. He has to inspect everything. He never has gotten over that time at the U.S. Open when he broadcast two sets without sound."

"I still say some angry female player cut the cables because her side wasn't getting enough coverage."

The two friends stood at the net to watch Carmen and Beanie Kittredge practice. Carmen waved to Jane from the backcourt.

Beanie's Aussie accent boomed out, "Hey, bitch, you getting any?"

Jane answered in perfect mid-Atlantic tones, "Beanie, I hear you put a yellow yield sign over your bed."

Carmen fluffed a ball. "No fair. Save your best lines when she's in her backswing."

Jane dutifully waited until Beanie's wrist was laid back for her murderous forehand. "Beanie, what's the definition of a macho woman?"

Beanie kept her eye on the ball. "I don't know."

"One who kick-starts her vibrator." The ball rocketed off Beanie's forehand toward the lights.

"Old joke!" Carmen called back.

The laughter thinned as Happy Straker, Alicia Brinker, and Susan Reilly walked by on their way back from a practice court on another level. Only Alicia waved a hello.

"An ulcerous presence," Harriet whispered to Jane.

Jane shrugged, "Assholes have to live, too. After Billie Jean King, Virginia Wade, and all those oldies but goodies, Susan came along and saved women's tennis. It was all Susan until Page Bartlett Campbell, Tracy Austin, and Martina Navratilova showed up. So she deserves her accolades."

◆ ◆ ◆

Susan steamed through the locker room in search of fresh tennis balls with Happy and Alicia still in her wake. The three planned to go back out and work on lobs even though they had just finished a grueling practice. Happy Straker and Alicia Brinker endured one another's company because Susan would have it no other way.

When Alicia looked at Happy she shuddered. She swore Happy took steroids because no woman could look that bad and be all woman.

In the best of situations, a new lover lacks charity toward the jilted lover. The jilted lover is usually seething with hatred.

It was a no-win situation for Alicia and Happy, but Susan benefited by having one docile lover and one eager doubles partner.

Happy replaced her soggy socks with a fresh pair. "You should ignore Harriet Rawls. You know Susan doesn't like her."

"Harriet never did anything to me." Alicia sat stoically.

"Susan feels she's a bad influence on the tour." What Happy didn't say was Susan thought that about everyone who didn't succumb to Susan's charisma.

"I never said I liked her. I don't see any reason to be rude, that's all."

Happy moved a step closer to the seated Alicia. "When you love Susan, her enemies are your enemies. Her friends are your friends. Why don't you do what she says? You'll last longer."

"Why didn't you last longer?" That arrow sunk up to the shaft. Alicia had some life to her, after all.

Happy lowered her voice. "Susan tired of her toy."

◆ ◆ ◆

"Señor Knipe, you know my sister is besieged with offers." Miguel larded on the Señor bit when he talked to Americans. The more he acted like a gaucho, the better they liked it. It was the year sportscasters discovered the words "awesome" and "relevant." Miguel decided to be an awesome and relevant South American.

"Yes, but it's for a good cause." Mr. Knipe headed Chicago's Easter Seal campaign.

"No doubt, but if Carmen helped out everyone who asked her, think what would happen to her game." He reassuringly patted the downcast man's arm.

"Won't you talk to her?"

"Of course, of course." Miguel's voice oozed understanding. "I've heard, Mr. Knipe, that you own a British Leyland, uh, what would you call it, franchise."

"A case in point against socialism!" Mr. Knipe loved Jaguars, MG's, and the other cars but dealing with the English drove him wild at times.

"I quite agree. We have our own troubles at home. The inflation rate is terrible, terrible. Have you any idea what one of your cars would cost in Buenos Aires?"

"Why, no, I never thought about it."

Miguel smiled his dashing smile. "Today it would cost one hundred thousand dollars. Tomorrow?" His hand spiraled into the air.

Mr. Knipe smiled. He was getting the picture.

♦ ♦ ♦

Harriet gave vent to a sudden urge to rearrange the cut flowers in their hotel room. It was the night before the finals.

"What are you doing?" Carmen was propped on the bed, working a crossword puzzle. Her English was better than that of most Americans.

"I'm throwing out these long-stemmed red roses. They've wilted."

"What's another word for misinformation?"

"Try bullshit."

Carmen smiled. "Nope. Not enough boxes for that one." She glanced up from her puzzle. "What do you think about when you're not with me?"

"History. I love history. Cat best-sellers. Baby Jesus is working on another one."

"What?"

"*Caterpillar*. This one's about kitty architecture."

Carmen laughed, but she was secretly miffed that Harriet hadn't answered the question seriously—seriously meaning that Harriet shouldn't think of history but of her. Harriet missed a lot of romantic cues. She was too honest to be romantic.

A few minutes of silence dropped on the room. The pencil scratched on the paper.

"Are you mad?" Harriet was a little bewildered.

"No."

Harriet rubbed Carmen's shoulders. She knew she'd said something wrong, but she didn't know what. "I was thinking about Rachel and Lawrence Burns today."

"Ugh."

"How do you think people get that way?"

"Practice." Carmen felt better. The massage improved her pout.

Rachel and Lawrence Burns were a middle-aged couple who lived in Cazenovia. Rachel wanted children but was never able to give birth to anything but a dermatoid cyst, a ball of unformed eyes, teeth, and hair. She kept this horror in an industrial mayonnaise jar, placed a Mets' baseball cap on top, and named it Gene. When you talked to Rachel she invariably brought up her "boy" and his love of baseball. Clearly someone shot the dots off Rachel's dice, but she was harmless enough.

"Odd, though." Harriet moved her thumbs between Carmen's shoulder blades. "People who perform the duties of life are apparently normal, but they all harbor a crazy streak."

"You haven't got both oars in the water when it comes to that ancient cat."

"I never said I was sane when it came to Baby Jesus."

Harriet kissed Carmen's cheek. "How do you feel about sex the night before a tough match?"

"You should have asked me that five minutes ago. It's too late to ask me now." They embraced, and Harriet bit Carmen's lower lip.

Carmen wrapped one leg inside Harriet's legs. Her arms, as strong as the average man's, locked around Harriet's waist. She licked Harriet's ear, her neck, and then returned to her mouth. She unbuttoned Harriet's blouse with one hand, a difficult feat. Using her leg, she rolled Harriet over on her back. She slipped her hand under her skirt. Carmen loved for Harriet to wear skirts. Following the curve of a thigh under a skirt was much more exciting than over a pants leg. With her index finger, she traced the edges of Harriet's silken underpants, then unexpectedly slipped her hand under the material.

Carmen liked surprises, especially when she was the source of the surprise. The palm of her hand slid over Harriet's wetness. Carmen plunged her tongue in Harriet's mouth and shoved herself inside her lover. She didn't have the time for a long night of lovemaking. She tightened her grasp around Harriet's legs and moved in synchronization with her. Slowly at first, then faster, she ground into her lover's bones.

When they came, they were as two moths caught in brightness. Finding the flame, they burned their wings and quickly fell to earth.

♦ ♦ ♦

Two floors below Harriet and Carmen, Alicia Brinker, she of the valiant vagina, was slinking stealthily down the hall. Two sharp raps and a door opened.

"Where the hell have you been?" Susan asked.

"I fell asleep reading."

"You've been sitting in your room reading? I've been sitting here biting my fingernails to the core. Do you know what time it is?"

"Uh, no," Alicia said, "I lost track of the time."

"You're two hours late!"

"Susan, I'm sorry."

"Sorry? I've got to play Hilda Stambach tomorrow, and you're sorry. I need you here with me."

"I'm sorry. I won't do it again."

"What did you read that was so important?"

"If we believe in Jesus, all our sins will be washed away."

"I heard that in first grade."

"I'm confused. Jesus loves me, but homosexuals are sick."

"I wish you wouldn't use that word."

"What do you want me to say? Lesbian?"

Susan's body went rigid. "That's worse. I don't want you to goddamned say anything. We're not lesbians, and we're not homosexuals."

"Then why do I have to sneak into your room each night? Why do I have to pretend we're just close personal friends? Why do I have to melt into the woodwork every time Craig and Lisa appear? And how come they're always just in time for the television cameras?" Alicia, formerly malleable, surprised Susan. Susan was not accustomed to being argued with.

"Because he is my husband and she is my daughter. I *am* a married woman."

"And you've had a lot of woman lovers."

"Life's lonely on the road. I'm not a lesbian. Except for you, the very few women I have been with, uh, have been mistakes."

"Will all Susan Reilly's mistakes please stand up?"

Susan slapped Alicia across the face. Alicia began to cry,

and Susan suddenly collapsed into repentance. "I'm sorry, I'm sorry. You made me do it. Alicia, don't cry. You know how keyed up I get. I've got to win tomorrow."

Alicia wiped her eyes with the back of her hand. "Yeah, I know."

"Besides, honey, it isn't just Craig and Lisa. Think what it would do to women's tennis. We're so young professionally, if you think about it. We can't afford any scandal. This would kill us."

Alicia didn't know whether public reaction would be negative or positive, but she certainly didn't want to find out. On the other hand, if love felt so good, why should she hide it? Why would God make her a homosexual and then forbid it? She didn't understand. "Uh-huh."

Susan plucked a tissue out of the box. Alicia blew her nose.

"I've got to rest. Let's not fight. If you love someone you don't fight with them."

Susan didn't quite know what was happening but she recognized a sense of loss. She slammed that feeling back into the darkest part of her brain. She was Susan Reilly, the world's greatest tennis player. Those other women were mistakes. She thought only about tennis, and people had to realize that tennis was her life. Those other women didn't understand her. They made demands. They were mistakes. After all, she wasn't perfect. She should be allowed her mistakes.

The trouble with Susan was that she made the same mistakes repeatedly. She'd fall in love with a woman and consume her. Susan thought that her mere presence was enough. What more was there to give? When she tired, usually after a year or so, she'd find another woman.

Unfortunately, Susan didn't remember what Jane Fulton once said. "Insanity is doing the same thing over and over again, but expecting different results."

A cigarette tray, gagging with lipstick-smeared butts, competed with a vodka bottle for space on the small coffee table. Lavinia, on her third vodka gimlet, was regaling Siggy Wayne with her version of her career. He'd heard it all before.

"Do you know one time we had a water balloon fight at Forest Hills? Oh yes, quite rocked the old fogeys. Those were fun days."

"Those were poor days." Siggy knocked back a Cutty Sark. His bottle squatted beneath his chair.

Lavinia's eyebrows, nearly bowed tonight, registered the remark.

"I think I've got the Chrysler deal." Siggy rolled the Scotch on his tongue. He was very proud of himself.

"Really?" asked Lavinia.

"Next year after the Tomahawk Circuit, we'll do a Citrus Circuit in Florida. Four cities in four weeks. It's good for Florida, too, since that will cover April. The tourist season slacks off a bit after March, and this can bring them down."

"I suppose cars go with the prize money?"

"We're working all that out, Lundy Grenshaw of Chrysler and myself."

"Do you think Chrysler is the right image? They're losers, to be frank."

"Old people stick to the old ways. They'll buy American cars in Florida. It's right. The players won't like the cars, but that's not an issue."

"How will it look for us to be backed with the taxpayers' money?" Lavinia didn't miss much.

Siggy paused a moment, and then said, "Tennis is a better bet than the cars."

They laughed and let the subject ride. When contracts were on the table, Lavinia would worry, consider, reconsider, and then do what she thought was best for the game.

Siggy poured himself another Cutty. His shirt sleeves were rolled up; his shoes were off. Over the years, his relationship with Lavinia evolved into an informal friendship. He appreciated what she'd done for the game and what she'd done for him. He made a percentage on every deal plus his salary. He pulled in enough for one lovely wife in Southport, Connecticut, and one loving mistress in New York City. He lived beyond his means, but that was the great American way.

Lavinia kept her cards close to her proverbial chest. Wendell left her well cared for when he died. She showed a flair for the stock market, and she made her own deals with sponsors. Lavinia was loaded, but she was never showy, never loud, and she'd die before she'd wear anything purchased at Gucci. She was a Peck & Peck woman, except there was no longer the old Peck & Peck or Abercrombie and Fitch, but there was Lavinia Sibley Archer. The future of shirtwaist dresses was secure as long as Lavinia Sibley Archer lived.

"Siggy, can you think of anything that would queer the deal with Chrysler?"

"Funny you should use that expression." His weasely smile appeared. "A homosexual scandal could hurt." He waved his hand a little. "Drugs could hurt. We faced abortion years ago, although with the New Right, it could become an issue again."

Lavinia rocked her glass back and forth to hear the ice cubes tinkle. "Yes, yes, we've seen a lot. But you think homosexuality would make them hesitate?"

"Not just Chrysler. I think Tomahawk might balk."

"Never! Howard Dominick and Tomahawk would never pull out on me, on women's tennis. Their image is cemented to our own."

"That's what I mean. Suppose a lesbian scandal did hit us? Tomahawk doesn't want their cosmetics, their image, associated with dykes. At least, that's how I see it."

"Lesbians use cosmetics, too." Lavinia raised her glass.

"You might be right, Siggy, you just might be right. Still, I can't believe Howard Dominick would chicken out."

"He's been running Tomahawk for about twelve years now. Clark & Clark is subject to a shake-up the same as any other corporation, and you know if a new man comes in, he'll remove all the old division heads and put in his own men. Corporate politics is like the days of Andrew Jackson, the spoils system."

She finished her drink and fixed herself another. "Are you hearing anything in the wind?"

"Rumors, but there are always rumors."

"Jensen Bainbridge is getting old." Jensen was president of Tomahawk's parent company, Clark & Clark. "When he goes, there goes our sponsor." Lavinia paused thoughtfully. "Siggy, I'm glad you brought this to my attention. I'll snoot around to see who might replace him. I still have some good friends at all the best country clubs. Wives know everything. I just might give Betty Bainbridge a call next week for old times' sake."

The two smiled.

"If the bubble ever bursts," Siggy said as he hunched over his drink, "do you think it will come from Carmen Semana or Susan Reilly? They are not our only lesbians, but they're the most volatile."

"Carmen." Lavinia's reply was immediate.

"Why?"

"Carmen's like a child sometimes. She leaps first and looks later."

Siggy rubbed the stubble on his chin. The night was getting longer along with his beard. "I don't know, Lavinia. Susan has a perfect cover, but she's hurt a battalion of people. Sooner or later someone will get her."

Lavinia said nothing. What she thought about and what she revealed were two different things. Even when drunk, Lavinia could babble on and still keep a watch on herself. That reserve had won her Wimbledon. But she sensed on some deeper level many things. She knew her varicose veins looked like lapis lazuli. She knew the players looked at her as a living reliquary. She knew they laughed behind her back as the young ever do at the old. She sensed that as she got older, all the events of her past became equally accessible. Her mind could call them up with as much freshness as the moment they happened twenty, thirty, forty years ago. But the events themselves ebbed away like shipwrecks sliding off the continental shelf to break up in the depths of the sea. The event was gone forever. There was only memory and the present, the eternal, chaotic, painful, pleasurable present.

Lavinia fixed herself another vodka gimlet.

◆ ◆ ◆

The finals were indeed final for Hilda Stambach. Her game deserted her, and Carmen waltzed off with the Chicago title. It was the kind of victory that made her giddy, for she had hardly worked up a sweat.

Harriet packed up Carmen's bags in the locker room so they could catch an earlier flight to Detroit. She liked to get in and settle in.

A burly youngster who'd just joined the tour that year was also packing her bags after winning the doubles. As she left the locker room, Harriet whispered to Carmen, "No more ugly dykes. We've got to petition straight people to stop breeding them."

◆ ◆ ◆

Miguel smoothed his black moustache, then straightened his $150 tie. He didn't own a suit under $1000. If Carmen cared little about how she appeared, Miguel more than made up for both of them. He proved the peacock principle.

Siggy Wayne eyed him with fascination. "I'm not a promoter."

"Not in America, Mr. Wayne. Outside of America, why can't you do as you please?" Miguel's eyes danced.

"I never thought about it." Siggy really had not thought about it. He received a hefty commission from the contracts he brought in. Although the sponsors on one end and the demands of the players on the other gave him ulcers, his base salary before commissions was $50,000 so he considered himself fortunate. A few times he allowed himself a special present under the table but nothing outrageous—no cars or girls or trips to Hawaii. The last thing Siggy wanted to do on his own time was travel. Cold cash, however, was different. Yes, he could take that, and Lavinia would be none the wiser for it. But promote a tournament?

"The terms of your contract with Lavinia's organization do not prevent you from free enterprise?" Miguel's soft voice carried the question.

"No." Siggy watched.

"My country does not enjoy a world-class women's tournament. The only great player we ever see is my sister." He chuckled. "Great as she is, she needs some competition."

"Carmen's the best, the best." Siggy waved his hand. The gesture would have been more complete if he was smoking a cigar.

"You are only as good as your opponent allows you to be. No?" Miguel said, repeating Hazel Wightman's famous line.

"Right."

"We have great interest in tennis at home but we do not have your great organizing capability." His dark eyes fluttered. Siggy blinked back, and Miguel continued. "You have so much influence with the girls and with Lavinia."

Ha, Siggy thought to himself. No one has influence with Lavinia.

Miguel lightly tapped the back of Siggy's hand with his forefinger. "Four big stars, the other girls will follow the leaders, and we'll get a nice draw. I'd like thirty-two players. We put up a $150,000 purse. The winner takes twenty percent, the standard agreement. You and I split the proceeds down the middle. You deliver the players. I deliver the stadium and the sponsors."

"There's no profit with prize money. Who will put up the money for operating costs?" Siggy trolled his bait.

"I assumed that was understood. We take a modest percent of the operating costs as salary, and then we split the profits from the gate."

Siggy found Miguel charming. Even if the gate was a total bust, all would not be lost. "What about the political situation?"

By now Miguel was wearily accustomed to American ignorance when it came to any country south of the Rio Grande. "Mr. Wayne, we are putting on a tournament, not a revolution."

"Yes, of course. I was only thinking of the welfare of the girls." Siggy rarely thought of their welfare in Cleveland or Detroit.

"Do you think the American market is saturated?"

Miguel was subtle. Siggy appreciated that. What he was really asking Sig was how many more commissions he could look forward to.

Siggy decided to answer directly. "Not only is it saturated, but the big boom is over. We'll lose ground gradually. To be blunt, Miguel, the women's game is a bore with few exceptions. And if the economic situation worsens, few people will pay to grow old during a rally between Page Bartlett Campbell and Rainey Rogers. Tennis could lose faster than anyone anticipates." He breathed deeply. "But I'm an optimist. I'm banking on the fact that men like to look at legs, and, well . . ."

"Won't cable tv help?"

"Some. Let's face it, Miguel, tennis lacks the sheer physical drama of football, the speed of basketball, the color of baseball. Individual sports aren't as exciting as team sports. If you don't like the shortstop on a team, you might like the pitcher. But if you don't like Susan Reilly, you really don't like Susan Reilly, and your choices are limited. Anyway, television tennis doesn't work as well, there isn't enough motion, and the court area is confining."

Miguel listened impassively. "Will you ever leave the game?"

Siggy's eyebrows involuntarily shot upwards. "Game? This is no game to me, Miguel. I'm a businessman."

Smiling, Miguel replied, "Which is why we should be partners in the Argentina Women's Invitational."

"I'll think about it. It's tempting." He then asked nonchalantly, "Can you guarantee your sister's participation?"

"But, of course." Miguel expansively stretched out his arms like a pastor giving a benediction.

Walking to his car, Siggy considered Miguel's plan. It had merit. But Miguel did not. Siggy didn't trust him although he liked him. Deep down he had the same reaction to Carmen. Charmers but lightweights. There was a piece missing. Miguel couldn't organize a Tupperware party. Why risk antagonizing Lavinia over what, at most, would be $20,000 profit plus a few extras? And what was that worth when translated into American money? Was Miguel talking Argentinian cash or U.S.? Siggy liked the barter, the strategy of business. It was not a lofty profession, but he liked it. He hadn't gotten as far as he had without trusting his instincts.

Looking up the side of a brick building, Siggy noticed the painted figure of a man who looked both somber and kind. Davidson Mortuary was printed under the man's folded hands. Davidson, no doubt. Siggy shook his head and thought to himself, "What are we coming to when funeral parlors advertise?"

The boom was truly over and Siggy knew it. The stars of

the game still held the fans; but women's tennis needed some fresh players to come on the scene. Fresh and pretty was what Siggy prayed for.

Tennis madness peaked in the mid 1970's. The average American couldn't wait to play tennis, until the average American learned it wasn't easy to play. Novice players found themselves chasing netted balls or sheepishly asking the players on the next court to hit back an errant ball. When it dawned on many that tennis was a sport that took years to learn, they switched to jogging. After all, how hard is it to run? Those people who needed competition as much as fitness discovered racquetball, a game that yields instant pleasure regardless of one's athletic ability or skill. Exercise workout centers claimed those people who didn't have the time for a long tennis match; exercising to music claimed even more ex-tennis enthusiasts.

The city of New Orleans served as a warning signal. Siggy didn't mention negative information to potential sponsors, but for his own planning he took heed. The use of public courts in that beautiful city had dropped by seventy percent. Local teaching pros were struggling to pay their bills as they had lost roughly half of their students. Sales in the pro sports shops nose-dived from twenty percent to forty percent, depending on location.

Men's pro tournaments never generated the profit New Orleans' promoters hoped. In fact, they flopped.

Even the oldest tennis club in the United States, The New Orleans Lawn Tennis Club, renamed Stern, felt the decline.

On a national level, Spalding and Wilson, two huge sporting goods companies, are looking into a cesspool of red ink when it comes to their tennis equipment. Bancroft, once an honored racquet in the game, is not seen around much these days.

Maybe New Orleans was an especially bad case. Tennis

was still in good shape in less enticing cities like Lincoln, Nebraska. New Orleans offers such riches of entertainment, tennis has heavy competition.

Still, Siggy worried. And he wondered if Lavinia bothered to acquire such municipal statistics or sales statistics from companies. She so identified with the game that she might ignore bad news. He couldn't afford to be so blind. If his income dropped below a certain level, he'd have to jump ship.

◆ ◆ ◆

Happy Straker, enjoying a streak of competence, beat Carmen in the Detroit finals. Carmen could do no right; Happy could do no wrong. Happy, puffed up like a toad, swaggered about. Carmen swallowed her anger and figured Happy wouldn't swagger long; there was always next week in Oakland, California. There was only one way to face a loss, Carmen reminded herself, and that was to learn what you can from it, then forget the rest. Otherwise you would eat yourself up.

For Happy, the victory was a final burst before the stately procession toward oblivion which is the future of all athletes. Happy had hovered in the top ten for the last five years, although history would not regard her as one of the great ones. History would not regard her at all. Not that Carmen thought about it either. That thought was to be avoided at all costs. Tennis was what she did best. It was her blessing and her curse that she was born in time to cash in on her skill. She could make a fantastic living doing what she wanted to do. The curse wouldn't stain her life until she left the pro circuit. Then she could hang on to the game like a tick, become a coach, found tennis camps, live on the fringes of her former famous self. Or she could sit down in her early thirties and realize that if she had studied to become a doctor, she would now be entering the high point of her profession. As a doctor she would be serving society and herself. As a broken-down tennis player, she would face a colossal identity crisis just as everyone else in her generation was finally getting hold of themselves. Carmen staved off this crushing knowledge with a steady stream of electronic games and crossword puzzles.

She did, however, allow herself to ponder love. What is it? How do you get it? How do you keep it? Why does it always start out great and end up shit? Carmen didn't know where the responsibilities rested, but she also didn't think it made much difference whether one was homosexual or heterosexual. She just wanted to be loved, to be happy, and she didn't want to suffer any pain for it.

On the road, life felt like a water lily disengaged from the stem. Instead of swaying in a pond, the Happys and Carmens of this world swept from bank to bank, hurtling ever onward. No one knew to what end until she reached it, but as she grew older on the tour, each woman knew she was born to that end on swift currents of sorrow.

◆ ◆ ◆

During the Oakland, California, tournament the players resided in the Roach Acapulco Hotel[1], or so they called it. The only night off that Carmen had, she and Harriet drove into San Francisco with Miguel and Beanie. Harriet loved the Hayes Street Grille so they ate there, went to a movie, and then drove back. Given Carmen's and Beanie's schedules, the little outing was a big event. The only other noteworthy event at the Oakland tournament, other than another Semana sweep to victory, was an incident involving an ice cream vendor. When the players would switch sides on the odd-numbered games, all the vendors would rush through the aisles hawking their wares. One ice cream vendor, his silvered box hung around his neck, tripped while coming down the stairs. As he fell, the lid to his box popped open, and ice cream spilled everywhere. The fans sitting around him scooped up the cups of fudge ripple and banana creme and grabbed the vanilla Popsicles. As spectators reached for the brightly wrapped ice creams, he stepped on their hands and finally lay down on the steps to cover his precious wares. Of course, his ice creams melted all over him. The fans handed him back what they picked up; no one ever intended to eat the stuff. His mistrust cost him an entire box of frozen delights.

Miguel watched this from his seat, tears of laughter rolling down his cheeks. The ice cream shouldn't have been sold after it fell out, so the vendor's investment was lost anyway. If he possessed any Argentine flair, he would have cheerfully handed out the Popsicles for free. What the hell, he might as well make other people happy. But not this guy. If he couldn't get what he wanted, then the spectators couldn't have what they wanted. How American.

♦ ♦ ♦

A tail flicked over Harriet's nose. Baby Jesus had positioned herself next to Harriet's face, then thrashed her tail wildly. In eighteen years this ploy had never failed.

"Good morning, Baby."

Carmen moaned, still sound asleep. Baby meowed.

Harriet's feet hit the floor, and as always when she was home, she went first to the window that overlooked the long lake. Frost zigzagged on the windowpane. The hills looked like purple breasts. Baby walked over and rubbed against her leg. Time to get up.

A door slammed downstairs; Miguel was up. Harriet felt imprisoned in her own home. On the road, tennis kept him in line.

Baby thumped down the stairs. Harriet walked into the

kitchen where Miguel smiled, bid her good morning, and returned to the newspaper.

Baby Jesus disdained Miguel Semana. Possibly it was his cologne that set her off, or perhaps she didn't like him as a person. In eighteen years, Baby had given Harriet her expert opinion on many people.

Harriet opened a can of cat food. Baby rubbed against her leg more frantically. She was hungry.

Baby smacked her lips when she ate. Her teeth were going bad. She walked with some arthritis in her hips but her ears and eyes were good. Her heart was sound and her senses were as keen as ever.

"If I have to grow old, I want to grow old like Baby Jesus," Harriet thought. "The human models stink."

"The coffee's hot." Miguel put down the paper and graciously poured her a cup.

"Thanks, Miguel." While he was pouring, the cat stole one of his link sausages. She raced into the pantry with her prize. Harriet said nothing.

"Do you know Seth Quintard well?"

"Not really. He's Carmen's agent."

"Where's my other sausage? I'm sure I had another sausage."

A triumphant puss paraded through the kitchen. She reeked of victory and sausage. Miguel observed her. "She suddenly looks fat." He laughed. He turned to Harriet again. "You don't know much about contracts?"

"Miguel, I keep out of it. It's not my business. If Carmen asks me, I'll give her my opinion, but otherwise I say little."

"I think Athletes Unlimited is cheating my sister." He laid down his spoon for emphasis.

"Oh."

"When she gets paid for an endorsement, they hold the checks up to three or four months. Of course, they deposit the money and earn a big interest!"

"I never thought of that."

He said magnanimously, "You're too pretty to think of such things. That's what I'm here for."

"Thank you, Miguel."

Baby Jesus burped underneath the table.

FIVE

L os Angeles, clinging to the Pacific, exerted a strange, erotic power over all who lived in its vast territory. Sir Francis Drake landed on the California coast on June 17, 1579. Since then, a flood of people made the same delightful discovery.

The tennis tournament was a big affair. The sponsors, players, and administration looked forward to the first week in March; there was time to get in and out before the smog destroyed one's eyes, nose, and throat.

With the exception of Page Bartlett Campbell, who wouldn't hit the circuit until the French Open, everyone showed up in LA. Susan Reilly would die before she'd miss it. Harriet uncharitably wished she would. Rainey Rogers was there and her mother was in evidence everywhere. Her oversized purse was on the coffee table in the players' lounge, her conservatively cut linen jacket was hung neatly on the back of a chair, and her game charts were stacked on the seat. Mrs. Rogers herself was chatting up reporters. She and her husband had masterminded Rainey's career from the time Rainey first showed promise. The kid was eight then. The Rogerses had sacrificed everything for their middle daughter. Their assessment of her skill was accurate; their contribution to her already developed discipline was valuable. The Rogerses never pushed. They trolled Rainey along by all those invisible hooks middle-class parents manage to sink into their children. Between Rainey and her mother, it was a toss-up as to who was the spider and who was the fly. Right now, it didn't matter. That problem would surface many tournaments later, many years down the line. For now the problem was how to win LA, how to give notice to Susan, Carmen, and the growing Hilda that Rainey would soon reign. The sportswriters played with that one ad nauseam.

"Going Hollywood?" inquired Harriet. Jane Fulton was wearing a glitter T-shirt, Donald Duck sunglasses, and jelly sandals. "Did you actually conceive of that outfit yourself?"

"Ricky helped. He's wearing a bicycle chain for a necklace. Did you see the draw?"

"Yeah, Carmen and Susan are on the same side of the draw."

"I worry about Susan off the court more than on." Jane took off her sunglasses.

"What can she do?"

"Call it a woman's instinct. She'll find Carmen's Achilles' heel."

"I still don't see what she can do."

Jane shrugged. "Damned if I know. It's just a feeling. If Carmen doesn't nail down the first two events of the Grand Slam, there will be no crisis. But if she gets close to that Slam, I tell you Susan will go crazy."

"I hope you're wrong." Harriet played with Jane's sunglasses. "How do I look?"

"I looked better. Here, you take Mickey Mouse." Jane handed her a blue pair of kiddie sunglasses.

"Thank you."

"Susan knows one thing."

"What, MizJane?"

"She knows that Carmen can take trouble on the court but not in her life."

"Carmen does have a propensity to stick her head in the sand."

"Or run away." Jane peered through her Donald Duck glasses. "You know, she's in a world that formalizes conflict and protects her from everything except tennis. That's not exactly preparation for life's continual assault on one's narcissism."

♦ ♦ ♦

Wearing enough gold to qualify as the legendary El Dorado, Lavinia Sibley Archer in a crescendo of bad taste held court in Los Angeles. Although she fancied herself to be above such tripe, she adored mingling with movie stars. Movie stars liked to be seen at sporting events. Movie stars liked to be seen, period. Everybody got what they wanted: attention. Lavinia fluttered over an aging male star with barely a body part left to call his own. He'd just completed another spy movie. He reposed in the box of honor, and soon Lavinia dumped herself down next to him and listened with exaggerated fascination to tales of his meager tennis ability. Her false eyelashes bowed as before a king.

The star graciously asked about the upcoming match. Was it really true that Carmen Semana and Susan Reilly hated one another?

"Hate? Let's say they have no love lost."

"Weren't they doubles partners? I know I've been on location for every major tournament for the last ten years, deary, but I seem to remember them being doubles partners a couple of years back."

"All the girls are like a set of junior high school kids. There's cliques, friendships, broken friendships. A tempest in a teapot."

"We live in the same teapot over at Warner Brothers."

"Saw your last film." She registered proper enthusiasm. "Very heaven."

"Thank you, but it takes more than one person to make a film, Mrs. Archer."

"Please, call me Lavinia. While it may take more than one person to make a film, it takes a star to bring in the public."

He shrugged in manly nonchalance over what he believed to be a total truth. The conversation was cut short by the usual parade of officials, ball boys, and ball girls in the required forest green.

"Excuse me, Mr. Ridgeback, I've got to be on court for a few moments."

"I shall eagerly await your return." He rose and guided her out of the box.

Once in front of the microphone, Lavinia displayed her loquaciousness. During this monologue, Harriet and Miguel positioned themselves in a local sponsor's box. Again, Miguel was asked to stand by a seemingly overjoyed Carmen. Miguel was getting into being a star-once-removed. After that touch of manufactured family love, Lavinia returned to her theme of the old days.

Finally the match began. Miranda Mexata steadied herself in the chair. Which way would the wind blow today?

Susan served deep and followed the serve into the net. Her strokes were fluid and solid. Susan was never a graceful player, but she was exciting. She moved well.

Carmen was far more graceful. She hurried only on those occasions when she was pulled wide or caught wrong-footed. Susan could destroy an opponent's rhythm, but today Carmen was loose. She'd eaten her usual breakfast and teased Harriet about another cat novel from the inexhaustible pen of Baby Jesus: Catnip, Great Catnappings in the Feline World. Both women ignored Miguel, the prematch tension, and their feelings about Susan.

Carmen had moments where she went into what Harriet called The Zone. Carmen, the Ozone Cookie, could float off into her own world. She did this when things really bothered her or when she was tired. Oftentimes, the higher Carmen's spirits, the more worried she was at a subconscious level.

Today, the escape worked. She was playing out of her head. Susan played well, but Carmen literally was in another world. Every shot felt like a hot knife through butter. Every serve left a shimmer down her forearm, a shot of coordination. She could feel the ball even when it was on her opponent's side of the court. Tight as the match was—Susan never gave away anything—Carmen possessed magic. Moving like a ballerina in time with beautiful music, Carmen hit winner after winner.

Susan clung on with her fingernails. She chased down each ball like a wild woman. She lunged, leapt, and lashed at the ball. She made returns that were impossible. Yet Carmen flicked her godlike wrist, and batted the ball away like an irritating gnat. It was an awesome display of talent.

Carmen put Susan down at six-four, six-four. The crowd was dazzled by Carmen's lyrical athleticism and amazed by Susan's concentrated will. As they walked to the net to shake hands, there was a collective intake of breath. Susan reached across and shook her opponent's hand. Relieved, Carmen genuinely shook her hand in return. Susan smiled a penetrating, unsettling gaze.

◆ ◆ ◆

Susan sat in her room and drank a Perrier with lime. Alicia sat silently on the sofa. It was not a good idea to talk to Susan after a loss. Susan played and replayed each point. She could recall points she'd played in high school. Had she ever shown any intellectual discipline, Susan Reilly would have forged a first-class mind. Now she forged her weapon.

"What are you thinking?" Susan asked Alicia.

"Nothing."

"What'd you think of the match?"

"No one could have beaten Carmen today."

"Every dog has its day?" Susan asked rhetorically.

"I guess so."

"It's the wheel of fortune. Did you ever see a tarot deck?"

"No." Alicia stuck close to the Bible. The occult was tainted with paganism.

"It's interesting, the tarot deck." Susan's eyes blazed like small laser beams. "It's another way to look at the world. Maybe it's a form of lost knowledge. Anyway, the wheel of fortune is a card showing a turning wheel. One person is up; another person is down. The wheel never stops turning."

"You'll be up."

"Yeah."

"If Carmen plays like that tomorrow, Rainey Rogers will get swamped."

"Maybe. Carmen has a curious habit of underrating her opponents when she's on top of her form. It'll catch up."

"The wheel of fortune?"

"Sometimes you have to give the wheel a push, I think." Susan swung her legs over the bed. She was back in the present. Alicia could breathe again.

◆ ◆ ◆

Gary Shorter, Rainey Rogers's coach, never had an idea above the waist. He fiddled with Rainey's many racquets; he checked the tension in the strings, the weight, the grip. Mrs. Rogers withdrew into her prematch trance. She fetched whatever her daughter needed, but she was rerouting her energy, preparing for the match the same as Rainey.

Rainey painted Tomahawk's Hot and Wild Pink on her fingernails. She brushed a thin layer of pearl over that. Her tennis dress was pale pink and edged with bugle beads to catch the lights.

Rainey thought about her game plan. Carmen at her best was unbeatable, but if Rainey could cause a hairline fracture in that confidence, then Carmen could be beaten. In two more years Carmen would be struggling to get into the finals. Rainey, like a duke defending his castle, withstood the assaults of Carmen. In her mind, it was the warfare of attackers and defenders. She stayed in the backcourt, her castle walls, while Carmen mounted wave after wave of attack. Rainey's bread-and-butter shot was a sharp, short crosscourt to Carmen's backhand. The cumulative effect of that shot was like a great boxer's left jab. Flick, flick, it looks as though it causes no damage. As time wears on, that flick wears down the opponent, kills his spirit, and he's open to the crushing finish. Rainey never took a match longer than she had to. She'd learned at eighteen if you've got your woman on the ropes, finish her off. In the end, it's a greater mercy.

"How's your blister?" Mrs. Rogers inquired. The blister was nothing more than a small red rub at her heel, but all athletes are hypochondriacs, so in Rainey's mind this was serious.

"I'm putting moleskin on it."

"Good." Mrs. Rogers picked up the shoe and pressed the back of it with her thumbs. "That shoe company! How many times have we told them exactly what we want? This is a little tight." She pressed on it some more. "There, that ought to help."

◆ ◆ ◆

Carmen hastened one busboy's nervous breakdown the morning of the LA finals. She snarled at the garageman who brought up the rental car. She glowered at her brother who for once in his life shut up, and she drove like an Indy 500 contestant on her way to the coliseum. Harriet, sitting in the front seat, tried to ignore the blur of buildings whizzing by. For Carmen, speed was a release and a feeling of power.

When they got to the courts, Harriet headed for her seat.

There was little to do for Carmen when she was in a mood, and as far as Harriet was concerned, Carmen had a right to her moods. But Harriet also felt she had a right to clear out. When Carmen fumed in psyching herself up, she spewed her venom on whomever was at hand. Rainey was a tough opponent. Carmen was infuriated by her style of tennis, she hated to play her, and her mounting discontent couldn't be contained.

The women's indoor surface was carpet laid over, in most cases, wood. This fast surface favored Carmen. Short of the flu, cramps, or disinterest, Carmen should win on carpet. If her first serve soured, life could be rough because she needed to get her first serve in deep so she could rush the net. Against a backcourt player of Rainey's caliber, the first serve was crucial. If Carmen couldn't get to the net, she couldn't win.

Her serve resembled a rocket. Carmen enjoyed such a good day that she squashed Rainey in two sets flat.

After the match, Rainey, her coach, and her mother dissected the defeat. Mrs. Rogers diagrammed each point for Rainey to study later.

Rainey used every defeat. She'd practice hours to widen the angle on her backhand crosscourt. She'd never own a demolishing serve but she intended to own the most accurate, which in the long run was more deadly anyway. Rainey believed that time was on her side. Her disciplined personality and the nature of her game would wear down the Carmens of this world, if not this year, then the next.

• • •

Exultant, Carmen drank a much deserved beer. A portable tape deck blared in the background. She lifted the beer bottle. "On to Dallas."

"Vulgopolis," Harriet toasted back.

"I don't know why, but that reminds me of what you told me once when I wanted to buy that Gucci chair."

"That awful thing."

"You said, 'Money without taste is like sex without love.'"

"How clever of me." Harriet kissed Carmen on the cheek. Someone knocked on the door.

"Who is it?"

"Miguel."

Carmen grunted and got up to admit her brother.

"Migueletta, my tiger."

"Where were you? I thought you'd come to the press conference."

"Business."

"Martin Kuzirian pissed me off. I wish you'd been there. He asked the stupidest questions." Martin Kuzirian, sports reporter for a huge Long Island newspaper, wrote a nationally syndicated column. In the sports world that spelled big cheese.

"Sports reporters represent the lowest form of journalism," Miguel commented as he sipped out of the beer bottle. "If they could be athletes, they would be. If they could be writers, they would be. In short, they can do neither."

Carmen punched her brother on the bicep. "That's right!"

Miguel scanned Carmen's dresser. "What are you doing, leaving your jewelry out like that?" He turned to Harriet. "How can you let her do that?"

"Miguel," Harriet coolly replied, "I am not her mother."

With his right hand he swept the bracelets, necklaces, rings, and earrings into his left hand. "From now on, I take charge of the jewelry! At each tournament, I'll put it in the hotel's safe deposit box. When you want a piece, you ask for it."

"That's too much trouble."

"Less trouble than being robbed."

"I'm insured."

He shook his head. "Little sister, why invite trouble? And since when has an insurer lived up to the policy?"

"He's right about that," Harriet agreed, even though she found this situation oddly repellent.

"There, see? The lovely Señorita Rawls has common sense."

"And I don't?" Carmen flared.

"You are God's gift to tennis. You don't have to do anything but play. We'll do the rest." He gestured to include Harriet, and she now felt this wasn't oddly repulsive, it was truly repulsive.

◆ ◆ ◆

If Miguel's intrusion into her business life troubled Carmen, she didn't show it. As long as she had money when she wanted it, she didn't much care about the details. The power to buy things fascinated her. The loss of geographic community and social stability was replaced with cash. What were roots compared to that glorified Volkswagen, the Porsche? The dollar was more important than the deed.

Modern professional sports rewards players for function instead of character. Responsibility is narrowly defined as doing a job better than anyone else. Emotional, social, or political responsibility is not even imagined. The fault lies not with sport. Sport is only a symbol of the fragmentation of life, a fragmentation begun with the industrial revolution which seems to pit each against all in a struggle for material goods. Spiritual, emotional, political concerns will fall by the wayside in this violent rush to get things.

Win and become a god. Lose and be forgotten. Carmen and Miguel had no resistance to the temptation of money and fame. Why should they? They'd never seen the alternative. Much as Theresa and Arturo Semana loved their children, they never bothered to supply them with any standards other than external achievement. Perhaps because they were young in the 1930's and remembered what the Depression was like in Buenos Aires they never got beyond material concerns themselves.

Every generation has a dark side like the moon. One is born into a time and has one's own experiences, but one also carries within herself the distilled experiences of her parents. Carmen and Miguel were truly the offspring of their parents. Winning was all that mattered.

♦ ♦ ♦

Whatever Lavinia's faults, an unwillingness to work was not one of them. She fired off orders to her staff and expected them to be obeyed. If anyone had cared to find out, they would have discovered Lavinia pushed herself harder than she pushed anyone else. As a player and now as a businesswoman, Lavinia demanded perfection.

Lavinia dialed Betty Bainbridge, wife of Jensen Bainbridge, head of Clark & Clark Pharmaceuticals. Betty was still a good club player, even though she was in her early sixties. Both women remembered tennis when men wore white flannel trousers.

"Hello," answered a voice from far-off Westchester, New York.

"Betty Bainbridge, it's Lavinia."

"Vinnie! What rathole are you in now?"

"Dallas."

"Poor darling. I had two sisters, you know. One died and the other lives in Dallas. It's so good to hear your voice."

"How's your health?"

"Just had a physical last week. No more problems. I still hate those damned examinations, Vinnie. I've been in the stirrups more times than Princess Anne."

Lavinia laughed. "How's Jensen's health?"

"He's fine."

"I heard a rumor that he was retiring."

Betty, silent, inhaled deeply. She spoke at a measured pace. "He loves the power, you know."

"Who wouldn't?" Lavinia asked.

Betty waited, then said, "Lavinia, none of us are getting any younger. He's eight years older than I am. We've seen too many friends die these last years. I want him to slow down."

"Yes, he works too hard."

"You might slow down yourself. There's more beauty in a sunset than in power, Vin."

"I'm not ready yet."

"I'll give a dinner party during the Championships." Betty changed the subject. "March twenty-seventh? Black tie."

"I'll be sure to wear one."

"Silly. Thanks for calling. I look forward to seeing you."

"The twenty-seventh. Bye."

"Bye." Betty hung up the phone.

Lavinia doodled on a notepad. Betty had told her everything she needed to know without once betraying a corporate secret. The Old Girl Network came through one more time.

◆ ◆ ◆

Susan Reilly's house in Pacific Heights, San Francisco, represented years of labor, but as she spent little time in the place, she was detached from it. The rooms were adequately furnished. It was her permanent rest place and not yet a true home. Susan took off this week while the tour was in Texas.

Craig and Lisa Reilly lived in Marin County. Susan saw as much of her child and as little of her husband as possible. Whenever she was interviewed by adult gossip magazines, the photos were always taken at the Marin County house.

She cradled the telephone to her ear. "That's a California law. Uh-huh." Pause. "Check it out. I'll be here until March twenty-second, then I'll be in New York for the Championships." Pause. "Okay, Jerry, talk to you later, thanks."

Alicia bounced into the bedroom. "Who was that?"

"Oh, nobody." A flicker of irritation showed on Susan's face. "Black cord fever. You know how I get."

Alicia did know that Susan could make phone calls to every part of the world at any time of day or night. This call did not smack of black cord fever. "It wasn't Happy Straker, was it?"

"No. I have nothing to say to Happy this morning." She rubbed her hands. The newsprint from the morning paper smeared her fingers.

"I think Happy's still in love with you."

"After all these years? Nah." She picked up the sports pages.

"Why hasn't she found anyone else?"

"Look at her."

"Susan, that's cruel. You loved her."

"I never loved Happy. Being with her was an act of mercy on my part. I couldn't look at those sad puppy eyes. I felt sorry for her. It was a mistake."

"Hm-m-m-m." Alicia stared out the window. They had a spectacular view of the bay and Alcatraz.

"Will you bring me another pot of coffee, please?" Susan didn't look up from her paper.

Alicia headed for the kitchen and the coffee maker. She filled Lucite cannisters with a variety of exotic coffee beans, priding herself on her brew. Alicia, caught in a web of needs, her own and Susan's, little realized how narrow her life was becoming. She was concentrating less on her own tennis and more on Susan's needs.

Susan accepted America's definition of work. That meant Susan's work was important, while Alicia's work, that of maintaining Susan, was insignificant. A married man might take his wife for granted, but on some level he did know her contributions existed. For Susan, women's work was so alien that she placed no value on it at all. She spent her life perfecting one, isolated skill. Her parents had given her no housework training nor had they even taught her that it was important.

Alicia, saddled with the shitwork, became invisible. If she had stood up for herself, saying, "What I do for you and for both of us is important even though I don't win tournaments," Susan would have blown her out of the room. Why did Alicia do these things? Had Susan asked for a wife? Alicia did them for love. Susan set it up so she need never comprehend what anyone did for her. If a person asked for equality, especially a lover, Susan unceremoniously terminated the relationship. She could not grant anyone equal status with herself. She resembled a lot of men in that respect. A wife, if a marriage broke up, could claim that her former husband be accountable to her. Alicia, when bounced, would get nothing. She'd keep her jewelry and the clothing Susan bought her in those moments of studied generosity. The house she cleaned, the secretary she organized, and the maid she directed would stay Susan's. Alicia was giving her life away with each breath and didn't know it. Susan paid the bills and asked for no money in return, not because she was generous, but because she wanted her own way. As long as she could look at her checkbook and know it was fatter than Alicia's, she felt powerful.

Alicia hummed as the coffee aroma filled the kitchen. If she felt Susan had calluses on her soul, she never betrayed it, but then Alicia betrayed very little. The only clue to her secret life was her fervent reading of the New Testament.

SIX ✦✦✦

✦ ✦ ✦   ✦ ✦ ✦

Madison Square Garden is a good arena for players and good for spectators. Arenas don't often provide one with the other. Harriet snaked her way through the crowd, a healthy number for an opening night, and sat next to Miguel, who dazzled tonight. He'd received the money from Dennis Parry at Amalgamated Interstate Banks, and he felt on top of the world. Harriet waved to Ricky and Jane up in the booth. Ricky stuck out his tongue. The Garden was full of high society and those merely high. One fellow in the same box as Harriet was so full of pills that if shaken, he would have sounded like a baby's rattle.

Rainey Rogers was on the first match. She bounced on the court like a graduated pom-pom girl. Lavinia Sibley Archer, shimmering in yet another yellow dress, performed the introductions. She brought it off in under ten minutes, a marvel for Lavinia.

Harriet usually watched only Carmen's matches. One could OD on tennis even when played at this exalted level. She left midway through the match because Miguel was trying to impress a sponsor with his fathomless knowledge of the game. For some reason, she couldn't stand to hear it one more time.

✦ ✦ ✦

Harriet wandered into the locker room.

"Did you call the accountant?" Carmen asked as she did her stretching exercises.

"Yes."

"I can't believe they're going to audit me again. Between your government and mine, I'm lucky I make a penny." Carmen was keyed up, but that was nothing new before a match.

"Passover's coming up mid-April. Maybe we could hire the Angel of Death for a return engagement. This time let's forget the firstborn and concentrate on IRS employees."

"Yeah." Carmen rotated her knee. "Know what Ricky told me today? He said Bill Tilden squandered his money producing plays so he could star in them. He also forgot to brush his teeth. Some people swear he never brushed his teeth." She rubbed her shoulder. "Isn't that weird? He was the greatest tennis player in the world, but he wanted to be something else."

"There's a running thread. He wanted to be looked at, whether on the court or on the stage. He had talent in one field and not the other. That happens a lot."

"All the halfbacks who go on to comment for ABC and last two shows?" Carmen grunted.

"It's a tough transition. Once you have all that artificial attention, which isn't to say you didn't earn it, it's hard to let it go."

"You as in me, or you as in general."

Harriet considered this. "Both, I guess."

"I am nowhere near retiring," Carmen stated quickly and emphatically.

"I never said you were."

"You can teach forever."

Harriet sighed. Sometimes the road even got to Carmen, the eternal gypsy. "We've had this discussion before."

Carmen snorted. "I fired Seth Quintard and Athletes Unlimited today."

The news caught Harriet off guard. "Why?"

"Miguel pointed out to me that they hold my money long enough to make interest on it. And, this I never thought of, I'm one of many to them."

"Hardly. You're the best player in the world."

Carmen acknowledged this with a smile. "Still, Miguel is taking over. With him, I'll always be number one."

Disturbed, Harriet said only, "Yes." She picked up a dog-eared deck of cards and absentmindedly dealt herself a hand of solitaire.

After watching one game, Carmen couldn't stand the quiet. "What are you thinking?"

As usual when Harriet was worried, she resorted to humor. "Oh, I was just stewing." She snapped the deck together and reshuffled. "Wages are down. Costs and unemployment are up. I can't find jelly-filled donuts. Gas stations don't give free glasses anymore. Telephone operators try to listen in on conversations, but discover the government got there first."

Carmen, her good spirits restored, laughed. She loved Harriet when she made her laugh.

◆ ◆ ◆

Rainey Rogers's game was as familiar to Miguel as his own. In analyzing people's strengths and weaknesses he was superb. Rainey had no glaring weaknesses. While not the quickest, she had speed. While not the strongest, she was tenacious. Her only real weakness was a tendency to avoid the net; the tiniest bit gun-shy, she blinked once too often when balls were rifled at her. Not that she fell apart at the net, but she didn't usually press home an advantage by swiftly moving in for the ball. She preferred to administer slow death from behind the baseline.

Miguel stayed in the ringside box because he wanted to

avoid Seth Quintard. Seth tromped in, however, sat beside him, and coldly waited for Rainey's match to end. Her matches seemed interminable but eventually they did finish.

Rainey had just reached across the net to shake the hand of her defeated foe when Seth started. "Mr. Semana, I have reason to believe you encouraged your sister to terminate her relationship with Athletes Unlimited."

Feigning surprise, Miguel replied, "I am close to my sister, true, but she makes her own decisions."

Seth leaned over. "It's a big mistake. We know what every other athlete gets for endorsements. No one can under-purchase her services because we know to the penny what the market value is on everyone."

"Of course." Miguel nodded.

"She belongs with us."

"She feels otherwise."

"Look, Miguel, cut the bullshit. You told her we invest her commissions and delay payment for the three- or four-month term of those investments."

Miguel did not appreciate the direct approach. "There is some delay in payments, Mr. Quintard."

"Even if that were true, and I'm not saying it is, we can do more for your sister than anyone in this business."

"Perhaps, but from now on I am managing her financial and contractual affairs."

Furious at losing the account, Quintard exploded. "I don't know what the brotherly version of a gigolo is, Semana, but you fucking qualify."

Miguel's face burned with hatred. He grabbed Seth by the necktie. "Get out."

Undaunted, Seth Quintard continued. "And further-more, you slimy spic, I know about the cocaine in the racquet handles."

Without releasing Quintard's necktie, Miguel leapt to his feet and dragged Seth up, too. He hauled him outside and hurled him down the back stairs behind the box.

Seth rubbed his neck. He scrambled to his feet and rasped, "You'll pay for this. If it takes me ten fucking years, you'll pay."

Miguel already turned his back and was walking away. Surprisingly few people observed the sordid drama. Those that did were unenlightened fans who assumed two guys had a little too much to drink.

Miguel stormed past the guards and walked outside. How in God's name did Seth know about the cocaine?

Miguel was a small-time smuggler. It was easy for him to acquire quality coke when home. He would bore out racquet handles and bring the drug through customs. When he accompanied Carmen, he was never searched. He didn't make a habit of it; it was an occasional sideline. Miguel always knew whom to contact if the right parties were looking. But he had no desire to be a full-time dealer. In fact, he only had two steady customers.

One of his customers, Ronnie Baldwin, a handsome male tennis player, would put the coke in a gelatin capsule and insert it in his asshole. The first set he would play relatively straight while his body heat was melting the capsule. For the second set and part of the third, he would be playing like a maniac. Of course, if his match went to four or five sets, he would be in trouble, so for emergencies he would keep some coke in a cup on the sidelines bench.

Then it hit Miguel. That bastard Baldwin belonged in Athletes Unlimited's stable. He must have squeaked. Why, Miguel couldn't imagine. Christ, he'd done this guy a favor by getting him such quality stuff. Someone must have put the screws on him. His game was on the way down. Maybe he lost a contract and was looking for a scapegoat.

Quintard couldn't have found out from Miguel's other customer. She was a New York socialite of impeccable origins. Seth didn't know people like that.

Miguel was shaking. He knew Seth wouldn't pin a coke rap on Carmen; she knew nothing. He couldn't pin a coke rap on Miguel either without jeopardizing men's tennis. If Seth was bent on revenge, he'd have to be imaginative. And from examining Carmen's contracts, he feared Seth could be just that.

◆ ◆ ◆

High above Central Park, ensconced in a friend's apartment, Susan listened to her lawyer. She had won her match handily, which put her in a good mood. He put her in an even better mood.

"You're at the office late. I thought everybody partied in San Francisco after sunset."

"All work and no play makes Jerry a dull boy," Jerry Hammer explained. "I checked out your problem. In some states where you play, homosexuality is a felony. An alien with a green card must abide by the laws of the state she resides in as well as by the federal laws."

"Which means what?"

"It means if your friend is caught in a homosexual act in, say, New Hampshire, and her homosexuality is known to the authorities, she could conceivably be deported to Argentina. Of course, you know homosexuality doesn't sit well in that country either. They're terrible on the issue. She's in a spot."

"She's only in a spot if people know. Is there any way around a fight if"—Susan halted—"if bad luck should strike her?"

"She could protest it legally, but her chances of staying in this country would be severely jeopardized."

"That's too bad." Susan reeked of concern.

"Susan, I'd be happy to help her out if disaster should strike. Is this a close friend?"

"An old friend."

"Tell her to be careful," Jerry counseled.

"I'll do that. Thanks, Jerry. I appreciate it." Susan paused. "You want a racquet autographed to Tiffany? I'll put it in the mail tomorrow."

"She'll be over the moon," Jerry said. "See you next time you're home."

"Thanks again."

"Bye."

"Good-bye."

♦ ♦ ♦

Jane and Ricky suffered a spat, during which he called the women's movement a home for aging Campfire Girls, and she said men grow old, they don't grow up.

Jane telephoned Harriet. "When the going gets tough, the tough go shopping."

Harriet, who knew better than to ask the details, agreed to meet her at 1:30 P.M. on the corner of 57th and 5th.

Jane greeted her. "He's such a prick."

"You, of course, are unimpeachable."

"Don't be reasonable, Harriet. I can't stand it when you're reasonable. He's getting like the players, you know? Those people never use toilet paper. Everyone is kissing their ass!" Jane put up her hand. "Don't say anything. What can we do?"

"We could think of twenty-three ways to decorate our uterine walls."

Jane struggled now to maintain her bad mood. "Well, I for one am going to spend money. Here, let's look at what I've got." Jane yanked a fistful of credit cards out of her purse. "American Express, we never leave home without it. Master-Card, Visa, Playboy. He's such a shit. Sears and Roebuck, can't use that. Saks Fifth Avenue, goody. I. Magnin, wrong part of the country. Garfinckel's, nope. Ah, ha! B. Altman.

Our Chase Convenience Card. The jackpot, Bloomie's! Let's hit Tiffany's first. We have an account there."

"All that colored plastic reminds me of the candy counter in the movies. Those cards are adult Jujubes."

"Saturday morning at the Ritz." Jane twirled through the Tiffany's doors. Harriet spun around twice. Jane pulled her out. "I bet you I can remember more candies than you can."

"I bet you can't."

"What's the bet, then?" Jane's mood improved immediately.

"A Tiffany stickpin."

"You're on, Rawls. There's a golden knot that I'm dying to have."

"I want the golden cube, and don't count your chickens."

"Ready?"

"Ready."

Jane recited her childhood sugar binges. "Almond Cluster, Almond Joy, Baby Ruth, Malted Milk Balls, Butterfinger, Butternut, um-m-m-m. Charleston Chew, loved that one. Hershey's Kisses. Fifth Avenue Bar, Clark Bar, Big Ben Jellies, Mary Jane, Milky Way, Payday." She slowed down. "Raisinets!"

"It occurs to me that you have the advantage by going first. It's like first serve."

"You should have said that in the beginning. You've got a mouth."

"Jane Fulton, you're a horse trader. Now let me try. How many did you get? I counted fifteen. You count for me."

Harriet closed her eyes by the stationery counter and pictured the glass counter next to the greasy popcorn machine at her childhood theater, The Southern. "Here goes. Tootsie Roll."

"How could I forget that one!"

"Jane, you'll break my train of thought."

"Sorry."

"Okay. Three Musketeers."

Jane moaned.

"Will you stop? I've only got two. Now, Sugar Daddy, Sugar Babies, Sugar Mama."

"Harriet, that's cheating."

"Oh, no, it's not. Each one of these was a separate candy."

Jane rested her elbow on the stationery counter and frowned. "You know, I've always respected you, Harriet."

"Shut up, Jane. I refuse to have you interrupt me one more time. Keep counting! Snickers, Red Hot Dollars."

Jane began to yelp.

Harriet put her hand over Jane's mouth and kept on, "North Pole, Nutty Crunch, Necco Wafers, Mr. Goodbar."

Jane bit Harriet's hand to make her let go. "That's literature." Jane wiped her mouth.

"That's a candy bar, and you know it. Baffle Bars and Bit-O-Honey, Black Crows, Pearson's Coffee Nips, Diamond Drops, Whirligigs, and Jube Jels. How many's that?"

"Eighteen." Jane jumped up. "Milk Maid. Sixteen. Eagle Bar and Poppycock. We're even! I've got to think of one more. Got it! M&M's."

"So I need two to win."

"Unless I think of more."

Harriet rested her chin in her hand. "Liberty Mints, Sour Balls, and Horehound Drops."

"Horehound Drops. Really." Jane thought hard. "Okay. Virginia Nut Roll."

"Chunky."

"You already said that one."

"Jane, I did not."

"You did, too."

"Goddammit, no wonder Ricky got pissed. Okay, smartmouth. Krackel Bar." She drew out her breath. "Orange Slices."

"Safe-T-Pops!" Jane shouted. People in the store pretended not to notice. The man behind the stationery counter, tied down by an elderly customer hovering between pale blue paper and hot pink, snobbishly ignored the two women.

"Fruit n' Nut Bar and Starlight Mints."

"Jujubes." Jane smiled.

"No fair. I said that to start us off."

"You didn't say it once we got under way."

"You're a sneaking fart."

"Do you eat with that mouth?"

"We all know whom."

"Oh, Harriet, must we lower ourselves to sexual banter? Either you know of more candies or you don't."

"What's the score?"

Jane innocently rolled her eyes. "I forgot."

"I didn't." Harriet tallied the marks on her little address book. "You've got twenty-two, and I've got twenty-six."

"You're so smug." Jane concentrated. "Pom-Poms, wait, don't rush me. Merrimints."

"York Peppermint Patties." Harriet resembled Ming the Merciless.

Jane thought. She thought some more. She walked once around the stationery counter. "You win."

"Good! I'll take that stickpin right now. Thank you very much."

Jane grumbled as the lady behind the counter handed the coveted stickpin to Harriet. "A moment of silence, please, as I honor my vanished income."

◆ ◆ ◆

A tide of feathers and tulips washed over the downstairs room of the expensive restaurant. Howard Dominick was introducing a new Tomahawk line: Pocahontas. Talcum powder in boxes shaped like tepees rose out of the center of the tulips and feathers. Tiny samples of Pocahontas perfume floated overhead; each sample was tied to a yellow balloon. The douche powder of identical fragrance was tastefully displayed in a corner. Not content with his new line, Howard lined one entire wall with other Tomahawk products. Autumn Plum nail polish vied with Mocha Maid lipstick.

Lavinia wore yellow. Until she moved, she might have passed for a very large tulip. The ice sculpture, a large tomahawk, was melting slowly.

Howard threw a huge party every year during the New York championships. Although the Washington, D.C., tournament was the culmination of the circuit in terms of player points, it was small potatoes in terms of business. In New York Howard made his deals, ran his division, and impressed or depressed his competition. Naturally he invited them to every party.

Miguel's white teeth glistened beneath his jet-black moustache. Tatiania Mandelstam, the empress of Tomahawk's fiercest competition, listened to him with rapt attention.

"Señora, how do you do it? You have discovered the secret of youth."

The elderly lady tossed her head. She was accustomed to homage. "Not at all, Mr. Semana. I simply practice what I preach—exercise, good food, and religious application of my cosmetics."

"Then I shall buy your magic potions by the case."

"I'm coming out with a men's cosmetics line this fall." Her dark eyes brightened.

"I was born at the right moment." He reached for a waiter's tray, picked up a glass of champagne, and handed it to the empress. "Why let Tomahawk have all the fun?"

She smoothly brought the glass to her lips and smiled. She was interested.

"Tomahawk gets free use of the girls. Youth. Health. Freshness. But not one of them is identified with a special line. For instance, Rainey Rogers doesn't represent Pocahontas."

Tatiania listened. She knew the industry, and more importantly, she knew her customers. "Go on."

"Wouldn't it be wonderful if my sister Carmen represented a new sports fragrance you might be developing?"

Tatiania appeared to consider this, then looked directly into Miguel's handsome face. "Wonderful for your sister, but not for us."

Perplexed, Miguel kept smiling.

She continued. "You see, Carmen does not have the right image for us."

"But she's young and the picture of health. Little girls and teenagers write her so much fan mail."

"About tennis, no doubt." She set her empty goblet down on yet another waiter's tray. "Tennis and glamor are two contradictory pursuits, my good man. Your accomplished sister may be the picture of health, but she is not the picture of femininity. Tatiania Cosmetics promotes woman as the ultimate mystery. You could paint Carmen's fingernails, dye her hair, uncurl it or keep it curled. Give her the best makeup artist in New York City and dress her in flattering clothes . . ." She paused. Miguel hung on every word. "And she'd still look like a dyke." With that, Tatiania grandly turned away to speak to another peasant, her emeralds and diamonds gleaming in the light. They didn't call her the empress for nothing.

◆ ◆ ◆

Gary Shorter was spreading cheer in lieu of VD. Rainey was to take on Susan Reilly within twenty minutes. Susan was a tough match. Rainey listened to his advice: play Susan inside, down the middle, and then unexpectedly pull her wide with a sharp little crosscourt. Since Susan would expect wide angles from Rainey, Gary figured they could crack her composure. Rainey, who had faced Susan on the court before, knew nothing would crack her composure if Susan was in the right frame of mind. If she was in the wrong frame of mind, line calls would get her before anything. Susan, like all the players, hated to beat her brains out for a point and then have some pudgy toad in a Tomahawk jacket determine the outcome.

"Deep. Keep those service returns deep. She's lethal even on her second serve." Gary patted his charge on the back.

"I've played her for five years now," Rainey snapped. Just because she was eighteen, everyone treated her like a kid. On the court she was a veteran; Gary Shorter could stuff it. However, Mother thought he improved her game.

Rainey was admirable but not likeable. She wasn't arrogant but she expected to get her way. She never gave orders but she'd repeat her request until it was filled. Her mother did the dirty work. Mrs. Rogers wasn't a venal, exploitative shit. She loved Rainey and, like plenty of other mothers, she lived through her daughter. That she pushed her child into the narrow, competitive tennis world could only mean either she didn't know a greater world existed or she did know it, but that world disappointed her.

Tomahawk used Rainey more than the other girls because she had recognition and because she was heterosexual. Tatiania Mandelstam was right in her own warped way. Rainey wasn't a great beauty, but she could be promoted as wholesome. Howard Dominick planned to offer Rainey a contract to be the model for a line of teenage cosmetics still being developed in Clark & Clark laboratories which would hit the market in another year or so.

Rainey would do anything for money, yet she wasn't greedy. Her family was large, and she remembered vividly the sacrifices her parents, sisters, and brother made on her behalf. She would pay them all back if it killed her, by becoming the greatest player in the world. She'd win the Grand Slam. Not this year, but soon. She knew she could do it even though only four players ever achieved it before. They couldn't have her motivation or her guilt.

Rainey had a reputation for being cold and aloof. She was neither. She was driven and had no time for superficial locker room friendships.

She feared the lesbians on the tour. She thought they were mentally unhealthy. She observed their desultory romances, their stark terror that they might be discovered, their eventual breakups. Sometimes the locker rooms stank with sullen emotions. Rainey wanted no part of it. She hated being thought a lesbian by association, and in a secret corner of her soul, she hated the lesbians for lying through their teeth. Why be something you are ashamed of?

As for her own mental health, she was sane enough to go along with Seth Quintard's publicity campaign to present her as the girl-next-door. Page Bartlett Campbell cornered the market as America's Sweetheart, so Rainey was the Junior Miss. She hated that, too. Being in *Seventeen* galled her. She would rather have been in *Vogue*.

Her future would be fabulous. Rainey believed her hand was firmly on the stickshift of life.

◆ ◆ ◆

Harriet, Ricky, and Jane squeezed into the tv booth. In another fifteen minutes the evening's two singles matches and two doubles matches would begin.

"Howard Dominick is so chintzy. He put all the tulips and feathers from yesterday's bash upstairs in the guest lounge. You need a machete to get to the bar." Jane fumed.

"I can't get over seeing Tatiania Mandelstam. A living

legend." Ricky fiddled with yesterday afternoon's party favor, a tomahawk on a key chain.

"A living lizard. She's two years older than God," Harriet observed.

"Wonder what she said to Miguel. Did you see his face?" inquired Jane.

Harriet shook her head. "No, Miguel never talks about who says what to whom or himself, come to think of it."

"Carmen used your old suicide tactic last night: Lob short and rush the net. Trixie Wescott was so ruffled she blew the return." Ricky tossed the key chain to Jane.

"How old is Trixie?"

"Thirteen. Harriet, I thought these facts were engraved on your heart."

Ricky noticed the golden cube stickpin on Harriet's coat lapel. "Very handsome. I heard all about the movie candy contest."

"Tiffany's hasn't gotten over it." Jane rubbed her temples. "Goddamned headache. I can't get rid of it."

"Want a B.C.?" Harriet dove into her purse for the magic powder.

"No. First of all, that stuff looks like cocaine, and secondly, it tastes rotten."

"It works."

Jane grumbled and then left to find tablet aspirin.

"Who do you think will win?"

Ricky leaned back in his chair. "Rainey should win. Of course, Susan can get rough out there, but Rogers is so methodical. She's the hardest kind of opponent for Mrs. Reilly."

Harriet peered down into the cavernous stadium. Seth Quintard snaked through the crowd. Miguel, already in the box, followed his progress with an ill-concealed look of contempt. "Seth doesn't care who wins, does he?"

"No," Ricky answered.

Since Athletes Unlimited represented both Rainey Rogers and Susan Reilly, Seth couldn't lose.

"Has it ever crossed your mind that some future day, say with a horrendously large contract pending for player X, and Athletes Unlimited represents player X and player Y, they might ask Y to throw the match just that once?"

"It's crossed my mind." Ricky sighed. "But I hope it hasn't happened yet, and I guess I hope it never will."

" 'Tomorrow, the Players Guild will hold their election of officers.' " Ricky read aloud from his schedule sheet.

Harriet giggled, "That ought to be rich."

Jane breezed back into the booth. "I never thought I'd live to see douche powder liberally sprinkled throughout the halls of Madison Square Garden. Howard's been a busy boy, Pocahontas piles are everywhere!" She grabbed the coffee out of Ricky's hand, knocked back two aspirin, and swallowed.

Ricky, a concerned look on his face, took the coffee cup from Jane. He put his hand on her forehead.

"My temperature's normal. It's just a bloody long headache, honey."

◆ ◆ ◆

Lavinia blossomed to her full glory during the annual guild meeting. She sat before the assembled players. Siggy Wayne, last year's president, was on her right. Rainey Rogers was on her left. Rainey was not elected because she was liked. She was elected because Lavinia wanted it that way.

The Players Guild was a puppet show, strings pulled courtesy of Lavinia Sibley Archer. The last thing she wanted was a union, so once a year management listened to complaints and suggestions. A slate of officers was presented to the players, although nominations could be made from the floor if one dared.

Siggy delivered the state-of-the-game address. Naturally the Guild's insurance plan was the best. The Guild, meaning Siggy in this case, was working on a pension plan. He also announced that because of their requests, another masseuse was being added to the roster. This met with applause. These girls were so easy, Siggy thought. We pay the masseuse a pittance and give her free transportation. Each player still has to pay $25 for a full body massage.

The Guild collected dues and paid for expenses from those dues. Siggy reported their finances were in good shape.

The Guild, supported by hundreds of hopeful pros, existed more for the benefit of the top players than for the rank and file. Although the top forty players were the heart and soul of the game, they got short shrift. Lavinia felt that stars were what tennis was all about. If a player couldn't climb that high, then she should be grateful to follow in their jetstream.

Polite applause greeted Lavinia. She walked to the rostrum, arranged her notes, and began. While her speeches differed from year to year, her theme was the same: Listen to Me.

"Last year forty-five million Americans paid their money and walked into the baseball park. The yearly total for all tennis tournaments, women's and men's, is a mere one and a half million. Even Wimbledon draws only three hundred and eighteen thousand for two weeks. Tennis is not a good bet for a promoter. That is why we rely heavily on local sponsors, and of course Tomahawk, for the prize money.

"Thanks to Siggy"—she nodded to him—"the press inflates our attendance figures, but if you stop to think about it, you'll realize we can never fill a ballpark like a baseball team can. Fifty thousand people can see the Dodgers. We only get that kind of crowd the last week of the U.S. Open when we're with the men. Besides, individual sports just don't draw the number of fans that team sports do.

"Without stars, a promoter will lose his shirt. The prize

money is only half of the expense. The promoter must rent the facility, pay the electric and heating bills for that facility, pay telephone costs, advertise, print and sell tickets. He must provide sandwiches and drinks in the locker rooms, as well as a lounge for your family and friends. Aside from the prize money, the promoter needs about one hundred and fifty thousand dollars up front just to put on a midsize tournament, a thirty-two player draw. And even then, if there's money to be made, it will only be made the night of the semifinals and the finals." She breathed deeply. "So you see, sponsors are the first priority of women's tennis. We must consider their needs because without them no one will promote a tournament, and you and I will be out of work. I know sometimes it's tedious to make small talk with sponsors at tournaments, but it is your responsibility. We can't assume that Tomahawk will underwrite us forever. We must meet them more than halfway."

She then thanked everybody, prophesied a good year, and indicated that Rainey Rogers had better be elected. Had she spelled it out, she couldn't have been more plain: The sponsor calls the tune. You dance.

◆ ◆ ◆

"Damn, Lavinia would ram Rainey down our throats." Carmen stewed in her hotel room.

"Rainey's an American," Harriet said.

"And straight!"

"That, too."

"She never gives me a break. I should have more . . ." Carmen couldn't find the word.

"Power."

"Yes!"

"You ought to run the whole Guild, but I think it's a blessing you don't have to."

"What do you mean?" Carmen ran her fingers through her curls.

"Do you really want to be the president of the Guild and listen to everyone's petty complaints, to say nothing of Lavinia's opinions on everything. Lavinia does have opinions. This way all you have to worry about is tennis. And since you'll win the Grand Slam, they can all go jump in the lake. Right?"

"Right." Carmen brightened considerably. "How'd you like a present?"

"My weakness! Goodies."

Carmen, impulsively generous, showered her lovers with gifts. She bought one woman a Corvette and another a chocolate brown Mercedes. She also put her lovers on the payroll by inventing job titles for them: secretary, coach, even manager until Athletes Unlimited came along. Now that Miguel won that title, she had to be more creative. Initially Harriet did not want to be an employee. Even after an exhaustive lecture from Carmen's accountant, Harriet still didn't want to be an employee. The problem was solved when they started a little real estate company as co-owners. Harriet actually took the company seriously, but Carmen stopped her. She never resented spending money on her lovers, or more accurately, she never resented keeping them until the affair was over. Then she would swear that the recent lover was a gold digger, yet promptly march off and repeat the process.

To have so much money so young is not a blessing. Everybody says yes. Lawyers, accountants, hangers-on, they all say yes because they want the money. But Harriet didn't always say yes, and while that angered Carmen, it also made her think sometimes.

"Well, what do you want?"

Harriet put her chin in her hand. "I want to go eat at Elephant and Castle."

"Is that all?" Carmen hugged her.

Later that night when they crawled into bed, Harriet found a beautiful pair of one-carat diamond earrings under her pillow. Carmen could take Harriet's breath away.

◆ ◆ ◆

That same night, Ricky and Jane were in bed under less happy circumstances.

"I've got to go back for tests." Jane clicked off the tv with the remote button.

"It may not be anything but sinus, honey."

"I hope so."

Ricky put his arm around her shoulders. "I'll go with you. We can both use an extra week off anyway. No use waiting. We'll go home right after the finals."

"Okay."

Jane didn't cry. There was nothing to cry over. She hadn't been given any bad news yet. Two years ago she had cancer in her jaw bone. She endured a new treatment; doctors would shoot a liquid into her jaw, and then she would sit under a localized radiation machine which shot "magic bullets" into her infected jaw. The doctor called the treatment "magic bullets," not Jane. She experienced very little hair loss and no nausea, but the treatment made her quite tired. She had three sets of twelve treatments. At the end of that period the cancer was declared cured.

Jane told no one except Ricky about the problem. She knew the prejudice and fear against cancer were epidemic. An employer was the last person to tell as far as she was concerned. She didn't want to be considered a bad note.

She routinely kept her checkup appointments. The last one was all clear. But these constant headaches bothered her. The fear that a cancer will recur is a fear only cancer victims understand. She tried not to worry, but it crept up on her.

Maybe the headaches were nothing but she knew, given her history, she'd have to submit to a battery of distasteful tests. For the second time in her life, she considered her own body an enemy.

◆ ◆ ◆

A white tin of Balkan Sobranie cigarettes, made from the finest Yenidje tobacco, rested on Miguel Semana's lap. The cigarettes were so strong, a smoker could chew the taillights off a dump truck after one week. He'd puffed through five. Miguel bet $20,000 on this match. Of course, his sister knew nothing of it.

Carmen split sets with Rainey Rogers and just had her service broken. The score was now four-three, favor of Rogers. Carpet was Carmen's surface, but Rainey's backhand was lashing. Her determination didn't waver. When Carmen followed a strong first serve, Rainey zinged the ball down the line.

Carmen was stronger. She was faster. Today she wasn't too flexible in her game plan. Carmen didn't like to change her tactics although she could if she had to. Rainey jerked her from side to side in the backcourt. Carmen stayed back to avoid the unerringly accurate passing shots, but staying in the backcourt was Rainey's game. Carmen grew up on red clay courts. She could stay back and win physically; temperamentally, she dried up behind the baseline. The trouble with Carmen today was in her head not on the court. Given her temperament, one reflected the other quite often.

Rogers grew more confident with each shot. Carmen wasn't giving up, but she wasn't having fun. Carmen was a woman who constantly read the temperature of her own pleasure. Living through discomfort or pain to reach a great goal was alien to her, especially emotionally. She could sometimes put off her immediate wants on the tennis court, but off the tennis court, if she wanted something, she wanted it now. She didn't care how much it cost, she didn't care whose boat she rocked. Not that she intended to disrupt anybody, but Carmen would leap and then look. To date she landed on her feet.

Susan Reilly was in the process of changing all that even as Carmen uncorked another shattering serve, a serve that rocketed off Rainey's racquet. The eighteen-year-old had drilled for six hours a day in order to handle Carmen's serve. She used Carmen's power against her like a judo expert felling a larger man. Increasingly frustrated, Carmen wavered between knocking the shit out of the ball and hanging back, trying to outbore the bore. This was not the way to win a tennis match.

Rainey punched her lights out, six-four in the third set. Harriet politely applauded. Miguel lit another cigarette and smiled wanly. What was $20,000? The clothing line would make him millions! Lavinia, Howard, and umpteen photographers milled on the court. Carmen, head wrapped in a towel, registered her private thoughts and pulled herself together.

When Carmen finally got into the shower alone, she cried. Why get to the finals to lose? "I'll win the Slam," she vowed. "I'll work on my first serve. I'll work on my second serve. I'll work on everything. I will win that Slam. No one can write me off after that!" She started to hit the wall and then thought better of it. No injuries. Not now.

The French Open would be the last week of May through the first week of June. It was played on clay, grueling red clay, a surface so punishing it could wear down even an iron man like Guillermo Vilas. A four-hour match was common on a clay surface. Cramps occurred like mayflies. Players had to abandon matches as they abandoned lovers: stay until it hurts so much you have to go. The French Open, the turf of Page

Bartlett Campbell, would be the hardest tournament to win. Rainey was waiting in the wings. If Page faltered, hard to imagine on clay, Rainey would be right there, a barracuda circling the blood. Somehow, some way, Carmen would have to harden her patience and prepare for the slower pace, the endless points, and the French themselves. Given the Parisian habit of insult, why weren't more of them murdered in their beds by angry Americans? wondered Carmen.

"I must win it! I will win it! I shall win it!" Carmen whispered to herself. If she won the French, she knew no one could stop her from the other three. Grass was her best surface. As for the U.S. Open, they slowed the surface down to get longer rallies out of the men's games. This was a disaster for the women, but if Carmen won the French, the Open was still faster than that molasses clay. She'd take the U.S. Open, Wimbledon, and the Australian Open on grass. She would win the Grand Slam.

◆ ◆ ◆

Relishing a cold glass of white wine, Susan conferred with Martin Kuzirian, a reporter and longtime acquaintance. She gave him special interviews over the years, put him in touch with other sports figures, and generally went out of her way to nurse him. Theirs was a symbiotic relationship to those who liked them, parasitic to those who did not.

Martin, a gluttonous smile across his face, said, "Beautiful view."

"Yes, the Simpsons know how to live."

"Where are they?"

"Tortola. They won't return until April."

"Can't blame them. After a while the weather wears you down, and if that doesn't get you, the people will."

"You look none the worse for wear."

"Life's treating me right." He smiled.

"I have a story for you."

"Susan, you are a continual source of inspiration. Maybe I'll get another promotion, although I'd rather have a raise."

"They don't go hand in hand?"

"Not these days. Haven't you heard? We've got a buoyant economy. It's kept afloat by inflation."

Susan draped her arm over the back of the freeform sofa; the Simpsons were very au courant. "The story is that Carmen Semana and Harriet Thorn Rawls are getting married next month."

"What?" He looked incredulous.

"Yes, they're getting married. I heard it from Carmen herself. She invited me to the wedding."

"Why on earth would they want to do that?"

"That's what I say. Living together for three years seems good enough to me. What's all this mumbo jumbo in front of a man with a smock?"

"I seem to recall that you did it." Martin resembled a badger.

"I was young."

"Not that young."

"Martin, at least I picked a man to marry."

He smiled, then said, "Still happily married to Craig, I take it?"

"Of course."

"Why are you giving me this story? I thought you and Carmen were friends."

"We haven't been friends since she met Harriet. Actually, she tagged after me. I think she had a crush on me when she was sixteen, poor thing."

Martin tried not to choke. Did Susan think he was that stupid? "Kids go through phases."

"I'm telling you this because I know you'll handle the story in a manner that places events in perspective. If those two dodo birds let it leak out and the gossip rags get it, it could hurt us all."

"Don't you think an isolated story about two women can hurt women's tennis?"

"It'll cause some feathers to be ruffled, but women's tennis is too big to be hurt."

"Yes." He rubbed his chin.

"Carmen's a fool. I told her not to get married, but then I told her never to become lovers with that teacher, too."

"People learn the hard way."

"If you ask Carmen if she's getting married, she'll lie, of course. That's no story unless you can catch them in the act." Susan had thought this out. The marriage ceremony was a complete fabrication to inflame Kuzirian's ambitions for a big story. "The person to attack is Harriet. Oh, I wouldn't ask her if she's getting married. That's too farfetched. I'd just ask her if she's a lesbian."

"Why?"

"She's an even bigger fool than Carmen."

"What exactly do you mean?"

"I mean Harriet couldn't tell a lie if her life depended on it."

Martin snickered nervously. This story could mean a big career boost. Too bad people had to get hurt, but that's life. "Any ideas about how to pin her down?"

"Pull her aside at a press conference. She hangs around Ricky Cooper and Jane Fulton a lot. They're the only people who will have anything to do with her."

"Why do you hate her? I'm curious."

"I don't hate her."

Martin knew better than to push. "When's a good time for me to hit her?"

"Hilton Head. There's a tournament there starting April sixth. The atmosphere is relaxed, easygoing, people milling about. By the way, the best way to bring Harriet out is to catch her with Carmen and attack Carmen in some way. Harriet hasn't a brain in her head when it comes to her lover."

"M-m-m."

"Silly, isn't it?"

"Love?"

She snapped, "I wouldn't call it that. I don't think women really love one another. I don't understand lesbians. I don't condemn them; I just don't understand them, that's all."

"Of course." Martin got up to leave.

As Susan closed the door, she smiled. So what if she made up the story of a marriage ceremony. Kuzirian didn't need to know that. All he needed to do was be motivated enough to provoke Carmen and Harriet.

Susan couldn't face the real reason she was hell-bent on obliterating Carmen Semana. Carmen was the one player who could overshadow her achievements. Carmen was the one player who just might win the Grand Slam. With her green card placed in jeopardy and the world in an uproar over her lesbianism, try, just try to concentrate on tennis!

Susan wasn't proud of herself. She didn't think of it in those terms. She acted in terms of survival. She was fighting for herself, for her achievements. She'd given her entire being to tennis, and she couldn't bear the thought that it might be over, that she might be getting older, that she might be soon forgotten. She only knew who she was when she heard the applause. How could she give it up? How could she step aside in favor of someone who only a few years ago was a kid who spoke broken English? As Susan saw it, Carmen was erratic, overemotional, and simple when Susan took her under her wing. She helped this young player reach her greatness. As for being lovers, well, Carmen was a mistake.

SEVEN

The plane lifted off. LaGuardia diminished below and soon resembled a toy set. Lavinia Sibley Archer and Siggy Wayne sat together in economy class. Siggy wore a spotted tie with his expensive navy pinstripe. The man was hopeless. Seth Quintard, his briefcase open, waited for a J&B on the rocks. The day was clear. The Tomahawk Circuit was over, but Lavinia, head of the Women's Tennis Guild, could attend any tournament she chose. Hilton Head was one of her brainstorms. April and May were slow times between the Tomahawk Circuit and the French Open. For the last three years Siggy and Lavinia lured sponsors for one-shot deals. Hilton Head was sponsored by a foundation garment manufacturer.

The two of them also cooked up the Futures Circuit which played midsize towns and developed the next generation of tennis stars. The Futures Circuit was good training for everyone, young players, umpires, and linesmen.

Lavinia and Siggy had good reason to be proud of their accomplishments, but at the moment, they were haggling over the Futures Circuit.

"This blonde girl—she's worthy of buildup." Siggy thought the kid was cute.

"She'd be a lot more worthy of buildup if she had a net game," Lavinia, ever the pro, countered.

"That will come in time. She looks great. The press will love her. She's fourteen."

"Trixie Wescott is thirteen."

"Trixie Wescott is a dog," Siggy said bluntly. "We need more pretty girls, Lavinia."

"If pretty girls aren't winning tennis tournaments, there's not much I can do about it."

Siggy breathed down her neck. "Sometimes all a kid needs is a boost, a shot of confidence. We need to select four stars of tomorrow. If we guess wrong, so what? The kids who win will get their fair share of the press. We've got to upgrade our material."

"All right, she gets to be one of the four. Who else do you have in mind?"

"The black girl."

"Annalise? Covers the court well. One more two-handed backhand. Such an ugly stroke. She's got the equipment, definitely got the equipment."

"We need a black star. Think of it, Lavinia. A whole new audience, the black middle class."

"Yes." Lavinia prayed nightly for a new Althea Gibson. "Siggy, I'm rather tired. Let's finish this off after I've had supper."

"All right." Siggy slid back into his seat. As far as he could remember, Lavinia was never too tired to talk business.

◆ ◆ ◆

Women who've graduated from Pappagallo shoes to Geoffrey Beene like places like Hilton Head. The condominiums are new, the high ceilings make them appear spacious, the grounds are planted to provide some privacy, and the island is overrun with birds as well as bicycles. The wildlife and quiet controlled surroundings help these women and their husbands in madras pants to surrender to a few moments of pinched rapture. Even if the middle-aged couples didn't have a good time walking amid the palmetto shrubs, they would go back home to New Jersey and swear it was wonderful.

Hilton Head provided a perfect setting for a women's tennis tournament. The biggest selling items were sunscreen, sun visors, and gallons of liquor. Hilton Head was definitely the land of the juice generation; they sought rainbows in their wine. Failing that, a round of doubles would do, or perhaps a round of golf. In the evenings couples strolled down the walkways enjoying the quiet. And then there was the ocean for those who wished to become acquainted with sand flies.

Carmen was practicing. A small crowd, dressed in the inevitable Lacoste shirts, gathered around. Carmen hit the ball behind her back. They oohed. She picked up a murderous shot on the half-volley. They aahed. She crushed an overhead. They laughed. Carmen's incentive was to show off and get paid for it. Like a dancer, her time was short, the applause was bracing, and the future was nonexistent except as an extension of the present. The truth would set in later, like arthritis. Carmen paid people to perform her everyday responsibilities; the tennis life left few other options. If she wanted a glass of orange juice, someone else picked, shipped, then squeezed the orange. Carmen squeezed life, and she thought there would always be juice.

Today she was blissfully happy practicing with her brother. He was blissfully happy, too. The bogus clothing line was selling. His partner in Hong Kong outdid himself in efficiency. Since his partner didn't have to worry about government interference, union regulations, or moral concerns, efficiency was easy. Dennis Parry had his $50,000. The next installment wouldn't be due for months. He knew the man in Hong Kong was skimming some of the profits but Miguel didn't mind. He'd already stashed away $100,000 from the original loan. Life was beautiful.

"I spoke to Baby Jesus on the telephone today." Carmen rubbed her sneaker against her calf. "Another novel, of course. *Catalyst*. This one's about secret love affairs."

Carmen was on top of the world ever since arriving in South Carolina. She even agreed to take a walk with Harriet.

"What else did Baby have to say?"

"She wants fresh chicken, fresh catnip, and one live mouse for her birthday."

"Her birthday isn't until July fourteenth."

"I know, but she's like her mother. She puts in her order early." A figure closed the door to a condominium. "Oh fuck, there's Miguel."

"Duck behind this shrub." Harriet yanked Carmen down. "Now let's go back the way we came."

"Good thinking." Carmen pinched her.

"Did you and Miguel have a fight?"

"No. Besides, I would have told you. I tell you everything. He got on my nerves a little bit by pressuring me to ask Ricky for air time."

"What?"

"You know, comment on matches. Miguel said it would land bigger contracts."

"I suppose it would, but you can't prevail upon Ricky that way."

"That's what I said. He huffed and puffed, but eventually calmed down. He also said I've got to get a new hairstyle."

"Lord." Harriet kept walking. "Susan seems to have quieted herself."

"Yeah, I think that punch in my face freaked her out."

"I think of Susan as a manic impressive."

"Whatever it is, she's definitely weird. It'll blow over."

"Well, I'd still like to put her in designer concrete boots," Harriet said.

Carmen wrapped her arm around Harriet's waist. "You're awful."

Martin Kuzirian had his moment. He'd been way back tailing the two. When they turned around, he was far enough away not to attract their attention. He took up a post in front of the little convenience store. Carmen's act was one of simple affection. It didn't have to be sexual.

"Hello." Martin hailed them as soon as their features were distinct.

Carmen dropped her arm. "Hello."

"Great match today."

"Thank you. Didn't I see you in the interview tent?" She knew perfectly well who he was.

Flattered by her noticing him, he said demurely, "Yes, I'm with *The Long Island Chronicle.*"

Carmen kept walking, and he fell in beside her.

Harriet bristled.

"Things are different today. There's such a permissive climate. I don't see why the two of you don't come out and relax. Everybody knows you're lovers and you're going to be married." He struck without warning.

Harriet almost choked. "You must be nuts."

Carmen wheeled on him. "Why don't you just fuck off?"

"You deny you're a lesbian?"

Harriet stepped in front of Carmen. "Leave her alone."

"Ah, yes, the mother lion defending her young."

"You son of a bitch." Harriet belted him. He rocked backwards.

"Honey!" Carmen put her arms around Harriet. When angry, Harriet was a handful even for Carmen.

"If you're not a lesbian why are you so mad?" Kuzirian wasn't letting up.

"Leave her alone!"

"Harriet, are you ashamed to love Carmen?"

"Lay off, you bastard. I do love her. I'm goddamned

proud to love her"—she caught her breath and tried to square it—"but that doesn't mean Carmen's a lesbian just because I am."

Carmen, sweating, pulled Harriet away. "Come on, forget it."

"Forget nothing." She turned back at Martin. "You leave her alone."

He pedalled backwards. "Okay, okay." He had what he needed to start his story. Time would give him the rest.

◆ ◆ ◆

Carmen hauled Harriet to the condominium. She handed Harriet a Coca-Cola. Harriet was ready to heave the glass, but thought about it, then took a drink. She was beginning to come down to earth. There was a string of expletives so miserable Carmen remembered only the mildest which was, "If a fart were a scab, that man would pick it off his asshole." The expletives and tortures of hell were followed by a kind of silence punctuated by outbursts of "Fuck, shit, damn." Finally she shut up.

Carmen was bone white.

Harriet sighed. "I blew it. I think I landed us in hot water."

"He won't print anything. You scared the shit out of him."

"No. I gave that asshole what he wanted. I told him I was gay. You'd better think long and hard about how you want to handle it."

"It won't come to that." Carmen couldn't face trouble theoretically, much less in the raw.

"I think it will."

◆ ◆ ◆

Ricky and Jane's beautiful white clapboard house sat right in the heart of Princeton. Because it was built immediately following the Revolutionary War, the measurements of the rooms were by human elbow to fingertip. Nothing was exact ,- ·ything looked exact. Uneven pine floorboards worn smooth by years shone the color of the syrup Ricky was pouring over pancakes. He made breakfast this morning, singing all the while.

Jane leafed through *Portfolio*, a magazine devoted primarily to painting. "Hey, hon, a Rosa Bonheur exhibit will be in Philadelphia this summer. Isn't going to be anyplace else in the U.S. We've got to go."

"Sounds good." He tossed off the front pages and dug into the sports pages. Suddenly he stood up, sat down, and then stood up again. "Jesus, Mary, and Joseph!"

Alarmed, Jane asked, "What's the matter?"

"Look at this."

Jane came and read standing next to him. "Holy shit."

"Kuzirian's a bastard." Ricky's hands began to shake.

"He doesn't say that Carmen's a lesbian, only her 'live-in friend with whom she shares a house in Cazenovia, Harriet Rawls, professor of religion at Cazenovia College.' He doesn't actually say Carmen is a lesbian."

"He doesn't have to."

The phone rang. Jane picked it up. "Hi, Frank." Pause. "Like hell I will." She slammed down the receiver.

"What'd your editor want?"

"He wants me to fly to Hilton Head for the story."

"Put out a piece of meat and watch the jackals gather."

"I'm calling Harriet and Carmen." She dialed their number. "Goddammit." She dialed again. "No one home. They must be down at the courts. Ricky, what can we do?"

"Wait until we talk to them first." He ran his fingers through his gray hair. "This could tear them apart."

Jane puzzled, "Do you think Carmen's a coward?"

"No, but she's young. All she's got is Harriet, and right now Harriet's the source of the problem."

Jane's eyes narrowed. "Not by a long shot. The source of the problem is a cobra on the circuit. This came from the inside. Who?"

Ricky sat down. "Who hates Carmen most?"

"It's too fantastic." Jane dismissed the face floating in her mind.

"What are you thinking?"

"Susan Reilly."

"That is too fantastic." Ricky stabbed his pancake.

"Women's intuition, honey."

"About the only thing we can do is write columns defending one's right to privacy."

"On the surface of it, yes. Sometimes our profession makes me sick. Martin Kuzirian calls himself a journalist." Jane pushed her food around her plate. "If I sit quietly like a doodlebug, sooner or later the guilty piss ant will fall in the trap."

"In the meantime, Doodlebug, I feel like we're rearranging deck chairs on the *Titanic*."

◆ ◆ ◆

Blissfully ignorant, Carmen walked on the court for her match. Since the condominiums were near the courts, she could bypass the locker room, dress in her room, and walk on court. When her name was announced the applause was healthy; there was a snicker here and there, but she didn't notice it. Trixie Wescott, beribboned, didn't look Carmen in the face but again, that wasn't unusual. Most players didn't want to look an opponent in the face, not right before trying to flatten her. Miranda Mexata was in control as always.

During the warm-up, Harriet noticed she was the object

of certain scrutiny. She told herself it was, of course, her celestial beauty that attracted the furtive as well as outright gazes. The only trouble was, Harriet was not a celestial beauty. Then she wondered if she evidenced signs of bubonic plague. Harriet sat there and wondered what in hell was going on.

♦ ♦ ♦

Siggy Wayne was all beshit and forty miles from water. Lavinia Sibley Archer, rattled but cool, spent precious energy on him.

"Chrysler. There goes Chrysler."

"Siggy, get hold of yourself. You're acting like Chicken Little."

"You don't think sponsors will pull out on us for this? Large ha. Who do I get now? Mack trucks?"

"Shut up and let me think." Lavinia rarely spoke so directly in the vernacular.

Siggy shut up. Lavinia paced the room. She tacked a Do Not Disturb sign on the office door. How long that would be respected she didn't know. The players would respect it for a while, but the press was another matter.

Unable to stay quiet for more than two minutes, Siggy spoke again. "Carmen must publicly deny she's a lesbian."

"I thought of that. She'll lie because she has to. Besides, I've never seen a lesbian yet ready to say she was one. Carmen's no different. She'll give us our press conference."

"What else is there to worry about? Sponsors are the game, Lavinia. The fans might come because they love tennis, but the sponsors won't. Oh, why did this have to happen now? I'm to sign the Chrysler contract next week."

She corrected him, "We're to sign the contract next week."

"That's what I meant."

"H-m-m." She examined him as though he were under a microscope. "You'd never have won Wimbledon, Siggy."

"I'm not athletic."

"What I mean is you've got to stay cool. The worse the situation, the more cool you become. Concentration, Siggy, concentration."

"This isn't fucking Wimbledon. This is business!"

"I won't have you speaking that way in front of me."

"Sorry, I forgot myself."

"We can contain the lesbian issue, I think. We've got to convince Carmen to throw it all on Harriet. I shall speak to her, and I'll see that Seth Quintard speaks to her."

"You forgot. She fired Seth. Miguel had a hand in that, you can be sure."

"Now, will Harriet accept the blame?" Lavinia put her finger alongside her nose, tapped it once, and then declared, "Yes. She loves Carmen. She can leave the tour and find a quiet job somewhere."

Siggy looked surprised. "A job? The woman is a college professor. She won't get hired in the heart of San Francisco after this scandal."

"She can always be a secretary," Lavinia sniffed.

"A secretary with a Ph.D.? The woman will be branded for the rest of her life, Lavinia."

"She can join the gay rights movement and be their leader." Lavinia drummed her fingertips together.

"The wages for martyrdom are zip."

"What's the matter with you?" Lavinia sharply demanded.

"It seems cruel, but . . ." His voice faded.

"You're the one screaming about sponsors."

"I know."

"I, for one, will be good and glad to get rid of Harriet Rawls. Since she was stupid enough to tell the truth, the rest is her own doing. We put the blame on her. What happens to a homosexual is of no concern to me—or you. She takes the blame!"

"You're asking a lot."

"I don't have to ask anything. Carmen Semana will do the asking. Tennis means more to her than Harriet. You ought to know that about tennis players. They sacrifice their mothers and fathers first, their husbands and wives next, and then they go for their children."

"Did you do that?" For once Siggy was taken aback.

"I married after my career. Times were different then."

"I'll call Chrysler and smooth things over. You call Howard Dominick."

"No, Siggy. Let it ride. Nothing may come of this. There's no reason in our calling attention to it by overreacting. If they call us, we'll discuss it. If not, let's act as though nothing much has happened. Remember it's Harriet who's in the electric chair, not Carmen and not women's tennis."

"Okay."

"Why don't you watch the match and see how it goes?" Before he could agree she announced, "We didn't have homosexuals when I played competitively."

"Lavinia, you can't believe that."

"If we had them, they didn't say they were. It amounts to the same thing."

◆ ◆ ◆

Carmen shook Trixie's hand. She'd beaten the thirteen-year-old without much trouble. Siggy Wayne stood at courtside. He grabbed her arm as she trotted off.

"Follow me. No press conference today. I'm taking you back to your condominium."

Harriet observed this and assumed he was taking Carmen to the press tent. She decided to return to the condo ahead of them.

"Did you read Martin Kuzirian's column today?" Siggy asked Carmen.

"No, but then I never read his column."

Siggy retrieved the clipping from his pocket. As they walked back to the condominium, Carmen read while he fended off people. Lavinia hadn't told him to escort Carmen, but he thought it was a good idea.

Carmen's expression changed from blank uninterest to fury. She crumpled up the paper and handed it back to Siggy. He put the ball back in his pocket. "Bastard!"

"All is not lost. We can work this out."

Carmen didn't hear him. She was thinking of committing the perfect murder.

"This doesn't have to be a scandal."

"What?"

These kids, Siggy thought. Airheads, every one. "I said this doesn't have to be a disaster." They arrived at the condo. "Let's go inside and talk this out."

Carmen reached in her racquet cover for the key. She couldn't find it. She knocked on the door twice. Harriet called from inside, "Who is it?"

"Me—and Siggy."

Harriet opened the door. Siggy was the last person she wanted to see, now or at any time. The brief walk she and Carmen took the other day was their only time together except for sleep.

"Read this." Siggy placed the ball of newsprint in Harriet's hand. Without being asked, he sat down. Carmen found her cigarettes and lit one.

Harriet finished the viperous article and returned it to Siggy in better shape than she found it. "The price of fame."

"As long as Carmen doesn't have to pay it." Subtlety was unknown to Siggy. "Think of her reputation in Argentina."

"What's that mean?" Carmen glowered.

"It means you've got to deny all this, and Harriet's got to pack off. Until things cool off, of course."

"Siggy, I think you'd better leave. We need to talk between ourselves."

"This is business, Harriet. I don't think you understand."

"I understand that you have no regard for Carmen and me as a couple. If we had two kids, one station wagon, and three pet hamsters, you'd never dream of sitting in our living room after a bomb like this had been dropped on us. Please leave."

"Oh." He stood up and headed for the door. As he turned the doorknob, he said to Carmen, "Call me after you two talk. We've got to decide what you'll say to the press. They won't leave you alone, that's for certain." He left thinking it was Harriet who had bad manners.

The phone rang. Carmen took the call, listened, answered with terse replies, then hung up.

"More bad news?" Harriet's voice was dead.

"George Gibson, my lawyer. He's worried about my green card."

"The article said I was a lesbian, not you."

Carmen stared into nowhere and said, "Would you love me if I didn't play tennis?"

"Yes. I loved you the day I met you, and I'll love you until the day I die. I don't care what you do, as long as you can look in the mirror and be proud of yourself. Isn't that what's important?"

"You're not going home. Fuck Siggy."

"I think we've had enough upset for one day. Let's play a hand of 500 rum. We can apply ourselves to my brand-new public lesbianism later."

"I wish I had let you beat the shit out of the creep," Carmen said.

"Then he'd call me a communist, a child molester, a dope

addict. Is there anything left in the lexicon of ills? In his little mind, I think homosexuality ranks with such horrors."

"I don't understand. I try to figure it all out, but I can't. We aren't hurting anybody. We work. We pay our taxes. But we're criminals? I don't get it."

"Neither do I." Harriet shuffled the cards.

◆ ◆ ◆

If bad luck follows its nose to the grave, Miguel had his first whiff of that foul odor. Sauntering back to his condominium, he passed Beanie Kitteridge. Normally buoyant, her behavior tipped him off. When he questioned her, he discovered the bad news. As soon as he was in his room, he read the column. It was a disaster by implication.

Miguel paced. He had to clean up his sister's act, but how? If a scandal of major proportions erupted, the clothing wouldn't sell. Miguel and an innocent Carmen would be staring down a $600,000 debt. If that wasn't bad enough, she could lose her legitimate contracts. They might not cut her off immediately; they simply wouldn't renew. He didn't know if he could rustle up new ones. Carmen could become endorsement poison.

Finally he picked up the phone. "Migueletta, come over. We need to talk."

"I'm relaxing."

"Get over here."

Carmen wanted Harriet to accompany her but Harriet knew this was strictly between brother and sister. Fearfully, Carmen opened the door to her brother's condominium. A breeze stirred the surrounding foliage.

"Is it true?"

"Yes," she said.

Miguel sighed. "I guess I always knew. I don't understand it. I don't know if you were born that way or if it's a disease like alcoholism, but I know this: it could cost you a bloody fortune."

Carmen started to cry. Miguel put his arm around her. He wasn't going to tell her how bad it could really be. Perhaps the chestnut could still be plucked from the fire.

"What do I do?"

"Lie."

"Christ, Miguel!" she sobbed.

"Everybody else does. Don't be a fool."

"What about Harriet?"

"I don't know." He stroked his moustache. "I suppose I could marry her. If she's good enough for you, she ought to be good enough for me." He tried to laugh.

Carmen was bewildered. His suggestion had a bizarre and unexplored psychological flavor to it. "What good would that do?"

"It would explain why you two room together on the road and live together in Cazenovia—she couldn't sleep openly with me. Now that Kuzirian is accusing her of being a lesbian, we'll tell the real truth."

"She told him she loved me." Carmen stated this with some pride.

"That was wrong."

"You should have been there. It's not like you think. She didn't ever announce it."

Miguel raised his hand to stop this torrent. "No doubt, no doubt. We can say he's trying to get a story that doesn't exist. She does love you as a friend and future sister-in-law. We'll make him look like shit."

"I don't know."

"Think about it. We've got to do something."

◆ ◆ ◆

137

Tomahawk's corporate offices were so high up in a Manhattan skyscraper that employees swore they suffered nosebleeds. Howard Dominick pulled at his thinning hair, a sure sign of advanced misery, since he usually took great pains with his remaining strands.

"I told Lavinia something had to be done about those girls."

Ruth, his long enduring secretary, nodded in agreement. "Tomahawk can't afford this. What will our customers think? Are they going to look at our salesclerks funny? They'll think we underwrite some kind of lesbian harem. Besides"—he lowered his voice—"we've sunk in so much money in order to become identified with women's tennis, how can we get out of it now?"

"It may not be as bad as all that," Ruth said soothingly.

"I can see the mail we're going to get, to say nothing about what the Old Man will say." The reference to Jensen Bainbridge caused him to shudder. "They'll say women tennis players are all a bunch of dykes." He yanked his hair again.

Trying to inject a note of humor, Ruth said, "What matters is, are they butch? If the girls look feminine, we can squeak by."

"Hell, even the straight ones look butch." Howard put his head in his hands.

◆ ◆ ◆

So rampant was Susan Reilly's public display of heterosexuality that Alicia Brinker fully expected her to wear diaphragms for earrings. Craig and Lisa were with her at Hilton Head while Alicia bunked out with a player who just qualified off the Futures Circuit. Susan, never bound by such considerations as sexual fidelity, banged away on Craig nightly. Every third word out of Susan's mouth was "my

husband" or "my daughter." Alicia read her New Testament.
There didn't seem to be an answer that applied to what she
was feeling. She knew that the person she loved had done
something unspeakably rotten. Alicia had not added two and
two together, but it was a matter of time. She was good at
math.

Initially she didn't believe Susan was the source of Martin
Kuzirian's column. Egoists don't go around talking about
other people. Susan wouldn't blow the whistle on Carmen.
Besides, if people started thinking the women's tennis circuit
was a hotbed of lesbianism, wouldn't Susan herself be in
jeopardy? It slowly occurred to Alicia that Susan's best defense was a good offense. Direct attention away from herself.
Maybe it was true that the people most vehemently opposed
to homosexuality were themselves closet cases. Alicia dismissed these thoughts. It couldn't be true. Nonetheless, she
felt as though bugs were crawling up her spine.

She closed her eyes, opened her Bible, placed her finger
blindly on the page, then read the following passage:

> Behold also the ships, which though they be so great,
> and are driven of fierce winds, yet are they turned about
> with a very small helm, whithersoever the governor listeth.
> Even so the tongue is a little member, and boasteth great
> things. Behold, how great a matter a little fire kindleth.

Alicia reread the passage. She closed her Bible and felt
worse.

◆ ◆ ◆

She couldn't have felt worse than Carmen and Harriet who
were still rocked by Kuzirian's disclosure. After a twenty-
four-hour interval, Lavinia made her entrance into Carmen's
condominium. Under the circumstances, Lavinia behaved ad-

139

mirably. She contained her dislike for Harriet and discussed the matter with both of them. She had brains enough to know she'd get nowhere by pitting Carmen against Harriet. Her argument was logical if one accepted her original premise, specifically, people don't want to know the truth and they don't need to know the truth. A tennis player is an entertainer whose job is to provide spectators with a few hours of pleasure away from the cares of their lives.

Lavinia cast no blame. She spoke for women's tennis as she saw it. Harriet grudgingly respected Lavinia. Lavinia made no bones about anything larger than her profession, and she was more than willing to compromise to advance that profession. However, Harriet squirmed when Lavinia requested that Harriet get lost, that Carmen vehemently deny all rumor of lesbianism, and that Carmen find a boyfriend fast and get a blurb in *People* magazine to that effect. Lavinia was good friends with one of the editors.

Lavinia zeroed in on Harriet. "You're older, Harriet. You know that Carmen has five years left minus injuries. Her career is a short one. What's a sacrifice on your part? The two of you can be together quietly at home. Life on the road is grueling. Take a much deserved rest, Harriet. Carmen can do whatever she wants when she retires. She can live more openly then, if that's how you see your lives, but for now, she must think only of tennis. I know a press conference may seem odious, but life isn't always what you want it to be, and people aren't always what we want them to be. America isn't ready for a lesbian scandal in women's tennis. Neither are the sponsors. There's more to this than the two of you. Try to think of the big picture." She paused. "Let me put it this way, Harriet, you have a different perspective so you probably think sports are not very important, but twelve-year-old girls look up to Carmen. You don't want them to think she's a lesbian, do you?"

Harriet found the lecture so beyond even a retort that she

listened without opening her mouth. Lavinia took this for acquiescence. After a few more well-chosen words, she exited, not without some style.

Carmen lit a cigarette after Lavinia left. Harriet was unusually quiet. That bothered Carmen.

"What are you thinking?"

"What?" Harriet jumped out of her skin.

"Thinking, what are you thinking?"

"I'm trying to balance what people say against what I feel and then balance all that against what's right for you."

"I'm not a liar." Carmen exhaled a dragon's breath of blue smoke.

"No, you're not."

"Everyone's asking me to lie."

Harriet tried not to pray her lover would be the woman she wanted her to be. She prayed instead that she would be able to love Carmen no matter what she did.

"I don't want to be a martyr," Carmen snapped.

"They're asking me to embrace amorous martyrdom, not you."

Carmen paced. "Yeah, yeah. They are sure dumping it on you. Everyone's dumping it on you."

"I'm an easy target. I told the truth and that makes me a sucker."

"Miguel says it has to do with advertising."

"Oh?"

"He says that we're bombarded by lies about products. You know, you buy an eggbeater that will last until eternity but it falls apart in a week. He says it makes all Americans liars. No one trusts anyone or anything anyone says."

"He might be right. We aren't what we were when I was a little girl." Harriet remembered when no one locked her doors.

"Why did this happen to me?" Carmen was bewildered.

"Damned if I know. I'm still trying to figure out why I

was born. Right now it would be better for you if I hadn't been born."

Carmen stubbed out her cigarette. "You're not getting enough oxygen."

"What do you want to do?"

"Run away."

"You can't!"

"What do you want me to do?"

"I can't make that decision. It's your life."

"No, it's your life." Carmen kept moving around the room.

"Honey, it's our lives, but it's your conscience and your career. I'll love you no matter what you do."

"Even if I lie?"

"If I stopped talking to people or liking them because they lied, I expect I'd have but one friend left, Baby Jesus. No, I'd have Jane Fulton. There are a few people out there who aren't chasing the bubble popularity."

"I feel so small. Do you think I'm a coward?"

"No, I think you're torn, and you're scared. You're human. You don't look small. I didn't say that I loved you because I'm a hero or Wonder Woman. I did it because I couldn't live with myself if my relationships with other people were predicated on falsities. Not direct lies exactly, but falsities. I still believe a person is only as good as their word. If a person lies about one thing, soon enough they'll lie about other things. I couldn't betray myself. I didn't know that when I barked at Kuzirian but maybe my whole life led up to that moment. I am what I am."

Carmen burst out crying. "I don't want to be pushed around. I don't want to be a piece of meat. I want to be my own person! I hate all this. I feel so trapped but you can't lose as much as I can. I could lose millions of dollars!"

Harriet felt the blood rush to her face. "What's the difference if it's three thousand or three million dollars? Is sorrow measured by the account book? Nothing is nothing, and after this, I have nothing. No job, nothing."

"I'll take care of you."

"For how long?"

"What do you mean?"

"I mean, you can't be alone, honey. If I'm hidden away in Cazenovia, and you're on the road eight to nine months out of the year, how long will it be before you find a new lover? For a while you can cover by calling her your coach or your business manager or your secretary. But how long will it be before you want to bring her to our house?"

This cut to the quick because deep in her heart Carmen knew it to be true. She exploded. "That's not true. I love you. And what is all this truth bullshit? I can do more good by being the best woman tennis player in the world than I can do by telling people the truth about you or lesbianism. I'm someone to look up to. I'm number one. I'm an example. Lavinia is right about the twelve-year-old girls. They need heroes."

"Is it so inconceivable that people might like you for just what you are? Whether you're a lesbian or not, you are still number one. No one can take that away from you."

"No one else is taking chances. Why should I? Answer me that! And if what you say is true, why are gay people still in the closet? America's two hundred and forty million people, right? How many accomplished people can you name who have told the truth about themselves? Americans are such cowards they import Quentin Crisp to do the dirty work for them!"

Harriet said nothing. Carmen continued, "This is one Argentine import who is looking after herself. And besides, I learned by what happened to Billie Jean King."

"Yes, I did, too." Harriet was angrier than she'd ever been, but she felt ice cold. "I learned that a woman's work doesn't count. I learned that the woman who acts like a man, the woman who does a man's work, is the important person.

The woman who nurtures, who puts her own career second, is viewed as a slut or a gold digger or an idiot. I learned that relationships between women are not supposed to entail emotional, social, or financial responsibilities. Lesbian hit-and-run. I learned that the only relationship that counts is one between a man and a woman. Unfortunately, gay people seem to support that view, since they let the press get away with that whole sad affair. I learned gay people are their own worst enemies. Each faggot and dyke out there believes she'll escape notice. She'll be the exception. We don't stick together. The battle cry of the anguished homosexual is: What I do with my life is my own business; no one needs to know. And I learned something else. It took me all these years to learn it, Carmen, but now that I know, I'll never forget it. I learned you are as sick as you are secret."

◆ ◆ ◆

Lavinia decided Carmen should play her semifinal match, and as normal, go to the press tent afterwards. If reporters wanted to bring up the lavender herring, they'd do so then. She vetoed Siggy's idea of a special conference because that would only underscore the problem.

Carmen tossed and turned most of the night. Since their fight, they dropped the subject. There was too much pain between them.

When they got up the next morning, Carmen said nothing about what she was going to do. Harriet wondered if Carmen even knew what she was going to do.

Miguel was nowhere to be seen, and under the circumstances, that was a relief. The crowd filled the makeshift stands. The weather sparkled. Harriet sat alone in the players' box. Directly across from her reposed the Reilly family, a tableau of father, mother, and child. Only the magi were missing. Susan beamed as reporters recorded this heart-warming scene. Heart worm was closer to it. Happy Straker, now on the court warming up with Carmen, shared secret smiles with Susan. Harriet began to consider Happy a Quasimodo—forever tolling the bells for Susan.

Carmen glided across the court, her forehand, that brutal quick shot, intact. Her racquet head was almost parallel with the court on her backhand backswing. Her volleys were so fluid they contradicted every coach's admonition to punch the ball. Carmen's volley was in a class by itself. She looked confident like the player she was, but as Harriet watched her walk back to the baseline, she knew how Carmen looked and how she felt were at odds today. Her first serve was long. That was the tip-off that the rest of her game would falter even though she looked great.

As Carmen took the court against Happy Straker, Harriet hoped for the best while nevertheless preparing for the worst. Should the worst befall her, Carmen would wriggle, squirm, twist and turn, break free and run if she could. Harriet could fight her own battles, but she couldn't fight Carmen's, on or off the court.

Happy played well. Carmen's timing was off. She was almost too eager. She overran balls, her service toss was too high, she missed the lines by inches—all out. But even on an off day, Happy wasn't getting a free ticket. The match went to three sets, raptly observed by Susan and her brood, less raptly observed by Alicia Brinker, high up in the stands. Carmen dropped it seven-five in the third set.

◆ ◆ ◆

Lavinia, Siggy, Seth Quintard, and Howard Dominick were sitting in the little press tent. They were as inconspicuous as polar bears. Behind the microphones, Happy pulsated all the charm of Idi Amin. Her terseness melted away in the rush of describing her win. It boiled down to a hymn of self-love. Since nobody else loved Happy, she deserved her moment of sunshine.

After Happy's performance, Carmen sat down behind the mikes. The questions centered on tennis. Why did she lose? No athlete ever believes she has really lost a match. She finds infinitesimal reasons why it happened the way it happened. It never happens because another player is better, although Carmen did manage to say, "Today, Happy was better." That's as far as it goes. If she doesn't make excuses for herself, if she does believe someone is better, she'll lose as sure as dew falls in morning. The ego defenses are elaborate, but painfully obvious to anyone who isn't playing the game.

Carmen's defenses were on red alert today. Martin Kuzirian was lurking in the fifth row. Harriet folded herself into a seat in the back. Her heart was pounded upon like Vulcan's anvil.

The polite facade crumbled as Martin called out, "Are you a lesbian?"

"No," Carmen lied. In her head, she thought this not too big an untruth. She technically qualified as a bisexual. If he'd asked her if she was a bisexual, she would have said yes. She had a boyfriend once years ago, so she clung to semantics.

"Why do you live with an avowed lesbian?" Martin bore down. The other reporters, too shy or too sensitive to attack, listened. They'd get the story while Martin took the blame as well as the glory.

"Because she's my friend. You can live with a dog and not be a dog." That was an unfortunate choice of words. Carmen's face looked like rice paper despite her tan.

The words felt like coffins. Harriet fought back tears. Damned if she'd cry in front of these vultures.

Another reporter asked, "Is it true that you own a house together in Cazenovia?"

"Yes, I also own apartment buildings in San Diego and property in Houston."

A diminutive woman fresh out of journalism school, her tape recorder in hand, asked, "But you don't live there?"

"I keep an apartment in San Diego in one of my buildings. I spend a lot of time in that city, but Cazenovia is home."

"So why live with Harriet Rawls?" Martin fired.

"Because I like her. Because she's fun. Because she's not like you."

That went over his head. "But you're not a lesbian?"

Mad, Carmen remembered a line Harriet used once. "Are you the alternative?"

Lavinia shifted feet. Siggy blanched. Still, she hadn't tripped over the line completely. The reporters laughed. They didn't like Martin. Seeing him being made a fool was as good as the story itself. He sat down, red-faced but full of himself.

Carmen said, "Are there any more questions?"

"How will this affect you in Argentina?" a reporter queried.

"I don't know," came the honest reply. "I haven't done anything wrong."

They quieted. She got up and left. Harriet sneaked out the side of the tent, just in time to run into that goddamned Martin Kuzirian and a colleague. Fat on self-importance, Martin ripped her, "Are you really a dyke, Harriet?"

"I rather thought of myself as the Hoover Dam."

Carmen wasn't playing doubles in the tournament. She and Harriet packed up to move on to Amelia Island. They'd get there a day ahead of everyone else, and that would give them some time. She packed quietly and so did Harriet. There wasn't much to say. Harriet knew Carmen felt horrible. And she also knew Carmen was scared. On the surface of her life, Carmen lived for love, but underneath it all, she didn't want to lose the racquet contracts, the clothing contracts, the many lucrative benefits of her profession that brought in more money than the tournaments themselves. Carmen lived high on the hog and she didn't want that porker slaughtered.

Seth Quintard called to give her fair warning. Get rid of Harriet or hide her in the attic. Why test it? This would all blow over.

Carmen felt ashamed. She felt she'd let Harriet down, although she pushed that thought back as much as she could. Harriet would become a living reminder for gay people, like a survivor of a concentration camp. Carmen felt guilty without Harriet saying a word. Well, fuck Harriet's pride. Some things were more important.

"You've got to call Miguel."

"Why don't I tell him to stay there for today and come down tomorrow? We've had no time alone."

"We'll have plenty of time alone now." Harriet hung up a dress. Seven years of hard wear and still it held up.

Carmen dialed. The conversation was brief. She hung up. "He'll come tomorrow."

Harriet wanted to hug Carmen, but Carmen had withdrawn from everybody and everything. Pack the bags. Go to the next tournament. Win the next tournament. Things will take care of themselves. She was hurt by Miguel's suggestion. The closer the pain got to her heels, the faster Carmen ran.

◆ ◆ ◆

Amelia Island is another instant resort. There are worse places to be than Jacksonville, but when there, one can't think of them. The island is dotted with the ubiquitous condominiums slapped together with plasterboard, plate glass, and plastic. Each group of condominiums has a pool. Then, too, there's always the ocean. One can rely on the Atlantic. It never moved although half the population of America seems to. The mosquitoes enjoy the atmosphere and so do people from Michigan, Wisconsin, and other cold places.

The interior of their condominium was a relief from avocado green and gold. This time it was dark blue and sea green. The interior decorators went for Fifties Restful. Harriet went for the john, wondering which would kill her first—the lesbian issue or bad taste. She decided the bad taste bothered her more.

Carmen drove to the grocery store and stocked up. She liked food shopping. When she carried the bags through the door, Harriet was on the phone.

"Hi," Carmen called out as Harriet hung up. "I'm making spareribs tonight. How hungry are you?"

"Not very." Harriet's head was up, but she looked tense. "What's wrong?"

"I was talking to Dr. Speicher, remember him?"

"Head of the religion department. Why were you talking to him?"

"I wanted to find out how bad it really is."

"Yeah?"

"He can't hire me back. He said forget teaching anywhere."

"Stop worrying about it! I make enough money to buy the fucking department. And I don't get it. They knew you were gay when you worked there."

"Well, I lived in a closet with an open door. I never said I was gay, but I never said I wasn't. Now I've said it."

"Forget it."

"Choosing not to work in order to follow you is one thing. Not being able to work is another."

"I told you to forget it. I pay all the bills anyway. It's no different today than it was yesterday."

Harriet was hurt. "You begged me to come on the road with you, Carmen. I never asked you to pay my bills, but who in God's name can afford to follow you all over the world? It bothers me that I can't get work now."

"If I win the Grand Slam, neither of us will ever have to worry about money."

"That's your life, not mine." Harriet smiled sadly.

This thought disturbed Carmen. Her life was her lover's life. Her lovers always accompanied her on the road, each yielding to the peculiar demands of Carmen's profession. In return, she paid the expenses. A life separate from her own seemed impossible . . . and it seemed somewhat traitorous. "When I'm on the road you can learn something new. Something where being gay won't matter. Don't worry about it."

Harriet, on the surface, brightened, "I guess I can audition for the telephone voice that says, 'At the tone the time will be two P.M.' "

♦ ♦ ♦

151

Carmen hauled her carcass through the first rounds of the Amelia Island tournament. Reporters buzzed around; a few proved obnoxious. Ricky headed them off when he could. Carmen and Harriet left their condominium in the middle of the night and moved in with Ricky and Jane. No one would dare mess with them there.

Carmen played golf every day. She played Boggle, Scrabble, cards, and darts when she wasn't playing golf. She'd practice tennis, play her match, and then hit the greens. Often Ricky would accompany her. He liked the pace of golf.

Jane and Harriet spent all Jane's nonworking hours together. The only players that would even nod a greeting to Harriet were the two married ones and Beanie Kittredge. The others, gay and scared shitless or straight and confused or sadly sexless, popped their bodies into reverse when Harriet was within sight. Harriet pitied them their cowardice, but she pitied Carmen even more. Carmen was running mostly from herself. There were moments when she couldn't look Harriet in the face. Harriet understood Carmen's dilemma. Carmen hoped it would all go away.

Harriet felt helpless and was helpless. She knew she'd have the unsavory experience of watching her lover run into a wall at eighty miles per hour. The question was, where and how? Some people can run until they're forty. Some fill up with bourbon. Some give up and die. Better to crash and crash so goddamned hard that you change yourself and change for the better, thought Harriet, but it was hard to watch. There was also the frightening possibility that someday Carmen would crash, period.

"Thanks again for letting us bunk out with you two," Harriet said as she and Jane sat down under a beach umbrella.

"Week's not over yet. You get the bill at the end or we take it out in trade." Jane put her fingers to her temples.

"Now, there's an idea." Harriet looked at her. "Another headache?"

Jane ignored the question, stared into the sky, and said, "Rawls, what are you going to do?"

"Live."

"That's never in question. You're probably immortal."

"Nectar and ambrosia."

"I mean it. Carmen's coasting over the lesbian issue. True, the tennis world gathered around to protect her. Did you read Susan Reilly's statement to the press?"

"No." Harriet turned so she could lie down facing Jane.

"She railed against the press for being bloodhounds. She said Carmen was not a homosexual." Harriet made a gagging sound. Jane pinched her nose with her forefinger and thumb and continued. "And she said people shouldn't be judged by their associations. Why, she, Susan Reilly, had gay men friends."

"Did she sign the statement, 'Your lying, fucking friend'?"

"It may help Carmen."

"Ha! It keeps the issue in front of everybody, and it keeps Susan in front, her favorite place, smelling like a rose."

"You're right, though, I hadn't thought of that."

"I miss Baby Jesus so much I could die."

"She'd rather be in Cazenovia than on the road."

"Yeah. What's percolating, Jane?" She wrote letters in the sand.

"American libel laws are one thing. British laws are another. You two are going to be roasted in England. That's what's percolating."

Harriet sighed. "I told Carmen I wanted to stay home from the French Open and Wimbledon for that reason. She went on a crying jag our first night here. A true jag. I can't leave her."

"Go with her and she'll cry, too."

"I know, but I can't let her down. I'm damned if I do and damned if I don't."

"Possibly." Jane smiled. "Harriet, I've known Carmen longer than you have. You may know her intimately, but I know her patterns. She's always got to have somebody. I'm not saying she doesn't love you or need you. But I am saying she's terrified of being alone. She ought to live by herself for one year to prove she can do it. You may not be helping her by running every time she calls. You can't make her happy every second of the day."

Harriet lay quietly for a few minutes. "Yeah."

"I'm only telling you what I see."

"How can I leave her alone for the first two events of the Grand Slam? They'll attack her whether I'm with her or whether I'm not. Better I stand by her and deflect what I can."

"Deflect or absorb?"

"It makes no difference."

"Harriet, I'm your friend, and I'm telling you you're being an asshole."

"For saying I was a lesbian?"

"Dense!" Jane threw up her hands. "No! If you go, you hurt both her and yourself, and if you stay, it's the same. You're in a no-win situation."

"Hell, I don't understand my life."

Jane put her chin in her palms. "Actually, I don't know if I understand mine either. Look, I'll be blunt. Carmen's easygoing, ready for fun, temperamental at times. She gets bored very easily and scared very easily. She responds to being scared by running away or by covering it with hyperactivity. She's running away from the lesbian issue—fuel supplied by ninety-nine percent of the circuit, thank you very much—and she could run away from you. Don't be fooled by these last few days of calm."

"Me! I'm the only person she can depend on."

Jane shrugged, palms upward.

"She loves me."

"I know she does as much as she can, given her profession and her age."

"Jane, why are you at me? So far, Carmen and I have been pretty good together. The only problem we had was my work."

"Resolved in her favor. Suppose something doesn't resolve in her favor?"

"I have faith in Carmen. I love her."

◆ ◆ ◆

At Amalgamated Banks, Dennis Parry read Kuzirian's column with more than curiosity. After all, they loaned Carmen Semana $600,000. If her corporation's profits depended on her popularity, Amalgamated's loan could be in jeopardy. Who'd want to wear her clothing line?

The phone call from a frightened Dennis Parry yanked Miguel's stomach into a knot.

"Dennis, don't worry. The next installment is due in two months. You'll have your seventy-five thousand dollars right on time."

Dennis hung up somewhat mollified.

Miguel was shaking. Would the scandal be reflected in the next quarter's sales? Miguel didn't bank on Amalgamated. He banked on his sister.

◆ ◆ ◆

Sitting in a golf cart watching the sunset, Carmen turned to Harriet and said, "Why is this happening to me?"

"I don't know."

"It's not fair."

"No." Harriet breathed in the salty air. "Florida sunsets are spectacular. Look at that orange and pink and purple."

"Yeah." Carmen touched Harriet's arm. "Do you think we'll ever have fun anymore?"

"I believe all things pass. This, too, shall pass."

"Sounds like something a nun would say."

"I'm no nun."

"Sometimes I look at you and wonder what you are."

Harriet, wanting to lift the mood, said, "Think of me as an angel with lice on her wings." But Carmen didn't laugh.

Mercifully, Carmen and Harriet had the week off after Amelia Island, and they returned home. Spring was flirting with Cazenovia. As it was so far north, the crocuses were only now blooming. Daffodils stuck their heads up in the flower beds around the lovely home. Even Miguel found himself charmed by the emergence of the town from its blanket of snow.

Carmen surrendered to the television. Hours of watching helped her unwind and escape the necessity of thought. Harriet launched herself into the attic closet in an orgy of spring cleaning. Unbeknownst to herself, she, too, began to put away her dreams.

The attic, cool and crisp, contained a huge cedar closet. Baby Jesus splayed herself across a shelf after making certain to nest in Harriet's prized cashmere sweaters.

Harriet loved the attic with its gables. The four-mile expanse of Cazenovia Lake lay smooth as a mirror. From the window she could see the lights in homes across the water. Legend had it that Hiawatha fished in the lake. A steam ferry sunk by irate citizens haunted one end of the lake.

Baby Jesus knocked a sweater to the floor. Harriet picked it up to fold it and, much to her surprise, found herself crying. The cat jumped on her shoulders and tried to lick her face. Harriet wiped her eyes and walked over to a gable window.

Must be all this tension, she thought.

Sitting perfectly still on the inside of the window was a giant luna moth. Its wingspan was easily seven inches. The wings and body were pale mint green with the shoulders and swallowtail edged in maroon. In the middle of each swallowtail pulsated a maroon dot that looked like the yin-yang symbol. The moth's fat legs were deep maroon while its antennae blazed like yellow ferns. Its iridescent eyes burned. The luna moth was early by nearly six weeks, but nonetheless, there she was.

Harriet and Baby Jesus, mesmerized by the creature, didn't move. At last Harriet opened the little window, and the giant moth fluttered into the dusk, seeking freedom or oblivion.

When the two of them thumped down the stairs, Carmen looked up from the tv.

"You were up there long enough."

"When Baby Jesus assists you, a job takes twice as long."

"I heard she wrote another novel." Baby listened impassively as Carmen continued, "*Catapult*, a novel about kitty warfare!"

"Baby, you pulled the wool over my eyes." Harriet spoke directly to the old creature, who blinked. "You said you were working on *Catatonic.*"

Carmen, now separated from the tube, said, "Oh, what's that one?"

"*Catatonic* is how to mix cocktails for parties and smart gatherings."

"Gimme a high five." Carmen put her hand over her head while Harriet smashed it with her own.

Harriet wondered, what did professional sportswomen do before high fives? When she was in school, girls didn't make such gestures. But then her generation grew up without many team sports, and as far as Harriet was concerned, she'd remain true to her generation. The world could have the high fives if she could dress to the nines.

Energized, Carmen slapped her on the back and challenged her to a game of gin. At that precise moment, Harriet realized something about her attitude toward Carmen. With all her glowing muscles and bulging veins, Harriet never thought of Carmen as a woman. Carmen didn't disappoint her. She rarely acted like one. She wasn't responsive or nurturing. All her energy was fixed on a goal outside herself. When it came to clothes, Carmen wore sweat suits or jeans. Now, with Lavinia's push toward femininity, Carmen could be cajoled into a dress and makeup, but she never really looked comfortable or womanly in that attire. She looked like a boy in drag. And maybe that was okay, Harriet thought. Sports have always been a male prerogative. If women get caught up in the violent competitive passions of sports, it's inevitable that they'll act like men. She laughed to herself as she thought, "Carmen is the only man I ever loved."

And Harriet did love Carmen. Her spontaneity, her carefree attitude and lack of concern for tomorrow, her animal good health, were intoxicating to Harriet who was anything but carefree. Carmen's strongest appeal was that when she loved, she withheld nothing. Her laughter was for Harriet. Her victories were for her, or so she said. Harriet became an important adjunct in Carmen's climb for success, cherished and adored. Adoration is habit-forming.

And so is the minutiae of daily life. How many spoons of sugar did she put in her coffee? Did she like Coca-Cola or Pepsi, potato chips or pretzels? Was she an early or late riser? Did she like the newspaper with breakfast? Such details seduce people into thinking they know one another.

Then a crisis strikes and the person one thought she knew so well can surprise the hell out of her. A quiet person can erupt in anger. A bombastic person can lapse into catatonia. A morally upright person can sink and become ethically sordid. A person on the fringes of society, a drunk perhaps, can become noble and strong. No one knows until it happens to her. Harriet didn't know what else Carmen would do, but she knew she'd find out.

About two hundred and fifty miles to the south of Cazenovia in Princeton, Jane and Ricky faced their crisis together. The tests came out positive. Jane had a brain tumor. The doctors declared it was inoperable, but chemotherapy might halt its growth.

Jane had seen the results of heavy-duty chemotherapy. Hair loss, nausea, spatial disorientation in some and loss of memory for others. Sometimes it did work; sometimes it worked for a while; and sometimes it just didn't work at all. She hated the thought of going through it. Chances were slender but even a remote chance was better than no chance at all.

She decided to begin the treatments immediately. Her doctor said she could probably go to the French Open and Wimbledon, but she should continue her treatments there. He made all the arrangements for her in France and England. Upon her return, she would undergo more tests and most likely more chemotherapy.

Ricky and Jane agreed not to tell anyone, at least not yet. As yet, too much was unknown, and why alarm friends and relatives unnecessarily?

As they lay in the bed, she rested her head on his chest. He stroked her beautiful hair.

"I always thought that Death was just my size, height, and weight. An invisible rope is tied around my waist, and the other end is tied around Death's waist. The younger you are, the longer the rope. If Death gives a yank, I can land flat on my face with injury, disease, or heartbreak. But if I tug on the rope with authority, I'll live. I always thought that as I grew very old, the distance would diminish until Death and I would blend and just walk away together."

"We'll both tug on the rope." Ricky kissed her hair, tears running down his cheeks.

NINE

The Peripherique encircles
Paris like an asphalt inner
tube. The various exits can take you back into centuries of
culture, into snarls of traffic, or into the urban sterility which
respects no nation. The Sofitel, the official players' hotel of the
French Open, was right off the beltway. Courtesy cars took
players to and from practice courts and matches. The French
pretended to give equal treatment to male players and female
players, but the reality was, ho hum, men first as usual.

Carmen and Harriet holed up in a tiny hotel not far from
the Sofitel. Pushing through the crowds of players, coaches,
reporters, and groupies in the lobby was bad enough. Given
their situation, they would sooner avoid crowds than plunge
into them.

Neither woman expected the press to let them alone.
Surprisingly, the French press was more restrained than the
English press. Harriet dreaded England the way Londoners
dreaded the plague of 1666. There would be no escape. She
pushed that into the back of her mind. They were in Paris for
two weeks; might as well make the best of it.

For Harriet, the tournament began as she was sitting
under the massive chestnut trees near the field courts. Two
male players on their way to practice observed Carmen's fluid
motion as she hit with Beanie Kittredge. The tall American

player said, "What has yellow balls and chases girls?" His practice partner shrugged. "Carmen Semana." Laughing, they continued on their way.

Great, Harriet thought to herself. Clay's her toughest surface. This is all she needs. Harriet closed her book, stood up and waved to Carmen. She might as well find Jane and Ricky.

The Stade Roland Garros was built in 1927 and named in honor of an aviator killed in action during World War I. Longchamps Racecourse was not far away. Harriet imagined Edwardians strolling the grounds, a very different crowd from those who attended racetracks or tennis tournaments today. The famous French skill at dressing wasn't in evidence at the Stade Roland Garros, especially in the west stand. The east stand habitués, sun behind them and money in their pockets, lived up to the fashion reputation a bit better.

The French Open reminded Harriet of Forest Hills. Forest Hills was now defunct, but in its day, it physically embraced the spectator as did Garros. Each was covered in ivy, built to human scale so one was not overwhelmed by architecture, and each bordered a city—accessible but not choked by the concrete octopus. Harriet hoped the French would never suffer a fit of building like the Americans. She still missed Forest Hills as the site of the U.S. Open. So what if locker space was impossible. It was beautiful.

A greenhouse was at the site of the stadium. Harriet wandered in. Lurking behind a potted palm was Jane Fulton.

"Palmy days, Jane."

"Hey, we got in late last night. How long have you been here?"

"Two days. She wants to get the feel of this clay, and Miguel wants to get a feel, period."

Jane kissed Harriet on the cheek. "How are things?"

"Hate letters arrive with alarming regularity. I zip to the mailbox before she does. She's had enough upset before a major tournament. Where's Ricky?"

"Lining up his ducks."

"What?"

"Getting everything under control. He's bad enough at an American tournament. Take him out of the country, and he's worse than his grandmother."

"How are you? Lest I forget my manners." Harriet touched a peach rose.

"Okay. Still bothered by headaches."

"My sinuses are rotten, but yours seem worse. Go to a doctor."

"They'll pump me full of some drug that's supposed to keep me awake, and I'll fall asleep. I always do."

The two emerged into the gray day. "Have you checked the draw?"

Jane replied, "Before I unpacked."

"Men's is a foregone conclusion." Harriet, unlike most tennis observers, was not a devotee of the women's game to the exclusion of the men's. She liked them both. In fact, she probably enjoyed the men's game more because she didn't suffer for anyone. She could relax and enjoy it.

"Despite your bias, wouldn't you say this looks like Page Bartlett Campbell's tournament?"

"With Rainey Rogers, the vacant heir, waiting in the wings." Harriet felt a drop of what she hoped was bird pee, not a shower.

Jane shielded her eyes and looked up. "It never fails—rain."

"The joys of an outdoor tournament."

"The French Open." Jane grimaced.

"Open season on Americans!" Harriet shouted, and they ran for shelter.

♦ ♦ ♦

So much rain dumped on Stade Roland Garros during that two-week period, it resembled the evacuation of Dunkirk. The crowds stayed home. A decent day brought them back again, but the players enjoyed no respite. If the court could take them, if the rain was over, out they went. Players stumbled back, red up to the knees. Inner thigh muscles ached from the sliding. On clay, it was so tempting to slide into the ball instead of moving one's feet. The grounds keepers would go out and tend to the court after every one of these gut busters.

Unless one was playing a paraplegic, there was no such thing as an easy match. Defeating even an unskillful player took time. A player who could be dispatched mercilessly on grass or even Deco Turf would hang on by his fingernails at the French Open. It was as though these low-ranking players became poisonous dwarfs. They were so exhausting to play that even the top-seeded players felt half dead.

Carmen was no exception. Her temperament, unsuited to anything or anyone slow, took a beating with her body. Her knee was sore; her torso, strong as it was, screamed after each match. She would rarely sweat, but the combination of rain and then heat brought the beads to her forehead. She hated headbands, but she wore one.

The early matches went her way. Trouble in the person of Susan Reilly lay in wait at the semifinals. Not that Carmen's quarterfinal match was a shoo-in. Justine Haverford, the English player, was good on this goo. Carmen's draw was tough, but Page Bartlett Campbell had Rainey Rogers in the semifinals, assuming they would both reach the semifinals, and of that there seemed little doubt. Harriet and Carmen were relieved Rainey was on the other side because facing Rainey for an eternity could knock Carmen down for Page in the finals. Carmen would need all her strength for Page, whose coolness was as hard to play as her game.

Page and Jeffrey Campbell, darlings of the European as

well as American media, bore it with good grace. Page liked the publicity more than she would admit, but then Page never admitted anything to anybody. The virtues of intimate silence covered up by general conversation were well-known to Page. At twenty-seven, she glanced over her shoulder and witnessed an army of little girls sporting two-fisted backhands, pigtails or pageboy haircuts, and questionable manners. Page worried about the manners. If these tykes were going to slavishly imitate her, they could also imitate her manners.

Page would always be mysterious to Jeffrey, because he had difficulty looking beneath the surface. Page, however, realized within the first year of her marriage that she tied herself to an extraordinary-looking man with an ordinary mind. She was more ambitious and brighter, more cynical. She cloaked the cynicism, but she'd observed enough to know what you see is not what you get. Jeffrey worried constantly: about her, about his football career, about money. Page was not one to hide from life or to puff off responsibilities, but she liked to have a good time. She rarely could meet anyone who didn't talk about tennis. She longed for association with exciting people. In short, she married a man who was not her equal. He loved her. He was honest, sober, and decent. She'd done better than eighty percent of this world. However, odds don't make up for the lack of mental stimulation and spontaneity. Page was a little lonesome. Given that their marriage had been trumpeted as the love match of the century, she certainly could talk to no one about her misgivings. Given the insularity of both the tennis world and the football world, she was in no position to make close friendships with people outside the sports world. Right now, Jeffrey would be hurt if she took any energy away from him. Their schedules were tight enough already without introducing new friends, new obligations. So she concentrated on her game. The French Open was her introduction back onto the circuit and she meant to win it.

Justine Haverford, fortunately for Carmen, was sluggish on the court. Carmen rolled over her, six-two, six-three. Next came Susan Reilly. Carmen needed to pull together for that one. It remained to be seen what would happen between Rainey Rogers and Page.

The larger the tournament the more wired Carmen became. Little things grated on her nerves. The tone of Harriet's voice could make her tremble with rage. Traffic infuriated her. The weather heightened her emotional state. Nothing was worse than having a match called during play because of rain, except perhaps losing the match. She'd get psyched up, then have to let down. Sitting in the locker room waiting for the weather to clear felt like waiting to be called to the tumbrels.

Lavinia, although she had no power on the European circuit, was much in evidence. She nipped at Carmen's heels and saw to it that Carmen was photographed in restaurants with a variety of men. Miguel stuck so close to Harriet, he could have been a sand spur.

◆ ◆ ◆

A small blue vein throbbed over Lavinia's temple. With difficulty she maneuvered Siggy Wayne and Seth Quintard out of this meeting. Seth could care less about Carmen thanks to Miguel but Athletes Unlimited wanted no trouble in women's tennis. Men lack the finesse for this kind of operation, she thought to herself. No one hailed her idea as brilliant for the simple reason that what she was about to tell Carmen Semana was done all the time. She'd been working up to this.

Lavinia picked up a tennis shoe; the bottom looked like a lunar landscape. Different treads were used for the different surfaces—grass, clay, carpet, and Deco Turf. As far as Lavinia knew, no one was planning a tournament on the moon. She laid the shoe down on its side on the floor. She was superstitious; it was bad luck to put a shoe on a table or chair. She'd need good luck today.

A knock on the door brought her to her feet. She crossed the room with a worn magnificence. "Carmen."

Carmen slipped through the door and sat across from Lavinia. The shoe on the floor did not escape her notice nor was it intended to.

"Would you like a beverage?"

"No, thank you." Carmen's hair was cut shorter than usual.

"When did you do that?" Lavinia pointed to Carmen's head.

"Yesterday. I got sick of blow drying my hair. I'll let it grow back after the Grand Slam."

"M-m-m." Lavinia thought Carmen's dream of the Slam perfectly impossible. "I'll come straight to the point, Carmen. This lesbian scandal must stop."

Carmen listened mutely.

Lavinia continued. "My left ear is red from the phone conversations I've had with tournament promoters, sponsors, and Howard Dominick who is sick, just sick. Women's tennis can't afford this."

"Neither can I."

"Miguel left his own legacy. You know, of course, you're going to have to pay off the Jaguar dealer in Chicago or perform a gratis advertisement for him."

Carmen shifted in her seat. She knew nothing about it.

"He got a white Jaguar, twelve-cylinder, in exchange for your services."

"I never saw it."

"He shipped it back to Argentina and probably sold it on the spot."

Carmen groaned.

"You're in a spot. I remember what these big four tournaments are like." How the old girl loved to go back into time. Like actors, athletes seemed incapable of moving beyond their applause. Perhaps Lavinia had no future, but Carmen still had one, at least until her game slowly eroded. Lavinia was addressing that future, or so she thought. "You know I liked the French Open. Most Americans don't, but I always did and still do. There's an ambiance, don't you think?"

"Yes. But then I'm not an American."

"Can't be helped." Lavinia smiled her ermine smile. "You could get bounced right out of America with this mess. If you admit to being homosexual."

"I don't think your government will pick on me. I'm not scared," Carmen bluffed.

Lavinia eyed this youngster. Homosexuality bothered her only slightly. What these girls did with one another was beyond her imagination. Seemed like such a waste, really. "Why take the chance?"

"I haven't said I am a lesbian."

"That will save you. There is a way out of this. You can save yourself, help women's tennis, and the sponsors and promoters will be happy, too."

"What's that?"

"First, can you give up Harriet?"

"I love Harriet."

"That's not what I asked."

Carmen shrugged her shoulders. "I don't know."

"I've known you since you were sixteen, Carmen."

Her face burning, the player replied, "What does that mean?"

"Homosexual relationships don't last. You people seem to have revolving doors to your bedrooms. If you leave Harriet, you'll find someone else." Lavinia was close to insult.

"I do not have a revolving door to my bedroom!"

"Well, your relationships don't last long, do they?"

"Harriet and I have been together three years."

"That's when the getting-to-know-you stage is over. You can't shift gears into the next level of love. I don't know any homosexuals who can. Is that how you want to live your life?"

"Lavinia, what I do is my business."

"You're wrong. What you do is everybody's business, most especially mine. My solution to this problem is simple. You are going to get married."

Carmen sat stunned. She reached over and took a swig of Lavinia's ever-present vodka. "Go on."

"Others do it." Lavinia discreetly avoided naming names.

"You have someone in mind?" Carmen's voice didn't sound like her own.

"Yes. An American boy. That will help you if things ever do get difficult at home. Oh, not just homosexuality, although marriage will take care of that; I mean politics."

Carmen listened as Lavinia told her how unstable Argentina was. Americans are all alike when it comes to South America, Carmen thought. It's hard not to hate them. "Who is this person?"

"He's the son of an old friend of mine. He lives in Los Angeles where he's a struggling actor. He's terribly good-looking and well-bred. He'll be perfect at social functions, and he's a nice person."

"Why would he agree to this? Is he gay, too?"

"I never asked. His profession is notoriously unstable. You will buy a house and run it. The prenuptial agreement will state that he cannot touch your money but aside from the new house which you'll own jointly, its running costs, and a car for him, you will provide him with sixty thousand dollars a year, adjustable for inflation. That's a cheap way out of your problems if you think about it." She paused. "He has good taste for his age. He'll help you make a beautiful house."

Carmen thought she already had a beautiful house, except that she owned it with Harriet. Lavinia, tireless in her devotion to tennis, offered Carmen a perfect solution. Carmen was not as strong as she thought she was. Her career had to come first. That's what everyone told her.

"When do I meet this man?"

"First week back in the States. You will like him. I think you should plan to get married on Christmas Day. Right after the Australian Open."

When Carmen finally left Lavinia, she walked back to her hotel. She didn't know when or how she would tell Harriet. She stopped on the corner, as she realized she hadn't even asked his name. The street lamp framed her head like a rancid halo.

◆ ◆ ◆

Susan Reilly liked clay no more than Carmen did, but she figured she could outgut Carmen. Susan held that opinion about all her opponents. She was often correct.

Alicia settled herself in the stands. Craig and Lisa would come over for Wimbledon, so until the last week in June, she had Susan all to herself. Susan shrunk from the world during a major tournament. Her every waking moment was spent honing strategy and studying the psychology of her opponent, her body, the weather. Unlike most players, she didn't watch television. She'd watch it during minor tournaments, but not during any Grand Slam event. Her trance lasted until she lost or won.

When Susan was a girl, playing in junior high school and high school, she loved the game. She hated losing, but she loved winning. She skipped college because the women's tour was established at the perfect time for Susan. Billie Jean King, Betty Stove, Virginia Wade, and others took the big risks. Lavinia Sibley Archer masterminded the tour; the players put their bodies on the line. Susan never took any risks except on the tennis court. There was nothing wrong with capitalizing on the labor of others. We all live off the work of the dead and of the living, older generations. She attended no meetings of the Players Guild. She sponsored no children for tennis camps; she taught no camps or clinics. Her entire being revolved around competition. Susan did only what was good for Susan.

Unfortunately, winning was no longer good for Susan. She hated losing more than she loved winning. What was a source of self-confidence and joy in her youth, became a contest for sanity at thirty. She willed herself to win. She had to prove to herself that she could win one more time. Each year further reduced her chance of winning the Grand Slam. Each year further reduced her.

Even her own love affairs became impoverished. In her twenties she loved them and left them. She still did that, but in her twenties, she experienced thrills, chills, highs, and lows. Now, though she experienced orgasms at regular intervals, she felt mounting irritation with any intrusion on her life and suppressed the secret horror that no one understood her. She suffered from spiritual anorexia.

The overcast sky hung so low it seemed pierced by the barbed iron fence that surrounded the stadium. Susan took the court. This was the first event in the Grand Slam. If she could stop Carmen now, she'd be content. She wanted to win the Slam, sure, but stopping Carmen consumed her. Hating to lose, Susan reduced herself further by transforming Carmen into her enemy. She cursed the day she took Carmen to bed. She was twenty-four and Carmen was sixteen. She must have been out of her mind. Carmen resembled an auto mechanic in those days before Harriet cleaned up her act. Susan wanted to forget that brief, ridiculous affair. She wasn't lonesome. She had a lover stacked away in the hills as well as Craig. It wasn't even lust. She let Carmen stay in her San

Francisco house during that tournament. One night Carmen crept into her bed and Susan didn't kick her out.

Carmen's recollection was substantially different. She remembered a great player paying attention to her when all she showed was potential, not accomplishment. She remembered Susan delighting in feeding her her first McDonald's hamburger, taking her to her first American movie, and unfolding San Francisco at her feet. She remembered being swept up by Susan's charismatic presence and believing everything Susan said. She was dying to sleep with Susan but it was fair to say that at sixteen she was dying to sleep with anybody. For the first three days of the week, she gave Susan a back rub every night before retiring to the guest room at the end of the hall. One night she stayed. Susan didn't throw her out. She rolled over and pretended to sleep, but with clumsy encouragement from Carmen, she woke up.

No one ever told Carmen that if God wanted to punish her, he'd answer her prayers. The person she admired most in the world was in her arms. It was a love too perfect to bear. After the tournament was over, Susan went on to Houston and Carmen returned to Buenos Aires. Every minute she relived those days, those nights, with Susan Reilly. Susan didn't call her, but then it's hard to call Buenos Aires and very expensive. Carmen didn't mind that. She had a calendar inside her address book. She crossed off each day with a red X. She'd be playing tournaments in America in three weeks. Those were the three longest weeks of her life. She made up her mind to leave Argentina in all but name only. She had a taste of America. She had a taste of Susan.

Susan refused responsibility for Carmen by dumping her the day Carmen appeared at her door. Since she refused responsibility by dumping her other lovers, that was nothing special. The only thing that kept Carmen from going over the edge those months alone in a strange country, struggling with a strange language, was her increasing mastery over her own body. Tennis kept her alive. Then, after months of silence and rejection, Susan asked Carmen Semana to be her doubles partner. Susan wanted to win as many doubles titles as singles. With this kid she could do it. When she asked Carmen at a Boston tournament, Carmen said yes. She hoped it meant more, but it meant doubles only. Resigned, Carmen played her heart out. She couldn't keep from loving Susan. Susan noticed only the tennis.

Over the years, the innocent love of a sixteen-year-old faded. The more Carmen saw Susan throw people aside like old shoes, the less she liked her. But she couldn't come to grips, even now, with what Susan had done. By virtue of being her first lover, Susan Reilly owned a ragged corner of Carmen's heart. Carmen would love those days in San Francisco even as she learned to hate Susan Reilly.

The two squared off. The match started slowly. Each player kept her serve. So far no surprises.

"Out?"

The linesman responded in French. Susan responded in foul English. The linesman, a true Parisian, pretended he couldn't understand a word of it. Susan stalked to the backcourt and awaited serve. Carmen won the first set seven-five.

The second set, peppered with a few more Reilly outbursts, picked up speed. The points weren't shorter, not on clay, but the pace was tougher. Both women were in splendid condition.

Susan became angrier and angrier at Carmen's exacting aggression. Why hadn't Carmen cracked into fourteen pieces, scattered about the court? Hadn't she been rocked by the recent scandal? Wasn't she mortified to show her face on the court, knowing everyone thought she was a lesbian? Susan's concentration shifted imperceptibly from the game to the inside of her opponent's head. Before Susan collected herself, Carmen broke her serve and was ahead four-three. Susan fought back, but she'd drifted a little too much and couldn't find her rhythm. Her increasing frustration sapped her game. Carmen soundly closed out the second set six-four.

Livid, Susan crawled to the net. She slid her hand across Carmen's outstretched palm. She couldn't look Carmen in the face. If she did, she'd hit her again.

♦ ♦ ♦

"I blew it!" Susan smashed a racquet against the bureau in the hotel room.

Alicia patted her on the back. "You'll catch her at Wimbledon."

"Goddamn me. That was my fault. I lost my concentration."

Alicia patted her again. Susan brushed her hand aside. Gloom settled in. "It can happen to anybody."

"Now I have to wait until next year to try for the Slam." Susan kicked the broken racquet.

"You're good for years to come," Alicia lied.

"I thought I had her. I thought this lesbian bit would take her mind off tennis."

A warning light flickered inside Alicia's head. "What?"

"The bad publicity—I thought it would wear her down. You know how emotional she gets."

"Yes, it does seem odd." Alicia meant that in more ways than one.

"Escape artist! I've known that creep for six years, almost seven. She won't face anything until it hits her in the face. She'll withdraw into tennis. Fuck. Well, the world will pry her out. Sooner or later, she'll be rocked. She won't win the Slam."

Alicia vaguely felt that Susan wasn't doing too badly as an escape artist herself. "You really hate her, don't you?"

"It's worse than that. She bores me." Susan threw her socks against the wall.

"Do you have any idea how that lesbian mess got started?"

Susan whitened. "Why would I know anything about it?" Her voice rose.

Alicia appraised her. "I don't know."

"Let's practice early tomorrow. I'm going to practice eight hours a day if I have to."

◆ ◆ ◆

Most people in Carmen's situation would have charged into Miguel's room and demanded an explanation about the Jaguar. They would have also suffered obvious anguish over the fate of their lover. But Carmen wasn't most people. She swept these issues out of her head and was concentrating only on the French Open. If at all possible, she wouldn't think about anything until after Wimbledon.

◆ ◆ ◆

Back in the United States, Howard Dominick of Tomahawk couldn't stop worrying. Lavinia Sibley Archer's reassurance that she'd haul Carmen into line didn't soothe his worries. Howard assumed sportswriters were hacks. They wouldn't criticize players or organizations because if they did, the controllers of those teams or individual players would cut off access. A reporter without interviews is like a tennis player without a serve.

In the past, the sportswriters could be counted on to weep, exult, chastise, and coo in unison with Lavinia or Athletes Unlimited. Martin Kuzirian burst that cozy arrangement wide open. Since Kuzirian couldn't get any more interviews, Howard figured he'd close up shop. But Kuzirian didn't. He got tougher. He began to dig around for the financial dealings among promoters, sponsors, and players. Not that the dealings were always dishonest, but more and more tournaments were losing money. That was worse than being dishonest in Howard's book.

Kuzirian was using the lesbian issue to advance his career as a hard-hitting reporter. If he was going to be hated by the front office, then he was going to be hated with style. More people read his column than ever before.

Disgusted though he was, Howard knew if one reporter showed some balls, others might try to follow. The role of sports reporters as shadow publicity men was drawing to a close. Howard's only consolation was that most of them still didn't know how to collect evidence, much less write.

That was his only consolation. Tomahawk couldn't afford a scandal in women's tennis since it was so heavily identified with the sport. Prestige once lost was usually not recovered.

In addition, the novelty of women as pro athletes had worn off. Continued sponsorship of Lavinia's girls would yield diminishing returns. It might be good for women's tennis, but was it good for Tomahawk? As head of the Tomahawk division of Clark & Clark, Howard clearly knew where his responsibilities were. The lesbian scandal would give him a good reason to get out without anyone looking into the books. His ass was on the line. If he discontinued support of women's tennis, he had to do so in a way that would preserve his authority. And if God were good to him, he'd find at that same moment the next Brooke Shields. No more tomboy look for Tomahawk.

◆ ◆ ◆

The morning of her finals against Page Bartlett Campbell, Carmen spat at Harriet, apologized, turned around and did it again when Harriet asked her a question about pressing a skirt. Harriet traveled with a portable iron and touched up Carmen's outfits. She couldn't stand for her to go on the court with one wrinkle.

"I'm taking a shower." Carmen slammed the door.

Carmen came back into the room after drying her hair and sat down to finish her cantaloupe. The silence continued for fifteen minutes.

Harriet finally broke it. "Is there something you want to tell me?"

Carmen stopped her spoon in midair. "Uh, not before the finals." She wondered if Harriet knew about her meeting with Lavinia. Crimson, Carmen gulped down the cantaloupe.

Harriet smiled, "I hope you win."

"I will." Carmen kissed Harriet. She walked into the closet and selected her outfit for the match.

Harriet fought off a throbbing headache and wondered what happens when a little lie becomes a reality or when reality becomes a lie.

◆ ◆ ◆

There are moments in sport when everything works. Chance magnificence because no matter how perfectly one plays his part, a thousand tiny things can go wrong. When they go right, no one ever forgets, neither the players nor the audience nor even the grounds keepers. Sport strips away personality, letting the white bone of character shine through. Sport gives players an opportunity to know and test themselves. The great difference between sport and art is that sport, like a sonnet, forces beauty within its own system. Art, on the other hand, cyclically destroys boundaries and breaks free.

Tennis, imprisoned within fixed boundaries, a patch of an acre, a green rectangle, tries the human soul. A tennis court is like a coffin, only larger. Someone can invent a new technique, but the lines, the rules, are fixed. Despite the mildewed intelligence of promoters and the industrial malaise that reduced tennis into just another vehicle for selling douche powder, beer, and automobiles, a fracture appeared in the commercial structure and the human spirit occasionally slipped through.

The women's finals of the French Open was such a moment. Page Bartlett Campbell versus Carmen Semana, the classic backcourt player versus the queen of serve and volley, gave people a glimpse of something beyond terminal greed.

The first set ticked off as odds makers expected. Page clung to the baseline and forced errors from Carmen. A great serve and volley player commits herself. Page knew Carmen would come in off a strong serve, off any deep, driving shot. The net was Carmen's domain. From that vantage point, like Archimedes, she could move the world. Hit into her body and she'd blast it back at a short angle. Hit wide and she'd leap into the ball and kill it. Page, a backcourt player, couldn't afford to hit too many slices. If she was going to pass Carmen Semana at the net, she would have to hit the ball flat and hard as hell or fire it past her with wicked topspin. Page would need pinpoint accuracy because even the quickest volleyer can't nick the blazing fury of a ball hit full force down the line.

The first set seesawed between the two women, but Page Bartlett Campbell could hit a dime from ten feet behind the baseline. She was better than a gunner in a Flying Tiger. Carmen, playing well, didn't let this rattle her. Only a goddess could keep up that deadly aim for the duration of the match. However, Page came as close as any mortal to that description.

Carmen had to win this final. No one thought she could win on clay. It was the beginning of her dream, the Slam, and it would terrify the other players to know she could put down the best clay court player in the world.

Carmen lost the first set in the tie breaker.

The second set opened up with Carmen pushing a little harder, taking chances but not foolish ones. Her opportunities were born of confidence. Coming up midcourt, she hit a half-volley that cut over the net and died. The drop shot brought applause from the crowd. Page waved—a great shot was a great shot—then dug into the baseline like an infantryman at Verdun. Campbell could not be beaten psychologically. The accuracy continued. Her short, backhand crosscourt ate away at Carmen's stamina. Page pulled her up, then passed her, if she could. She jerked her from one side of the court to the other. Carmen, a panther, increased her vocabulary of movement. It was as though her body extended that extra inch. She was there.

If they were goddesses, Page was Athena. Her game was the essence of rationality, planning, and flawless execution. Carmen was Artemis, goddess of the hunt. She sprang, leapt, and twisted in a ballet of power. Her game plan was secondary to her phenomenal athletic prowess. Page thought through every shot; she could gauge the degree of spin and height of bounce before the ball was on her side of the net. Carmen understood strategy, but at her best, she seemed guided by divine inspiration.

The contrast of personalities electrified the crowd. Spectators chose sides as to which woman was the greatest player alive in the world today. Seeing them at their best, head to head, was like watching Man O' War or Secretariat. Spectators knew they'd not see the like again for decades. Between Page Bartlett Campbell and Carmen Semana, competition reached its highest level and became a sophisticated form of cooperation.

Carmen won the second set seven-five.

Jeffrey Campbell devoured four packs of gum. His wild swings of emotion were either blood sugar rushes or total identification or both. Harriet, face impassive, prayed the muscles in her midriff would not constrict further. She could scarcely breathe, and sweat poured from under her armpits. Before an important match, she would sandblast her armpits because of nerves. It was one thing to be nervous. It was another thing to stink. Her mouth was dry. She never took her eyes off Carmen. Her radar, usually activated the night before a match, told her the outcome. She literally woke up in the mornings and knew if Carmen would win or lose. She awakened this morning thinking Carmen would win, but after watching Page on her best surface, at a tournament she repeatedly conquered, Harriet was questioning her prediction.

By now, the women had been in the afternoon sun for three hours. Every game went to deuce, ad; deuce, ad. Each point was an arabesque of struggle. The third set was at five-all, Page serving.

Page's serve was deceptive. She lacked the booming power of Carmen. What she possessed was that deadly accuracy, coupled with enough power to hold an opponent back. Her feminine appearance belied her strength. When necessary, Page had a surprisingly flat, forceful service. She usually conserved her energy, opting for placement and fair speed. Her ground strokes depended on torque. The twist of her body sent the ball winging over the net. Those who played her often never underrated her power. The Sunday coaches in the stands thought Page Bartlett Campbell was all brains and no brawn. Too bad they didn't have the opportunity to play her. She'd grind them into hamburger.

Thirty-all in the game and Page rocketed a serve to Carmen's backhand, then followed it to the net. Page only came to the net to shake hands after the match was over. She caught Carmen off guard and cracked a forehand volley neatly into the corner.

At forty-thirty, Carmen rocked back and forth awaiting service. She didn't know what to expect. Page hit her standard speed serve. Carmen ripped a forehand down the line. Deuce. Page coolly called for a ball from the ball boy. She took a deep breath, steadied herself, and hit that flat serve again. Carmen was surprised once more, and Page danced up to the net; she never seemed to be clumsy or heavy footed. Carmen returned the ball across Page's body. Page had a reputation of being afraid of the net. Carmen figured instead of going down the line, she'd bore into her and perhaps force an error. Without batting an eye, Page met the ball with her racquet head open, no slant. The ball ricocheted back, Carmen's power turned back on herself. Carmen scrambled for the wide return, and with a superhuman lunge and a flick of her stainless steel wrist, she hit a clear winner down the line.

Her advantage. Carmen's steady rocking motion to receive the serve gave no hint of her own fear. She'd been in the sun, on grueling clay, for over three and a half hours now. She was tiring, and she knew it. Page was tiring, too, but neither one could slacken the pace. A whiff of indecision, a hint of exhaustion, and one would tear the other's throat out.

Page served hard to Carmen's backhand. The steady slice returned the shot over the net. Page's two-handed backhand meant she had to take more steps to get to the ball. She barely made it, but she got off a decent return. Carmen took advantage of the chance and laid everything she had into that ball. She drove it back on the baseline. Page reached up almost at shoulder level to return the ball, but the return was weak and in no-man's-land. Instantly, Carmen was on it. Page hovered in the backcourt waiting for the tremendous blow sure to follow. Carmen caressed the ball over the net like an artist stroking the canvas. The ball dropped over the net, spun backwards, and was impossible to reach. Carmen broke Page's service. She had only to hold her own to win the match.

Holding her own took another twenty minutes. No one could believe the punishment those women inflicted upon one another. Each point was an agony. Page called upon all the reserve and courage she had. Her murderous, line-catching shots would have broken the back of a weaker player. Carmen ran until she thought her lungs would burst. She made one backhand volley at the net where she leapt a foot off the ground, hit the shot, spun around completely, and hit Page's return on her forehand volley. Yet after all that, she still lost the point.

The audience was on emotional overload. Jane and Ricky, hypnotized by the quality of their play, commented very little on the points. The tennis was so fantastic, it was best left to view in silence. The audience held its breath. All that could be heard was the ping of the ball on the racquet and the groans of the women, by now in obvious distress.

Finally, on ad in, Carmen used her last ounce of power for a blazing serve. Page's serve return was crisp but short; Carmen moved in. Page shot down the line. Carmen, displaying a sixth sense, catapulted her body parallel to the net, blocking the shot. Page raced to it but couldn't get it over the net.

Carmen Semana won the French Open. She won the first of the big four, the tournament no one thought she would ever win. What or who could stop her now?

TEN

A fter the French Open, there were two warm-up tournaments on grass in England. Carmen always skipped the first, preferring to practice on the private grass courts of English friends.

Miguel, Harriet, and Carmen slipped into England on the last hydrofoil. The reporters hanging around the airport were fooled, but when the Eastbourne tournament began, there'd be no escape.

Cold, damp, the weather did not tempt Carmen to practice, but she knew she had to. Miguel was especially demanding as he drilled her on the court. His analytical mind made him a good coach.

Before returning to the house, Miguel wrapped a towel around her neck and put her sweat jacket on. "Migueletta, you must send Harriet back or force her to marry me this week."

"I don't want to talk about it."

"We've got to talk about it. Lavinia calls me every day." He didn't mention that Seth, the shit, called once to gloat.

"Lavinia's planting an article about my marriage."

"What marriage?" Miguel was thunderstruck.

"She found me a man in Los Angeles to marry."

Miguel tempered his voice. "Who is this man? What kind

of man would marry you without knowing you? A man who needs a cover of his own! And money!"

"Lavinia has arranged a reasonable sum."

"Without consulting me? I forbid it!" He forgot to control his fury.

"You forbid nothing. You took a Jaguar in exchange for my endorsement of a charity I knew nothing about, as well as the car dealer. I never made the endorsement, Miguel. You forged it!"

He winced. She'd better never find out what else he forged. "You must never make a business decision without me, never," he said.

"It's a good deal."

"I'll be the judge of that after I investigate your mail-order husband."

Carmen explained why Lavinia thought it would work. Miguel listened impassively. He saw the sense of it, but he just hated to pay this jerk a yearly salary. However, that was preferable to losing all the endorsements. The plan was not without merit.

"I still want to investigate. It may be a solution, but never again commit yourself to anything before coming to me. You didn't sign anything, did you?"

"No."

"This is insane."

"Harriet can stick close to you or Jane and Ricky. We'll be in a private house, so who will know what room she sleeps in. And I want her with me."

"No."

"The article about my marriage will throw people off the track."

"Oh, Migueletta." He threw up his hand in disgust.

"I love her and I want her with me. I need her. Don't fuck around with me during Wimbledon."

His face softened. "I'm trying to protect you. You're pinning a lot of hope on this marriage article."

"Lavinia will back me up and so will the sponsors."

"For now, perhaps." He stroked his chin. "But we're in Europe and this is Wimbledon. The sponsors aren't in the driver's seat for Wimbledon."

"I love Harriet."

"I know you do, but you should send her home."

"I won't do it." Carmen was torn. She didn't want to be alone. She needed Harriet. What she couldn't admit about herself was that she couldn't be alone for over a week. If she shipped Harriet back, what would she do? Many athletes, like other entertainers, rely on reaction. Without an audience, even an audience of one, they become frightened. They need other people to approve of them, to tell them who they are.

Carmen met Harriet three years ago. She'd gone to Syracuse University to see a doctor of sports medicine for stiffness in her elbow. Harriet was a guest lecturer and she wandered into the hall and that was that.

Carmen was impulsive about love. She thought each lover would last forever. She quickly disengaged from her lover at the time, a pretty girl her own age. And when she met the pretty girl she left an older woman lawyer who cared for her. After Susan Reilly dumped her, Carmen vowed to herself never to be dumped again. Her affair with Harriet lasted three years, and Carmen wasn't tired of her although she was getting there. The tension of professional tennis, the pressure of Kuzirian's article crept in. Harriet was exciting when she was a professor, but in following Carmen, she lost some of her excitement. Carmen didn't exactly know that, but she did know things weren't as intense and passionate as when they were first lovers. But she wasn't ready to give Harriet up just yet.

♦ ♦ ♦

In England, the men are very masculine, but then the women are, too. Harriet liked the people, but found them perverse. The English have a natural impulse toward kindness and spend the rest of their lives brutally restraining it.

Devonshire Park in Eastbourne glittered an inviting green. The grounds of this Wimbledon warm-up tournament outclassed the Big W itself. Pink, yellow, and red flowers dazzled passersby. Elms lined the edges of the court. The desire under those elms was purely athletic.

Eastbourne, a favorite with the players, was also a favorite tournament of the cucumber sandwich set. Out they trooped in their natty dresses, sensible shoes, carrying the ever-present symbol of British life, the umbrella.

If the greatest minds of the nineteenth century controlled the All England Lawn Tennis and Croquet Club, Wimbledon, then the promoters of Eastbourne were to be congratulated— or scolded, depending on your attitude—for having advanced to the twentieth century.

Eastbourne was Carmen's nemesis. She often lost in the early rounds, although a few times she did make it to the finals. Instead of pitching a fit and falling in it, she began to think, if she lost Eastbourne, she would certainly win Wimbledon. Anyway, it was a tune-up, so why get bent out of shape?

The British press warmed up at Eastbourne as well. Harriet, ever accompanied by Miguel when she went out in public, became adept at melting into shadows. Both women knew the reporters would save the big guns and their store of potent venom for Wimbledon.

Reporters wrote snide little articles about the "undesirable element in tennis," namely Harriet, but really Carmen. Photos of their home in Cazenovia made the papers, which soon would wrap fish and chips but not soon enough for Harriet. These would be laid out next to fawning articles declaring Page Bartlett Campbell as a "credit to her sex." Page hated it, too. If one is to be praised, one would like it to be for something one has achieved. Page was born a woman. Why praise her for that? She liked Carmen, and she loathed being used against her.

Lavinia did plant the marriage news. She eagerly awaited for it to appear and the reporter promised it would be before the end of Wimbledon.

♦ ♦ ♦

"Do you want to stay with us?" Jane asked while driving the Rolls-Royce she and Ricky rented. Ricky, Harriet, and Jane shared a profound weakness for English cars. They couldn't afford a Rolls in the U.S. so it was great fun to rent one in England.

"I don't think so."

"There's plenty of room."

"Thanks for the offer, but we'll stay farther away from London. Carmen's a maniac at Wimbledon. This is my third one, and it looks like a killer. Between the press and the pressure to grab number two on the Slam, I think she'll be bouncing off the walls."

"She has been unusually tense, except she goes back and forth. She's either loose as a goose, or she's not there."

"I've seen a lot of the 'not there' lately."

They passed a smooth pond with two black swans majestically sliding on the surface.

"Oh, juicy gossip." Harriet's face brightened. "You have to guess."

Jane whipped around a curve. "Sex on the circuit?"

"Uh-huh."

"One of the players?"

"Of course."

"Rainey Rogers' coach?"

"That's right. Gary Shorter and fill in the blank."

"Harriet, I can't stand this. Tell me right this minute."

"Alicia Brinker was seen leaving that hulk's room late, very late, last night."

"No!" This was scandal too good to be true. "How'd you find out?"

"Happy Straker."

"Happy Straker doesn't talk to you. She hates you."

"Well, I know it, but she does talk to Susan Reilly and Happy made the mistake of telling Susan what she saw last night while a third party was changing for practice."

"Who heard it?"

"Carmen, my precious peach blossom."

"What?" Jane sheered another hairpin curve.

"She was in the can, heard them come into the locker room and drew her feet up on the seat. She said she didn't know why she did it, but she did it. Carmen heard every syllable."

"Alicia Brinker! Being in his room doesn't mean she slept with him."

"Ha. He'd fuck a dog if it shook its ass right. If she walked in that room, she'd not get out intact."

"What's she up to? Susan will kill her."

"I always thought of Alicia as a limpet. I may revise my opinion."

Jane slowed the car. "Before this year is over, we'll all have revised opinions."

♦ ♦ ♦

Bonnie Marie Bishop was a senior in college. She and a group of girls from American colleges were touring Europe during the summer. Bonnie Marie was tall, skinny, and nondescript.

She had no athletic ability of her own, but an appreciation for it in others.

Despite administrative cries to the contrary, most gifted athletes take basket-weaving courses, get shoveled through the schools, and are then left in the world with no skills other than dribbling, hitting, or running. Bonnie Marie was spared this. She did want a good education in business. She burned to set up her own company immediately upon graduation. Of course, it would have something to do with women athletes, but just what, she wasn't sure yet. What she was sure of was that she wanted to be rich. She was true to her generation in that way.

She was also a lesbian. Her fear over being discovered was intensified because if women are at a disadvantage in business, then a lesbian is at a double disadvantage. Poor Bonnie Marie. One had only to look at her to see a storybook dyke. She manfully tried to be a lady, but femininity was not her strong point, good looks not her blessing. However, she possessed a pleasing personality. She publicly hung on the arm of whatever man she could dredge up and verbally her heterosexuality was reassuring. Not that anyone believed her, but people went along with it to make her feel better.

Bonnie Marie showed up at Eastbourne along with some of the other girls. They were conspicuous by their American T-shirts and their sneakers. English ladies do not wear sneakers. English dykes may, but English ladies don't. In this world, there are lesbians and dykes. The two have nothing in common. Lesbians are women who love women. Dykes are women who imitate men.

Harriet and Miguel passed the pack as they sneaked back from Carmen's match. Carmen was now in the quarterfinals, sharpening her grass game with every stroke. Harriet inwardly groaned, whisked past them, and didn't look twice. Sadly for Harriet, Carmen did look twice.

True to form, Carmen whiffed Eastbourne. She won the doubles, a pleasant sensation but singles brings in the endorsements, not doubles, and her endorsements were in enough jeopardy. No one noticed that Carmen was a better doubles player than a singles player. She liked teamwork. Singles was for pride, doubles for the love of the game.

The two of them stashed their clothing in a little rented house in the London suburbs. The decor approximated English cozy—old furniture and damp as hell. Harriet preferred it to tinted Levelor blinds, fake Bauhaus furniture, and wall-to-wall carpeting. Harriet declared she could never love a woman who believed in wall-to-wall carpeting.

Wimbledon started out as usual with schedule snarling before half of the first day was up and bickering among players, coaches, and staff. The actual powers-that-be at Wimbledon rarely engaged in these daily pabulum pits since they thought themselves deified. As they were dead and too dumb to fall over, this attitude was not far off the mark.

Wimbledon is only as impressive as one cares to make it. It's not the cathedral of tennis, but it's a decent enough English club clinging to the days of the British Empire and kept alive because every foreigner in the world wants to be there and win it. Obviously the English don't want to win it. They haven't bothered with tennis in decades with the exception of Virginia Wade. Uganda has a better tennis development program than England, but by now half of Uganda is in England so perhaps things will pick up.

Fans queue up for hours, not because they are raving tennis fanatics, a few are, but because there aren't that many tournaments in the country and this is their national tournament.

The physical structure itself isn't imposing. The grass varies from year to year and that's not the grounds keeper's fault. The weather would try the patience of all the giving saints. Once, in an act of Australian defiance, Beanie Kittredge dragged her toe on her serve to hear one of the "limey bastards," as she called them, groan.

If Wimbledon were not Wimbledon, it would be regarded as a pleasant enough tournament, badly run and over-crowded, but with definite charm. But it was and will ever remain Wimbledon, so every sportswriter in the business genuflects annually, newscasters fabricate stories, ossification masquerades as tradition, and the players fight tooth and nail to win the Big W.

For the opening day of Wimbledon, Carmen drew a bye. She didn't have to play until Tuesday. Tuesday came and went with a Semana victory, a wobbly one at that. If she could get through the early rounds, she'd be fine.

The grace period from the press abruptly halted after the next match. Carmen, Harriet, and Miguel were converging on Carmen's car by separate paths. Miguel lent his car to Beanie Kittredge. A gray piece of putty with legs was in hot pursuit and followed by other similar creatures, the reporters.

"Shit, get in the car," Miguel commanded.

Harriet, stupidly, stood on the driver's side. She forgot the steering wheel was reversed, another example of English perversity. Carmen got the door open, jumped in, and realized Harriet was still standing outside the car. "Get in on the other side!" Miguel threw her in the car.

In America velocity is confused with achievement. Carmen drove as though velocity were achievement. In England she got away with it. The suburb of Wimbledon flashed by. Tense, she snapped, "Why did you have to tell Martin Kuzirian? Nothing would have ever happened. Everything would be all right."

Rattled, worried, Harriet held her head up. "If you're ashamed to be a lesbian, you're ashamed to be a woman."

Carmen drove home in silent fury.

Miguel considered what Harriet said. For all his slippery deals, he was not completely insensitive. Harriet had a point. He hoped other women didn't agree with her.

◆ ◆ ◆

Susan, herself a silent fury, prepared for Wimbledon, flanked by her husband and daughter. Did Alicia sleep with Rainey Rogers's coach, Gary Shorter? Just what the hell was she doing, coming out of his room at that hour, then slipping back to her own room? At major tournaments Susan and Alicia became more circumspect than usual, if that's possible. Susan wanted to rip into Alicia, but she didn't want to know the answer until after Wimbledon. Nothing must intrude on her focus, on the mantra chant, "Win, win, win."

If Susan had been sensitive to anyone outside herself, she might have noticed that Alicia was in torment over lesbianism. Sex with men was bad enough. The young woman was a terminal Puritan. Her body did one thing; her mind screamed another. What she needed was compassion, acceptance, and, if need be, counseling. Alicia would never go to a psychiatrist. But Alicia would have spoken to a minister, and many of these individuals, competent as counselors, were alert to crisis. If Susan had any heart at all, she would have helped Alicia help herself. Instead, Susan plotted how to dynamite the information out of Alicia. It never occurred to her simply to ask Alicia what she was doing in Gary Shorter's room. Unlike Susan, Alicia generally told the truth.

◆ ◆ ◆

The tidbit about Carmen's marriage did make the papers. Harriet didn't see it because she was grounded. Newspapers weren't delivered to the rented house. She spent her time in the garden or in the library reading. She felt miserable. She was about to feel worse.

Jane pulled in the driveway, honked the horn and walked around to the back of the house. "Yoo hoo."

The door flew open. "Hi! Come on in."

"I had to get away from the zoo. Anyway, I did my work for today. Valerie Virtue."

"Coffee?"

"No, thanks." Jane plopped in the kitchen chair. "They call this summer. Maybe I will have that coffee."

Harriet puttered over to the stove. "Anything exciting on the job today?"

"Hell, no. The seeds progress in order. So far, it's predictable. Couple of the men's matches were good."

"They've got so much depth."

"Yeah, I know. I asked for coffee, Harriet, not a twelve-course dinner."

"Kitchen maid I am not."

"Here." Jane measured out the correct amount of ground beans. Slowly the aroma of percolating coffee filled the tiny kitchen. "You look blue. Lavinia's at it again."

"She's been on Carmen's case. According to her standards, she's doing the right thing."

"You're being generous. False stories of marriage aren't the right thing."

"What are you talking about?"

"Didn't you read the paper?"

"No."

Jane put her hand to her mouth. "Oh."

"The coffee's ready." Harriet poured a cup as Jane repeated the story.

"And that's it." Jane smiled wanly.

"That's enough. I guess it will save her for now. If I stay out of the way, things ought to be better. Maybe I should go on home to Cazenovia now."

"It's not my place to advise you. In your own way, you

work for Wimbledon, too." She propped her leg up on an empty chair. "Sometimes I think this is a tempest in a teapot. Women's tennis has some lesbians." Jane rolled her eyes. "Big deal."

"It's a big deal to Lavinia."

"If someone farts in the dressing room, it's a big deal to Lavinia. Remember that pig, Claire Schick, and the time she barfed in a potted palm courtside in Seattle?"

"Oh, yeah." Harriet laughed.

"Lavinia still hasn't gotten over it."

"There's always Tomahawk and the local sponsors. It's a big deal to them."

"Fuck 'em." Jane gulped coffee. "The game's too commercial anyway."

Surprised, Harriet said, "What got into you?"

"I don't know. This is one of my waffle iron days."

"Perish the thought!" Harriet laughed, remembering the day at Princeton when Jane's waffle iron wouldn't work. Jane fiddled with it and fiddled with it. Finally, she got so mad she threw the goddamned appliance across the kitchen.

"You must be stir crazy out here in the suburbs without a car. Don't you want to see the matches?"

"I watch Carmen on tv."

"I'll sneak you in tomorrow. The last place anyone will look for you is the television booth; your face isn't exactly a household item."

"England's loss."

"Feel pretty rotten, don't you."

Harriet toyed with her spoon. "Does it show that much?"

"No, but I'm not stupid. I'd hate to be in your shoes." She looked under the table. "Even if they are size six."

"Jane, do you think Carmen knows about this marriage story?"

"I don't know."

"It must be Lavinia's brainstorm. Carmen would tell me."

"I would hope she'd tell you, but people are strange at Wimbledon."

"Not that strange."

"I wouldn't ask any questions until after the finals. No point in upsetting her."

◆ ◆ ◆

Down another hallway in a small but clean room in a medium-priced hotel, Carmen Semana was humping the hell out of Bonnie Marie Bishop. Carmen had arranged her schedule with care. Harriet rarely made sexual demands during a big tournament, so Carmen would have enough energy. Bonnie Marie melted in her arms. There was a lot to melt. Bonnie Marie would never admit to being a lesbian. She was new. No past. No problems. She was wonderful.

◆ ◆ ◆

If the All England Lawn Tennis and Croquet Club directors were an abomination, the English spectators were a glory, especially the older citizens. They could distinguish a forehand topspin from a flat forehand whilst sitting in the remotest seats. And when they watched a match, it was not an isolated point in time but a running thread throughout their lives. They remembered Lew Hoad versus Ken Rosewall and if they didn't see Anthony F. Wilding versus Arthur Gore in 1912, their mothers and fathers did. Wimbledon was one more sonorous note in the symphony of English life.

Ball boys in purple and green, looking like pages who walked into the wrong century, moved out on the court. Yesterday one of the ball boys winked at Carmen. Pretty cheeky, but nice.

"What do you think?" Jane, a little farsighted, held the draw sheet at arm's length.

"Carmen will win it in two sets. Rainey Rogers will be the bitch in the semis. She ought to make the quarters against Justine Haverford okay," Ricky predicted.

"Except the entire country will be pulling for Justine."

"Oh God, look at Lavinia," Jane exclaimed.

Lavinia Sibley Archer, only one vodka gimlet to her credit, floated through the crowd. Encased in yellow, she moved with the solemnity of a person marching to "Pomp and Circumstance." Older spectators recognized her which sent her into a transport. Heads leaned together as people informed one another about who was whom. Lavinia shone today. She had been relieved to see the gossipy item in the morning paper about rumors of an upcoming marriage for Carmen Semana. She dearly hoped whatever happened in England would have no effect on her baby, the Tomahawk Circuit. She would do her best to make certain it had no effect. As she sat down at last, she pretended to be absorbed in the two women taking the court. She was really listening to the buzz behind her. Yes, they remembered her.

"An old firehorse." Ricky shook his head.

"She earned it." Jane was fair.

"Success recalled may be as sweet as success newly won."

Harriet curled up behind them, out of range of cameras, and picked up the discarded draw sheet. If Carmen smacked up against Rainey Rogers, then Page Bartlett Campbell would draw Hilda Stambach, assuming the seeds won as expected, but with Susan on Page's side of the draw, there was a question. Susan could never be counted out. Hilda was vicious on the grass. Her forehand topspin resembled Bjorn Borg's forehand. On grass you might as well be facing a bazooka.

"Few women have the courage to go all out for achievement. That's one thing I like about the tennis world. The women on top aren't afraid to show their skill." Ricky rubbed his hands.

Carmen won the match six-three, six-four. Jane noticed Carmen glancing into the stands. Carmen always looked for Harriet that way. Jane watched her awhile. Carmen was sure zeroing in on somebody. Jane hoped Harriet wouldn't notice, but Harriet noticed before the first set was two-one.

◆ ◆ ◆

Miguel was ready to substitute Valium for potato chips. His Hong Kong partner flew in for Wimbledon. The news, while not fatal, was depressing. Sales were down. Miguel had made the last loan payment on time, but in three months he would face another one.

Miguel wasn't cheating Carmen. He planned to set aside ten percent of the profits and put it into her account. He hadn't gotten around to it, but then he told himself he couldn't realize a profit until after the loan was repaid.

He hated giving ground to Lavinia, but her plan might save them all. The last thing he wanted to do was tell Carmen what he'd done.

Walking back from a distant court, he spied Ronnie Baldwin. Quick as a cat, he grabbed Baldwin by the arm and pulled him out of traffic.

"Miguel." The tennis player was scared.

"Why the fuck did you tell Seth Quintard about the coke?"

"Hey, man, I didn't tell him."

Miguel, a strong man, tightened his grasp. "The hell you didn't."

"Let me go."

Miguel grabbed his throat. "Why?" Then he released the startled player.

"My game was shit and he was on my tail. So finally I told him—too much blow. It just sort of happened, you know."

"Baldwin, I'll break every bone in your body if you don't shut up."

"He was the only person I told. Honest."

"He was enough. I took risks for you, you son of a bitch."

"I know you did. I know you did, Miguel, and I'll make it up to you. I will. I swear I will."

Miguel turned his back in disgust and walked away.

◆ ◆ ◆

The small change of emotions, the nickels and dimes of love, the kisses on the cheek, the sections read aloud from newspapers, continued unmolested. Carmen woke up each morning, reached for Harriet, hugged her, got up, brushed her teeth, took a shower, and then fixed herself a giant ham sandwich in the kitchen. She'd fix one for Harriet, too. They'd chat after Carmen read her paper. Harriet made up love letters from Baby Jesus and read them. Carmen laughed.

But Harriet sensed weeds growing in her paradise patch. If Carmen had been older or less emotionally erratic, she might have carried on this affair with the dignity they both deserved. Harriet wasn't fool enough to think Carmen would be faithful physically to her until death do us part. She did, however, believe the companionship and the common goals they shared would cement them for life. Once Carmen, on her knees, sobbed that she'd love Harriet until the day one of them died. Harriet believed her.

A true partnership meant good times, bad times, and in-between times. If one hurt the other, she'd heal. It made little difference whether one married a man or a woman. What made the difference was the ability to love someone when she was unlovable. Marriage eventually thrusts that harsh test upon every partnership. Most don't make it.

Carmen was sneaking around. Harriet hated that. She knew, her every instinct was heightened. If Carmen slept with another person, she'd live. But she felt Carmen backing out, slipping away, abandoning her. She didn't know if she could live without Carmen. Harriet was unaccustomed to even the mildest dependence, and that thought slashed through her like a bayonet. And she once laughed at people who felt like dying when their spouse or lover walked out.

"How great that you've got a day before Rainey." Harriet studied the book review section of the *Times*.

"I think I'll practice twice today. Doubles this afternoon. Might as well stay out there."

Carmen carried on her life in what appeared to be a routine manner, but already she and Bonnie Marie confessed they loved one another instantly. After being together two weeks at Wimbledon they had mentally bought a house, picked out furniture, and met one another's friends. No one understood Carmen like this new woman. Carmen quite forgot she said the same thing to Harriet three years ago.

◆ ◆ ◆

The next day Jane stretched out on the beat-up sofa in Harriet and Carmen's house. Carmen had a day off before meeting Hilda Stambach, who tipped over Page Bartlett Campbell. Page was suffering from a swollen knee tendon, but she said nothing to the press. Hilda was good and grass was not Page's best surface. However, Page could win on anything. She'd have to wait another year for Wimbledon and that meant another year of putting off a family. She wondered if it was worth it.

Jane briefly interviewed Page and was telling Carmen and Harriet that Page was staying over a few days after the finals.

"Jane, would you like a drink?"

"Twist my arm."

Carmen pretended to twist Jane's arm. "Wine, beer, or hard stuff?"

"White wine. It's too early in the day to go heavy duty."

Carmen poured Jane some wine. Jane felt the tension. She knew Carmen; her worry was for Harriet. Ever since Susan Reilly jilted her, Carmen made sure no other woman would do the same. Jane thought of Carmen as a lovely person in many ways, but your basic love junkie.

Jane also thought a little about herself. Change. Life seemed nothing but change, even when the surface was most placid.

As Carmen handed her a glass of wine, Jane asked, "What would you die for?"

"I don't think about dying."

"Not during Wimbledon." Harriet sipped a Coca-Cola.

Jane said, "But I wonder if life is worth living, if there isn't anything or anyone you would die for?"

"No," Harriet answered.

"No, what? You have something you'd die for?" Carmen questioned.

"I hope I'd die for you or for a friend; a child, if I had one; my country, depending on the circumstances; an idea, if it were great enough, although it's easier to die for flesh and blood."

Carmen didn't reply.

"Sometimes I think we get up in the morning because we haven't managed to die in the middle of the night." Jane fluffed up a pillow.

"It's easier to live if you've got a purpose."

"The Grand Slam," Carmen said.

Jane, comfortable now, said, "External purposes fail. Not that they aren't wonderful, they give us a sense of accomplishment, but it's not enough."

"The Grand Slam will be enough for me." Carmen didn't cotton to Jane's line of reasoning.

"I don't mean it's not important," Harriet said. "Sports do give us examples of courage. I guess I was hoping there's a purpose beyond things, certainly beyond my ability to describe it. Maybe I'm groping for the spirit, for collective consciousness."

"Wouldn't that be something?" Jane sipped her wine.

"One planet with one heartbeat." Harriet clicked her glass against Jane's. Carmen clicked her Perrier glass with Jane and felt guilty because she put off telling Harriet about Lavinia's plan.

"To Carmen's Grand Slam and to revelation," Jane toasted anew.

"I welcome revelation," Harriet said. "Logic is too time-consuming."

◆ ◆ ◆

Hilda Stambach, a client of Seth Quintard's, made the finals. Athletes Unlimited should have had both women as clients, except Miguel screwed that. But Seth got his revenge.

The day before the finals, usually reserved as a day of rest for the two finalists, he waited patiently for Carmen as she practiced. A payoff to an English woolens manufacturer guaranteed that Miguel would be out of sight. Miguel and the fake manufacturer were currently discussing Carmen's possible endorsement of socks.

Seth pounced on her as she left practice. He had the phony Hong Kong clothing with him. When he carefully explained what was happening, she almost passed out. Seth didn't know about the forged signature for the Amalgamated Banks loan, but he was smart enough to know Miguel had to have gotten the money from somewhere.

Carmen examined the garments in disbelief. Seth reminded her that her name was being misused on a shoddy product, and then he walked off, triumphant.

"Miguel!" Carmen burst in upon his meeting.

"Migueletta, how was practice?"

"Excuse us." She put her hand under her brother's armpit and lifted him out of the chair.

Protesting, but worried, he was dragged behind her until she jammed him in the car. She tore out of the parking lot, almost forgot to drive on the left-hand side of the road, adjusted, and then flew toward the Thames. She parked the car as close as she could to the river, slammed the door, and pulled him out. From her flight bag on the seat, she produced a shirt and a blouse.

"What's that?"

"You know what it is."

Miguel took the clothes. He said nothing.

"Miguel, goddamn you, don't lie to me!"

"I made a deal." He breathed deeply and then told her about Hong Kong, the distribution network, the genius of the plan, and most important, he was putting ten percent of the profits into her account.

"What else?"

"That's all."

She had one card, but she played it smart. "Seth Quintard told me you borrowed the money."

Miguel assumed she knew about the forged signature. "I'll kill that bastard. How did he find out about Dennis Parry?"

"Athletes Unlimited has friends everywhere."

Miguel reached for her hand. She snatched it from his grasp. "So I forged your signature—no harm in that. This was a good deal. I paid off Parry, the loan officer. He's a weasel, but he did get me the loan. Who's going to believe that you didn't know about this?"

"So how much do you owe?"

"We owe about five hundred thousand dollars plus some interest. I've made a few payments already or it would be worse."

"You know that Seth Quintard will probably sit down with the American manufacturers. If he gave me the phony clothes, he'll give it to them."

"I'll kill him."

"But they'll know about all this. There's no way to sell this stuff, not anymore."

"Not in America." Miguel's face was stark white. "It's sold in Southeast Asia."

"Enough to pay off the debt?"

"I don't know. I doubt it. If you don't become an instant Mrs., the stuff probably won't sell there either."

"Jesus Christ, Miguel, how could you do this to me?"

"Everything would have been fine, Migueletta. You'd have had more money in the bank, and I'd have been a rich man in my own right. How was I to know you were a lesbian?"

"What's that got to do with it?"

"Your hot crotch will cost us a fortune."

Carmen hit him in the stomach. He doubled over. "Slippery. Papa always said you were an eel. You forged my name, and you used me."

He straightened up and pinned her arms to her sides. "You might be half a man, sister, but I'm all man and I can still beat the shit out of you."

"Let me go."

"Not until you listen."

She spit in his face and brought her knee up between his legs. He howled.

"I can hurt you pretty bad while you beat me up, stupid."

"What good will this do us? We're both in trouble. We've got to stick together."

She stood over him. "Why?"

"Because I'm your brother. Yes, I got you in a mess, but it could have been great. What good will it do you or women's tennis if a marketing scandal erupts? Seth Quintard had his revenge. He won't make it public. The last thing Athletes Unlimited wants is more trouble in women's tennis. So you pay off the loan and no one will suspect anything. We'll stick together. Not all my investments were bad."

She listened impassively. "Okay, Miguel. But you make no more deals. Not ever. Once I'm in the clear, you go home."

Miguel's eyes filled with tears. "Forgive me. Please forgive me."

"Shut up and go home. I've really got to win tomorrow."

♦ ♦ ♦

The morning of Wimbledon's women's finals was clear, an unexpected blessing. Carmen, more wired than a Con Edison turbine, sprinkled pepper on her breakfast steak.

Harriet put up the tea. "Telegram from Baby Jesus arrived while you were in the shower."

"Let me see."

Last night after Carmen went to sleep, Harriet sneaked out of bed and cut apart all the telegrams Carmen had already received, added a few letters herself, and made a telegram from the cat. She handed it to Carmen.

Carmen smiled and read aloud. "Carmen. CATastrophe for Hilda Stambach. Stop. Win. Stop. Would like kippers for celebration. Stop. Come home. Stop. Peed in your tub. Never stop. Baby Jesus." She folded the telegram and tucked it inside her racquet cover.

"Even the animals are on your side." There wasn't much else to say, since both their minds were on Centre Court.

Harriet's prediction was accurate. The final was anti-climactic for everyone but Carmen, Harriet, and Bonnie Marie, who was buried in the stands. Carmen strung together the points like pearls. Hilda's first appearance on Centre Court may have rattled her nerves, but even if she'd been hardened to Wimbledon, she wouldn't have slowed Semana.

Carmen was high. A lock lifted on her control canal. She was free. Her body was loose. She didn't think about the points so much as she felt them. The game was instinctive, fluid, magical.

After the match, she held the silver plate high over her head and turned around for the crowd. Now people were taking her run for the Grand Slam seriously. If she could pace herself and keep well, Carmen Semana might do it.

◆ ◆ ◆

As Jane and Harriet sped away from Wimbledon, unobserved in all the celebration and confusion, Harriet said, "Carmen's having an affair. I know it."

"How do you know?"

"I just know. Jane, what am I going to do?"

"Can you take it? Her having another lover?"

Harriet was silent.

Jane halted in front of a jewelry store. "If your heart is breaking, you're allowed to cry out and crawl on all fours while you put your life back together. God knows I did."

"You did?"

"When my first marriage came apart at the seams, I didn't know which end was up. I'd built my whole life around that bastard. Oh, he's not really a bastard. We were two unhappy kids who found a moment of happiness, an illusion called The Future."

"Probably it's the same for Carmen and this—what's her name?"

"Bonnie Marie Bishop. As near as I can gather she's a senior in college."

"Bet she graduates summa cunt laude."

Jane ran her hands through Harriet's hair, a big sister prettying up her little sister. "This may get much worse before it gets better. Don't be too proud to call on your friends. And remember that old phrase, 'Leave her to heaven.'"

Harriet's eyes moistened. She hated crying, and she couldn't bring herself to cry on a public street. "Maybe lovers are like radio stations. As you cross the country, they come in clear and then fade out."

ELEVEN

Athletes, like fireflies, gathered at tournaments and then dispersed at play's end. They lived in eternal summer until winter caught up with each individual. As the species was ritually replenished with aspirants, the fallen comrades were rarely missed. When a giant of the game retired, the news stayed in memory for a day, two at the most, then sunk like a stone.

With the passing of Wimbledon, the shining bodies packed their bags and headed to the next tournament or home for a week or more off. Soon city tournaments would start again, each one sponsored by an aggregate of banks, car dealers, and other local businesses. Lavinia, back at the helm in her own country, would command the women's tournaments until the U.S. Open, another site of her former valor.

The women players went off in one direction, and the men players went off in another. Anyone who nurtures fantasies of endless sex between male and female tennis players is smoking opium. The male players disdain the female. These fellows want starlets and models, not athletes. Only a few of the girls met with their approval. The male players thought the female players were a pack of dogs. The female players thought the male players were stupid pricks. So much for love games at tennis.

The Wimbledon crash flattened everyone: players, spectators, even linesmen. It was a two-week lawn party which, like all lawn parties, was better in the reliving than in the living. The British rightly turn their attention to cricket. The tennis players, less impressive in street clothes, faded into the year like sunlight fading into twilight until next year, same time, same place, most of the same faces.

At least when a player dropped away now, it was usually due to retirement. Some fans remembered men like Joseph Hunt of the United States or Henner Henkel of Germany, up and coming stars who were obliterated in World War II. Others remembered the blond presence of Karel Koseluth, the great Czech star of the 1930's. He was born in the wrong country and at the wrong time. And then there was Anthony Wilding himself, the golden god of Wimbledon, destroyed in the World War I. Maria Bueno still played doubles, but a car crash cut short her amazing career. She was the most beautiful player anyone had seen since the days of Suzanne Lenglen, in the early 1920's. A graceful, luminous presence like those two women comes once every forty or fifty years. Maureen Connolly, who should have presided as the Grand Matron of Tennis, was dead of cancer. Others, great names best left great by not ratting on them, lost to drink or drugs, were no longer part of Wimbledon's roll call, no longer part of the functioning human race either.

Another year. Three hundred and sixty-five days. To those athletes in their prime, that seemed so long. To those past their prime, next year's Wimbledon would arrive in the blinking of an eye, and the ghosts would crowd the memory once more with the flood of what was once young, beautiful, and strong. It befalls each generation to claim its own ghosts. The Medusa of time works her will on us all.

◆ ◆ ◆

Carmen loved Chinese food. Harriet arranged a sumptuous feast at their rented house, catered by the best Chinese restaurant in London. The owner of the restaurant set the table and brought food on chafing dishes. As he walked out the door, Carmen walked in.

"My hero." Harriet rushed forward to kiss her.

Carmen was ecstatic with her win. "What's this?"

"Dinner is served. Are you starved?"

"This is great." Carmen sat down.

As they ate the delicious food, Harriet told Carmen how proud she was of her victory, how she was halfway to the Slam, and how she loved her. Carmen commented on the food and a few memorable points from the match.

"Isn't it funny to be eating Chinese food in England?" Harriet mused.

"Yeah."

"Today I was thinking that society is like a Chinese vase, one of those giant vases. Each generation puts on a layer of lacquer. The older the society, the deeper, richer, more beguiling the texture of the vase, but if little hairline cracks aren't repaired, then one day the whole structure collapses."

Abruptly, since she didn't know how to work up to it, Carmen blurted, "I'm not coming out."

"I haven't asked you to."

Harriet's pride in Carmen's victory evaporated. What was to be a lovely supper was turning into sour grapes. "I can only tell you that I must answer to myself. I wasn't born to be a liar."

"Oh. And I am?"

"In a word, yes."

"Why the hell should I take the risk? Why my neck on the block? I want a nice house, a lot of fun, no hassles. I've hurt no one, and I don't want anyone to hurt me."

"Sometimes a few of us must take great risks so many of us will take small risks."

"You can be the Messiah. And losing your job is not as important as my losing mine! You and your truth kick. It's nobody's business how I live my life."

"As to the truth, current feeling is that no one side should possess more than fifty-five percent of it."

"I thought you owned it all."

"Listen, smartass, you win Wimbledon and come home spoiling for a fight. I try to tell the truth as best I can, but no one sees the whole picture, no one even sees the total truth about themselves."

"I'm worried about my career. I can't have anything interfere with the Slam. Can't you be quiet for six months?"

"The damage, as you might put it, is already done. I can't take back what I said."

"You don't have to say it again."

"No, I don't." Harriet couldn't eat. She played with the silverware.

"Maybe you should go home and think it over. I'll go on to Los Angeles alone."

"I have nothing to think over, Carmen. I will not base my associations with other human beings on lies. It took me my whole life to come to that conclusion. I won't say that you're gay. I'll say nothing but I can't lie about myself. I wish to God we'd all stop lying. I wish every gay person and bisexual person in America had a blue dot in the middle of her forehead so she couldn't devour herself with deceit, anxiety, and fear, that's what I wish!"

"You're nuts."

"Maybe I am. I think people should live their lives as they see fit. Do I want to be loved for what I am not or hated for what I am? Is that the only choice? Surely there must be some heterosexuals who don't hate us."

"This isn't philosophy, it's survival," Carmen sneered.

"Survival is philosophy."

"You're so clever, Harriet. You can twist anything your way. I'm sick of it."

"You're sick of me."

"Don't tell me what I feel. I don't need you to define everything for me, thank you very much."

"You have Bonnie Marie Bishop."

Carmen's face curdled. "How'd you find out?"

"You left a secret trail of guilt. You've been banging away for the last two weeks. God knows, I haven't been getting any."

Carmen composed herself. "She's very nice."

"It's not for me to approve your lover. You can't expect me to feel good about her or you right now."

"If I'm with someone else, it's your fault."

"I hope not."

"You only go looking when things aren't good at home."

This cut Harriet to the quick. First of all, she didn't believe that. People need various things at various times. When lovers are used as weapons, that's different from one person needing another. Right now everything was mixed up worse than a dog's breakfast. Harriet was hanging on by her fingernails. She alternated between rage and horrible grief, and she didn't want to let either emotion out.

Throwing her shoulders back, Carmen sat straight in her chair. "This is as good a time as any. I've been meaning to tell you about Lavinia's plan."

"What?"

"She's found a man I can marry."

Stunned, Harriet gripped the edge of the table. "You can't be serious."

"I am serious." Her dark face betrayed no emotion.

"Is he gay?"

"I don't know. His name is Timothy Meeker. I'll meet him next week. He lives in Los Angeles."

"It's cruel to pretend to be something you're not to a heterosexual man. He has a heart, too."

"This is strictly business. He goes on salary." Carmen already committed herself to this course of action. There was

211

no turning back. She would have to find it within herself to justify what she was doing.

"It's crazy."

"It makes perfect sense."

An enormous amount of information had just been dumped on Harriet's head, all of it bad. "What about your new girl friend?" This was said with as much defiance as curiosity.

"She thinks it's great. She doesn't want anyone to know about her either."

"Two liars are better than one, I guess."

"That's not fair!"

"By no stretch of the imagination can what you are doing be called fair." Harriet bristled. "What are you doing? You're entangling yourself in a web of deceit."

"People want to think of me a certain way. They'll believe what I tell them. You know that. People are stupid." An edge of bitterness crept into her voice. "Anyway, movie stars do it all the time."

"That doesn't make it right."

"Why don't you shove it? You're not my conscience. After my career, I can do as I please."

"After this, you won't be the same person."

"What do you mean?" A flicker of comprehension flared in Carmen's eyes, then subsided.

"Every act a person commits in her life marks her. What you do, you carry. It's like a stain on the soul."

"Oh, bullshit."

"Actions have consequences, Carmen, even though they may be years or decades down the line. What you are doing will haunt you the rest of your life, and I don't give a shit how many cars, furs, jewels, homes, or women you buy."

"What you need is a pulpit," Carmen sneered.

"You put a price on yourself. You sold out, plain and simple. For what, Carmen? The good opinion of people you wouldn't like if you met them? For money? Even if it is millions of dollars, your integrity is worth more than any amount anyone can pay you. How are you going to look at yourself in the mirror, knowing what you've done? You've squandered your integrity."

"You're so out of it. You're such a silly idealist. I'm going to have a wonderful life! I can do anything I want. And I can do it with someone who appreciates me. You always tried to make me what I wasn't."

"I tried to help you find yourself. The Carmen I love wouldn't lie."

"I knew you never really understood me."

"What kind of person would ask you to erode your self-respect?"

An uneasy silence settled over the sumptuously appointed table.

What neither of them said was that Carmen was panic-stricken to be alone. Her career concern was a cover for deeper issues. One can only succeed if she embraces that which she fears most. Carmen was nowhere near facing her loneliness, which could change into solitude, then self-knowledge. She needed her personality tossed back to her just as she needed the ball returned from the other side of the court.

"Why are you doing this?" A tear ran down the side of Harriet's nose.

"Because I don't trust you anymore. If you loved me, you wouldn't have told everyone you were a lesbian. You don't care about me or my career. You only care about yourself."

"I've fucked up my career. I've tagged along from one country to another, one empty place to another empty place."

"I didn't ask you to do it."

"Then why did you cry and tell me to resign my post? Why did you call me five times a day and cry when we were apart? Was that not asking me?"

Carmen became red in the face. "I'm not asking you now."

"But you did, and I'm thirty-six years old, and altering my life at this stage is scary as hell. At twenty-four you think you can always start over. Life is an invitation to beginnings. I'm at a different place in my life than you are, and you're playing fast and loose, not just with my head, but with my career. God, I was a fool to think you meant what you said. You said you'd take care of me."

"I pay the bills."

"How dare you use that against me after you begged me to stop working!"

Carmen hated knowing that she broke her word. "I have no control over my heart. I'm allowed to make a mistake."

"But which one of us is the mistake? And what about the other women who were your lovers before me?"

She couldn't take this. Carmen wanted everything easy. Yesterday was yesterday and it didn't apply to today. Past lovers were forgotten or fondly remembered on occasion. She changed the subject. "Miguel is in big trouble. He owes Amalgamated Banks over six hundred thousand dollars."

"What?"

"He took out a loan for six hundred thousand dollars plus interest and forged my signature as his cosigner."

"What's that got to do with us?"

"I'll lose a lot of money if I don't go straight. Miguel has been in on a counterfeit clothing deal. Oh, don't even ask. The point is, if sales drop and he can't pay the loan, I have to come up with the money."

"Carmen, I liked you better when it was your heart you worried about."

"You don't care about me or my career. Anyone else would be frantic. Bonnie Marie is sick over Miguel's mess."

Harriet slapped her. That was the straw that broke the camel's back.

Rubbing her face, Carmen said, "I never did trust you."

"Why don't you just shut up?" Harriet got up and walked out the door, closing it behind her.

Carmen raced for the phone, hysterical. "Bonnie Marie, I told her. She hit me! I hate her!"

The conversation then took the predictable turn. Bonnie Marie loved her. Yes, Harriet was an awful person. They'd be together within twenty-four hours, and everything would be all right. It had to be.

◆ ◆ ◆

Ricky massaged Harriet's feet. It was his cure for everything.

"I don't understand why I feel so bad. I've seen friends go through this."

"It's new to you." Ricky pointed out the obvious.

"Here, drink this." Jane handed her a vodka gimlet.

"I don't drink."

"We all know that, but there's always a first time. You'll spend the night here. Tomorrow morning I'll go back with you to pack your stuff, and we can all fly back to New York."

"It's all been too much for her." Harriet did drink the gimlet.

"Sweetheart, you paid the price of love. Now you're paying the tax. The sooner you forget it, the better off you'll be."

"My God, Jane, we own a house together. We made a life together."

"So have plenty of others. Divorce ain't no free ride on a pink duck."

"What's that supposed to mean?" Harriet quizzed Jane.

"Just that it's a bitch. It's a bitch for her, too, but Carmen won't find that out for years."

"Lavinia wins one more Wimbledon." Ricky brought in a

pillow and blankets for Harriet, already drowsy from the vodka. "I hope the sofa's comfortable."

"It's fine."

Jane put the covers around her. "Night."

"Night, you guys. Thanks for this."

"Come on." Ricky kissed her cheek.

Before she conked out, Harriet said, "In God's army, I'm on latrine duty."

◆ ◆ ◆

Mount Desert Island of Maine was a crystal mecca. The water was pure, the air sparkled, the rugged landscape cleansed the soul. The people, whether summer or year-round residents, were solid. Susan Reilly and Alicia Brinker repaired there after Wimbledon.

The two weeks after Wimbledon were the only two weeks out of the year when Susan stopped her obsessive practicing. She declined World Team Tennis even though the money was good. This vacation was her treat to herself.

Skimming across the deep blue waters in a small sailboat, the two chatted amicably. The weather was perfect, and Alicia was a good sailor. Susan was fixing to dump Alicia if she could find an adequate replacement. Alicia was a bit too passive. What was she doing in Gary Shorter's room? And besides, it was time to get a new model. Like people who've suffered entirely too much graduate school and measure each year by the beginning of fall, so Susan's internal clock told her it was time for someone new.

"Great day." Alicia expertly handled the rudder and the big sail.

"I love Maine."

"Me, too."

"Susan?"

"Yes?"

"I have something to tell you."

Here it comes, Susan thought. "What?"

"I think you tipped off the press about Carmen Semana and Harriet Rawls."

"What makes you think that?" Susan lay flat on her back soaking up the delicious sun.

"The story about the marriage ceremony. It was so out-rageous only you could have thought of it."

Susan's billowing ego took over. "Don't be silly."

"Reporters aren't that smart. You cooked that up. You can't stand the thought of Carmen winning the Grand Slam."

Susan's teeth gritted slightly. "She won't win it. No one will ever win it again."

"She's halfway there. Just wait."

"What's this to you?"

"Curious. You will always fascinate me." Alicia's gentle voice floated over the water.

"H-m-m."

"It was a rotten thing to do, Susan, rotten but funny in a way."

A forbidden smile crept over Susan's lips.

"The other thing I want to tell you"—Alicia tacked the sailboat—"is that I'm pregnant."

"You're what?" Susan sat up.

"I'm pregnant."

Susan's face was splotched. "How could you?"

"I want a baby."

"I have a child."

"So why can't I have one?"

"Alicia, you're forever reading that Bible. You worry about us. How can you go out and breed?"

"I want a baby. I want one thing or one person I can love, and I don't want to spend a life hiding."

"You can love me."

"Not really. I don't think you let anyone close enough."

This was not the conversation Susan prepared for. She hoped for a tearful confession. She would comfort Alicia and forgive her for her one night out with the boys. Then she'd feel perfectly justified in finding a new lover posthaste. "That's absurd."

"I'm not getting married. I know this will kill my parents, but it's something I have to do."

"You don't have to do anything but die." Susan heated up.

"There's something else I have to do."

"What?"

"Leave you." Alicia dove off the boat and swam to the shore. It took an inexperienced Susan two hours to maneuver the craft back to the basin. When she got to the room, Alicia had cleared out. Susan sat down on the bed. It was the first time in her thirty years that she was left by a lover.

♦ ♦ ♦

Lavinia Sibley Archer was left, too. Howard Dominick got sacked. Tomahawk wanted a new big chief and women's tennis was unceremoniously dropped in the corporate trash can.

"I never thought this could happen."

"You've had your way for twelve years. I'd say you came out ahead."

Lavinia turned to Siggy, "What did you say?"

"I said you ran the show for twelve years. Maybe it's time for new concepts and new people."

Empurpled with fury, she yelled, "Are you implying I'm over the hill?"

"Over the hill? You ought to be under the sod."

"You're fired!"

"Great. I quit. But before I go, let me tell you I don't give a shit that you won Wimbledon. Nobody gives a shit that you won Wimbledon or the U.S. Open. The sun does not rise and set on Lavinia Sibley Archer and women's tennis."

Her outrage led to paralysis. Lavinia stood riveted to the spot.

Siggy, now unleashed, ripped on. "The women's game will never bring the revenues the men's game does, and men's tennis ain't no bed of roses either. If you want to survive, you'd better target your market, babe, because it ain't Joe Six-packs. If he's going to watch women, he's not going to watch preteen kiddies and sweating dykes. Your market is the married, middle-aged female, the club player and her husband, if she drags him to the tournaments. And she's not thrilled with dykes either. She comes because she wants to watch good tennis, go home, and hit a backhand like Susan Reilly. She doesn't want to be Susan Reilly. Get it?"

"Get out!"

"I'm giving you dictatorial court. I'm going with plea-sure."

"You're wrong about the tennis market!" she screamed.

Siggy was heading for the elevators.

Lavinia recognized a crisis when she saw one. She swallowed her ego and ran after Siggy. "Wait a minute, wait a minute. I lost my head. Come back and let's talk this out."

Coolly Siggy backed away from the opening elevator doors.

They talked for five hours. Siggy Wayne proposed a reorganization of the circuit. Everything would be scaled down. Next he promised he'd get a new sponsor, one not identified with femininity or women's products specifically. And lastly, he'd be made her full partner or he'd walk.

Lavinia hedged until he could produce the new sponsor. This he did. A liquor company wanted to release a new drink, an alcoholic milkshake called "Avalanche." They decided to take the chance for one year. The contract could be canceled if any scandal erupted. While Avalanche would be aimed at the new drinkers, those aged eighteen to twenty-four depending on the state, the company would also push its staple line, gin.

Siggy was a full partner. Women's tennis would have a future under his reign. Promoters, once given tournaments on whim, were now subject to sets of rules handed down by Siggy Wayne. Tennis, although slightly diminished, was centralized under Siggy's control. It was now truly a business and would steer through economic waters like any stable corporation. In his way, Siggy was more important than Wimbledon.

◆ ◆ ◆

Carmen's wedding, a gala Los Angeles affair, made all the papers and sports magazines. Lavinia, although no longer certain of her media pimps, knew no one could resist this. The joke was that Bonnie Marie Bishop was Carmen's maid of honor. Arturo Semana gave away his daughter while Theresa, her mother, sat in the front row weeping copiously. Miguel wept, too. He knew this pretty actor would get involved in a power struggle with him sooner or later. Miguel and Carmen patched things up as best they could. She still loved him, but she'd never trust him again. She'd never really trust anyone again except Bonnie Marie—and whoever came after Bonnie Marie.

Christmas was the original date for the wedding but the events of midsummer shook Lavinia to her core. This was a shotgun wedding with women's tennis as the baby.

Before the wedding, Happy Straker, along with most of the other girls on the circuit, organized a bridal shower. Movie cameras were in abundance. Afterwards, the gay players took a vow of silence. No one would ever admit she was gay, and no one would ever be seen with a publicly gay person. Of course, that meant Harriet. Lavinia saw to that. All her press releases referred to "the unfortunate friendship." After Carmen's marriage, when her girls were safe, she'd stop trashing Harriet.

Susan Reilly was conspicuous by her absence. So was Alicia. That story was whispered behind closed doors. Happy policed the silence now. It was a role for which she was well suited.

Now married to an understanding Timothy, Carmen was secure and wildly happy with Bonnie Marie. Bonnie Marie was stashed in a pretty house in Westwood while Tim and Carmen inhabited her new huge Bel-Air home complete with tennis court.

Carmen's only concern was winning the U.S. Open. She practiced with Miguel with a holy fervor. She was going to win the Grand Slam, and that was all that mattered.

◆ ◆ ◆

Feverish as Carmen's practice sessions were, they couldn't match the intensity of Susan Reilly's. Susan placed herself under the tutelage of Marvin Wheelwright, one of the great coaches of the game. He'd been a fine doubles player in the fifties, but he really found his niche with coaching. Marvin could rebuild a game more accurately and faster than anyone in the sport. He was expensive, and his pupils worked eight hours a day.

Susan was up at 6 A.M. Since Marvin lived in Florida, they worked from 7 A.M. to 11 A.M. They broke for lunch, followed by weight training and strategy sessions, and then were back on the courts from 4 P.M. to 8 P.M.

Marvin drilled her on Deco Turf, the surface of the U.S. Open, and grass for the Australian Open. He was one of the few pros in America who maintained a grass court.

Marvin wasn't sure about Susan and the U.S. Open. Her impatience with the artificial surface could hurt her, but on grass, if she remembered what he taught her, especially about her approach shots to the net, on grass she'd be a killer.

Susan was already a killer in her own fashion. Devoid of love, such as she knew love, Susan's maniacal streak ran without restraint. On her own after eight P.M., she would head for the weight room to further punish her body. She was a woman obsessed.

◆ ◆ ◆

Harriet found herself in dire straits. She couldn't afford the upkeep of the Cazenovia house, but all her savings were tied up in it. She never thought Carmen would be petty about money, but she discovered otherwise. There is probably no such thing as a good parting, but the wrangling with Carmen's high-powered lawyers over the New York property was not a happy way to spend the summer for a woman who'd been dumped by her lover and dumped without a cent. The beautiful presents Carmen gave her were useless in this situation and only further served to make Harriet hostage to Carmen's wealth.

Finally the house was sold. The settlement was held up while Carmen's lawyers declared Harriet hadn't put in half the money for the house. She never said she did, but then money wasn't the basis of her relationship with Carmen. They were lovers, not accountants.

Divorce is the one human tragedy that reduces everything to cash. Harriet hated every minute of it. Carmen, if she cared at all, never offered to alleviate this distress. When it was finally settled, Carmen foamed at the mouth about how she was taken to the cleaners by Harriet, the lesbian gold digger. Harriet took her half of the house money and tossed it in a high interest certificate and rented a house in town. She wanted time to think.

Aside from the house money, she had no income. Friends at Cazenovia College and Syracuse University arranged for her to tutor doctoral students and advise them on their dissertations. It about paid the rent and bought food. Harriet found out that being a lesbian was a very costly proposition. She regretted Carmen's leaving her, and she regretted Lavinia's smear campaign. But she didn't regret telling the truth.

◆ ◆ ◆

Lavinia and Siggy set new policy for the Women's Tennis Guild by sweeping through the employees like a white tornado. All dykes were out. All female employees must wear nail polish, nylons, fragrance, and skirts. A player didn't even have to be gay, she need only be suspect. It was tennis's version of the McCarthy period. Unfortunately, the homosexuals were accustomed to the paranoia. Only the straights complained.

TWELVE

Flushing Meadows, site of the U.S. Open, is aptly named. People filter through the turnstiles for the first two weeks of September to witness flamboyant tennis stars as well as umpires with egos that belong in the Met's production of *Aïda*.

The U.S. Open is a loud, brash tournament, ready to destroy any tradition as long as the profit sheet merits it. Sponsors fought over exactly where their banners would be placed. Tomahawk, a tangential sponsor still committed through the end of the season, solved the problem by painting the name of the latest fragrance, "Moccasin," on the backs of the toilet stalls.

The crowds were good this year. The rich still hung on in Bar Harbor or sailed around Newport. The U.S. Open attracted the middle classes who had to return from summer vacation if they wished to remain employed. A smattering of lower-class Americans attended, but truthfully, tennis would never be their sport.

Lavinia darted everywhere. The only place the bright yellow dress was never seen was at the top of Louis Armstrong Memorial Stadium, an arena which seats twenty thousand people. She didn't want to pass out from lack of oxygen.

Carmen was the number two seed. Page Bartlett Campbell was the number one seed. She'd won the U.S. Open the last four years in a row. Carmen smoldered over the ranking. She tucked two of the Grand Slam events under her belt, and the committee still stuck behind Page.

Siggy Wayne and Seth Quintard wore out a pair of shoes daily running from players to corporation executives. The U.S. Open, a fertile ground for deals, had both men in hog heaven.

Bonnie Marie strolled in and out of the locker room, usually forbidden to outsiders. She was at home in locker rooms. The female guards at the gate must have thought she was another player. She was, in her way.

The players raced through crowds to get to their matches if their matches were played on outside courts. The soaking heat trapped in the artificial surface of the courts flamed up their legs like napalm. The landing gear of planes approaching La Guardia Airport threatened to impale more than one tall player. The subway noise at Forest Hills seemed a lullaby compared to squealing airplanes.

◆ ◆ ◆

Harriet didn't want to go to the U.S. Open but Jane begged her to come down for a few days. She could stay in Princeton and visit old friends. Lonesome, Harriet agreed.

The first night at Jane and Ricky's she received a strange phone call. "Alicia! How did you know I'd be here?"

"A wild guess. I bet you're wondering why I'm calling you."

"Yes."

"You know I left Susan."

"Five will get you ten that's not how Susan tells it." Harriet had no quarrel with Alicia but she did wonder what was up.

"The Hitler of the tennis world."

"Oh, she's not that bad. Maybe Ivan the Terrible?"

Alicia giggled. "I'm going to have a baby. I'm not getting married though. I'm having this baby all by myself."

"That takes courage. Why are you telling me this, Alicia? It's not like we're bosom buddies."

The high-pitched voice hesitated. "No, but I never took sides openly. I never disliked you, but Susan did. You know, ever since you said what you said in Hilton Head, I decided I liked you. At least you weren't afraid to love. Susan was always afraid." She paused. "What do you think about my having a baby?"

"I wish you luck, Alicia."

"I've got to tell you something. I don't know why. There's nothing you can do about it."

Harriet plumped up a pillow in the bed. If she was going to hear true confessions, she might as well be comfortable. "Okay."

"Susan Reilly tipped off Martin Kuzirian about you and Carmen. She set you up. She's smart that way. You walked right into it."

"Carmen walked right out."

Alicia bluntly said, "She'd have done that eventually. She turns in her lovers when she's tired of them."

"For a new lube job?"

Alicia giggled again. "Kinda. Harriet, I wish you wouldn't be a lesbian. There's no stability in those relationships. You'd make a good wife and a loving mother. You need a man to take care of you."

"Right now, I think you need the man more than I do." Harriet had heard this argument all her life. She knew it was said with the best of intentions. In Alicia's case it was said as much to convince Alicia as to convince Harriet.

"Think about it."

After hanging up the phone, Harriet jumped into her

robe and tiptoed over to Ricky and Jane's bedroom. The door was open, and they weren't asleep.

"You'll never guess what Alicia told me!" Harriet related every syllable.

"I'll be damned."

"I knew it." Jane smacked her thigh.

"No point in telling Carmen." Harriet sat on the edge of their bed. "You look tired, Jane."

"Old age."

Harriet looked at her. "Not you." But she couldn't fail to notice the dark circles under Jane's eyes.

"Well, this proves my theory." Ricky put his hands behind his head.

"Go on, Einstein." Jane waited.

"You can't judge love by its results."

◆ ◆ ◆

In an electrifying semifinal, Susan Reilly defeated Page Bartlett Campbell. Susan now faced Carmen in the finals. Carmen had a slightly easier time of it in her semifinal, for Rainey Rogers pulled a groin muscle.

The early September day sweltered. Before the first serve was tossed both women were drenched.

Susan, playing strongly, won the first set six-four. Carmen fought back to take the second set, seven-five. If they could have changed their sticky clothes before the third set, each woman would have felt better. The men can peel off a shirt between sets, towel off, put on a fresh shirt, and charge back out. Not the women. Their clothing hung on them like chains. Their tempers, like their bodies, were boiling. It was only a matter of time before someone blew.

Timothy regally imposed himself in one of the reserved seats behind the baseline. Bonnie Marie folded herself into a much less conspicuous seat. Miguel sat next to Timothy and ignored him.

At three-two, after a particularly vicious rally, Susan charged the net. She had Carmen forty-thirty, and it was Susan's serve. She bristled with confidence. Carmen rifled a ball down the side. Susan reached it, and it flew back on the baseline. The ball was clearly on the line.

"Out," called the linesman.

Carmen walked over to the line and looked at it. She knew to shut up. Miranda Mexata, the sun in her eyes, could not have seen that ball and Carmen knew Miranda couldn't, in good faith, override the linesman.

Susan flamed by the net. "That ball was in by a mile."

The tv camera for the viewers at home also showed that the ball hit the line squarely. But the video meant nothing on that court. The situation was agonizing.

Susan howled, and the fans howled with her. The linesman was obstinate. The heat fired him up, too.

"Carmen, do you want to win the match this way?" Susan pleaded.

Carmen said nothing.

"We've played for years! We've never cheated one another." Susan stretched the point.

Carmen wavered.

"Just tell him what you saw."

Miranda said, "Ladies, next point please."

"Tell him."

"I saw the ball good," Carmen hoarsely told the uncomfortable linesman.

"Miss Semana, I saw it out."

"See, even my opponent knows it was good."

"Susan, if you don't serve the next ball, you will be penalized a point which will make it Miss Semana's advantage."

Something snapped. Too much tension. Too much heat.

Too much left unspoken between two former lovers heading for disastrous fulfillment. Susan vaulted over the net. She raged before the linesman. Carmen sensibly walked over to the deuce side.

The crowd fumed. Everyone was mad. Susan kicked the linesman out of his chair.

"Guards, remove Mrs. Reilly from the court. This match is over, ladies and gentlemen. Carmen Semana wins by default." Miranda Mexata had seen officials ground into mincemeat at the U.S. Open. This was one time the promoters couldn't dilute her authority. The situation was clear. No player is bigger than the game. Susan Reilly committed a hideous offense against the linesman, her opponent, the spectators, and the game of tennis itself. Out!

It took four guards to get Susan off the court. One of the promoters miraculously appeared at the foot of Miranda's high chair. She leaned down and told him to put it in the shit can. There was no way this match would continue after Susan calmed down. Hell, they'd have to force-feed her Thorazine. Panic-stricken though he was, the promoter knew he had to back Miranda Mexata.

The next day, journalists bellowed in an orgy of outrage over Susan's assault. Curiously, Martin Kuzirian remained silent.

So Carmen won the U.S. Open. A cloud would hang over that victory and for that she'd curse Susan to her dying day . . . but she won it. One tournament remained. Just one.

THIRTEEN

J ane told no one about her condition. By the end of September she experienced a serious slide. The chemotherapy affected her horribly. She rallied but did not travel. Harriet, ignorant, called her every other day. Jane explained the fact that she wasn't on the road by saying she really was writing that long-promised novel. She promised to visit Harriet soon.

She was admitted to the hospital the second week of October. Ricky broke the news to Harriet. Jane swore she'd recover, but he knew she was never going to walk out of the hospital alive. When Harriet came through the door Jane threw a glass at Ricky. Her anger subsided as quickly as it came. Ricky left them alone.

"I've brought my portable typewriter. Thought you might want to dictate."

"Later." Jane sighed. "I didn't want anyone to see me like this."

She looked awful. In the last three weeks, she lost a dangerous amount of weight. Her vision was blurred, and the headaches were worse. Medication eased the pain, but it made her groggy.

"I don't care how you look."

"Pretty bad."

Harriet shrugged her shoulders. "I'm sorry if I've upset you by coming. I wish you'd told me."

"It's not you. I didn't tell anybody. You can understand that, can't you?"

"Yes."

"I've been thinking a lot. You'd be amazed what you think about when you're sick. Of course, half the time I'm so doped up, I can't think at all."

"Is there anything I can do?"

"Watch out for Ricky."

A convulsive shudder shot through Harriet's body. "Jane . . ."

Jane waved her hand. "Pull yourself together. I might be well tomorrow."

"Of course, you will be!"

"Yeah, well, I might become a Girl Guide to the cosmos, too."

"Lighting celestial campfires." Harriet smiled. She felt dreadful.

Jane leaned forward and took Harriet's hand. "I'm sorry for your troubles."

"My God, Jane, my troubles are nothing!"

"I don't believe in comparative pain. You're having a rotten time. Now that Carmen's married, maybe they'll let up on you being the lesbian Svengali."

"After a while you get numb to it."

"Do you know what I've been thinking about?" Jane continued to hold Harriet's hand. "I was raised a Christian."

"Me, too."

"Well, I do believe Christ died for my sins, tell that to Baby Jesus. But you know, I think throughout history, there were thousands of sons and daughters of God, unnamed souls, who suffered and died for us also. Rebirth is a collective process. We chose an individual to symbolize it, but we really must do it together. Understand?"

"I'm trying."

That was the last conversation the two friends shared.

Jane Fulton died suddenly the next evening. She was talking to Ricky as she died.

Passing down a corridor of long darkness, Jane rushed toward the unknown, spilling finally into blinding light. Perhaps this was a memory of the journey down the birth canal and into the world. Maybe the memory is in each human, and death recalls it, like a stored tape, to soothe the process of death. Or maybe it was true rebirth. Whichever, Jane Fulton smiled at the end.

◆ ◆ ◆

"I missed covering the Melbourne Olympics. I was just out of school and working for a tiny paper in Charleston, West Virginia." Ricky and Harriet strolled around the Olympic Park, hard by Fitzroy Gardens in Melbourne, Australia.

"I read the scores in the papers and dreamed I'd grow up to throw the javelin."

"Pipsqueak." Ricky shaded his eyes and looked at the names carved on the outside of the stadium. "Thank you for coming with me. I know it's hard for you to see Carmen, to be around the tennis crowd, but I couldn't face this tournament alone. It's the first major tournament I'll cover without Jane." His voice cracked.

"I'm not doing you a favor, you're doing me one. I love Australia and you generously paid my way."

Ricky read more names carved on the white, somewhat crumbling stadium. "Hard to believe less than thirty years ago this park was filled with people from all over the world. This was the center of sports for two weeks."

◆ ◆ ◆

Kooyong Stadium, an emerald jewel, sits outside Melbourne. Truck drivers zooming by on the raised highway honked their horns for the sheer hell of it. More than one player was undone by merry tooting.

The grass glittered this year. Because the seasons are reversed on the other side of the equator, Harriet did her Christmas shopping in a halter.

Over the back of Kooyong Stadium, the clouds resembled Thor's clenched fist. A burst of water sent people streaking for cover. Just as suddenly the sun returned, the schoolchildren in uniform got to their seats first and then the Melbourne matrons waddled into the club seats.

One lady, tainted with Victoriana, observed a young woman in a bikini. She snorted, "What's left for her husband?"

Multicolored tents, pitched outside the stadium, housed various charities and benefits. Each day money was raised for some worthy cause, and the attendants had the pleasure of gossiping while they saved.

Sponsors vied for attention. A giant tennis ball the size of a balloon hovered over the court site. The ball supplier thought of that one. Everyone deplored his lack of imagination, but everyone noticed it.

The week provided good tennis. Beanie Kittredge made it to the semifinals and put up a marvelous fight against Susan Reilly. Susan threw her down but it took awhile. Susan was fined $5,000 for her behavior at the U.S. Open. She paid up, made copious apologies, and was out to prove she could behave on the court. Carmen's semifinal was less dramatic but satisfying to her. She punched out Rainey Rogers in two sets.

The media made much of the face-off between Carmen and Susan, former teammates, now bitter foes. No one ever knew why they became bitter foes although speculation abounded in Australia as elsewhere.

Susan ensnared a lovely girl with red, curly hair. She

would have made a good team mascot. She was perfect for Susan because she thought Susan was perfect. They planned to ride off into the sunset together.

Ricky buried himself in his work. Sometimes Harriet stayed in the booth with him, though not during Carmen's matches.

Harriet found that she missed the American tennis crew. Miranda Mexata wasn't there. She had no authority in any country other than the United States. Too bad, for the officials could have used a little help. Harriet didn't miss Seth Quintard or Siggy Wayne. But what the hell, she once caught herself thinking, they've got to eat, too.

She especially missed Lavinia Sibley Archer and her speeches, breathtaking in their irrelevance. Lavinia, bundled up in Connecticut, would be putting the finishing touches on the revitalized women's circuit which would culminate as always in Washington, D.C.

The morning of the finals, Harriet struggled out of bed. She had progressed to a time zone somewhere in the Pacific, but she hadn't progressed as far as Australia yet. She pulled open the bureau drawer for her bottle of vitamins. Underneath was a Bible, King James Version. A prior tenant had placed a red ribbon on a page. Curious, Harriet opened to Corinthians and read the following passage:

Though I speak with the tongues of men and angels, and have not charity, I am become as sounding brass, or tinkling cymbal.

And though I have the gift of prophecy, and understand all mysteries, and all knowledge; and though I have all faith, so that I could remove mountains, and have not charity, I am nothing.

Ricky rapped on the door. "Are you coming to the finals?"

"I just this instant made up my mind to go, thanks to the Bible."

He tapped his knuckle on the door between their rooms. "So, you're coming on Noah's Ark, after all."

"Why, you think it will rain?"

"No, I wondered how long you could hold out before watching Carmen."

"I'm coming on, as you put it, as a unicorn, a dark unicorn."

He laughed. "Let's go."

• • •

Carmen and Susan walked out on the court to warm applause. By now the sports world was in a tizz over the Grand Slam. Reporters gave up the word "awesome" and now used "miraculous." One would have thought it was the Second Coming.

Harriet looked at Carmen for the first time since August. My life used to lay within her arms, she thought. How could people who knew one another so well become strangers?

Timothy lounged in a seat right behind the baseline. Bonnie Marie was discreetly tucked away in a sponsor's box. Miguel was back in Argentina, disgraced again. A stone fell out of Carmen's necklace a month ago. When she took it to be repaired, the jeweler told her it was rhinestones and paste. Miguel didn't put her jewelry in safety deposit boxes, as he said. He had the stuff copied and sold the originals.

Carmen warmed up. Each woman hit with authority. The returns boomed back on the baseline. They both looked relaxed. Susan's new honey practically blew kisses every time Susan met the ball.

Carmen glanced around the stadium. She automatically looked up for Ricky. She'd heard, of course, that Harriet was there. She hadn't seen her. When she looked up this time, Carmen saw her. For an instant it was as though nothing had changed—Harriet was squinched against the wall out of camera range, Ricky had his earphones on, and . . . no Jane. Carmen blinked and hurriedly looked for Bonnie Marie to reassure herself. She pushed her thoughts away and faced her oldest opponent, aside from herself, across the net. Susan had the look of eagles.

The first set, hard fought, went to Carmen. The second set saw Susan, a madwoman, take it down to the tie breaker and bag it. Each successive point, drenched in hatred, permeated the crowd. The Australians were like the Italians; they quickly seized the drama in any situation. They handled it differently, but they vibrated like tuning forks. Carmen hit one forehand crosscourt so hard her racquet shivered like a struck lance.

If smoke wafted up from the court, no spectator would have been surprised. These two despised one another with savage intensity. Every point was a challenge, a duel. There was no defense in this match, it was all attack and counterattack. Even the drop shots seemed edged in venom.

Neither woman could break the other's serve. Surely one would have to slow, tire, falter. Susan grew maniacally stronger with each point, whether she won it or lost it. If she heard the crowd, she never seemed to. Carmen's lips were drawn tightly across her teeth. Deep furrows ran alongside her mouth. She looked ten years older than her twenty-four years. The tension redoubled her concentration.

In war, there's a killing zone. Tennis has one, too: no-man's-land. On either side of that zone, midway to the net, a player might live. In the middle, she greeted death. Speed and a carbon-steel half-volley might save her ass. Otherwise, lights out.

The third set sped by even though the points were long. Susan deliberately blasted away at Carmen's adequate but unspectacular backhand. It was the only weakness in her arsenal. There are two theories in tennis and only two: Either break down the opponent's weakness or break down his strength. Breaking down the strength is harder, but if accomplished the results are faster, since the opponent's game will fold quickly. Susan chose the longer but surer route. The body loses one percent efficiency each year over twenty-five. Susan was a split second slower than when she was in her prime. She was calculating enough about her abilities to know that. At her own peak in her mid-twenties, she would have tried to crush Carmen's forehand. Now she utilized her years on the court, and she planned every point. She wouldn't blow Carmen away, she'd pick her apart.

Carmen, physically at her peak, was everywhere. Even the unrelenting Australian heat couldn't wilt her. Susan's nibbling at her backhand didn't frighten her. She'd slice the ball and keep it low. Since they were on grass, the ball often skidded with a slice. Carmen could live without a supercharged, topspin backhand.

High overhead, Harriet watched what she and everyone else knew: This would be reckoned one of the greatest matches in tennis history. It was a pleasure to see two evenly matched combatants. The heroic proportions of the struggle compensated for the lack of depth in women's tennis. The tedious, lopsided early rounds were forgotten in the splendor of the final.

Carmen looked so powerful on the court. Odd, how athletes are assumed to be mentally strong because of their physical prowess. In truth, they are usually people unable to cope with the outside world. Physical strength has never corresponded to emotional strength. Perhaps Harriet expected too much of Carmen. How could the Argentinian be an adult when she was surrounded by children, pursuing the goals of youngsters? Games are glorious, but they're for kids. Carmen could only be what she was—basically a good person with a short attention span, no ability to face emotional conflict or disappointment, and one who only wanted to be happy.

The people around Carmen most emphatically did not want her to think about anything but tennis. She lined their pockets. How could she grow up when fifty-year-old promoters, tight-faced from cosmetic surgery and hair transplants, also echoed the same childish concern—to be happy. Why wasn't every day Christmas? It should be, or so they thought, as they put one more contract in front of her.

It takes an extraordinary person to withstand the seduction of professional sport. Carmen's skill was extraordinary. She was not.

The last game of the third set, Susan's serve held true to form. Each point was a marathon. Susan closed out her serve with a murderous forehand crosscourt that nicked the corner line and scudded across the grass. Magically, Carmen was there and sent the ball crosscourt with a flick of her wrist. Susan, caught off guard, was pulled wide.

Courageously Carmen tore up toward the net. In a fury at what she thought was an untouchable shot, Susan twisted her whole body into the ball and followed it into the net as well. No one could believe what they were seeing. Both women were caught in no-man's-land. Defiant, each held her ground and pounded the shit out of the ball. Neither would retreat and neither could advance. The point was played like a doubles point at the net. People sat motionless in their seats, awestruck.

Carmen fired a ball at a sharp angle past Susan's reach but Susan was there, and she hit the ball at Carmen's feet. Carmen picked it up a trifle too high, and Susan returned it sidearm down Carmen's backhand side. Susan held her serve.

The tie breaker went into effect. Neither woman lost her serve in the tie breaker. Sudden death turned into lingering death. One woman had to win by two points. Carmen broke Susan's service. The crowd went insane. Susan, reaching to Mount Olympus, broke back. The score was even again.

Carmen had another serve. If she could only get one up

and break again. She thundered a serve, spiraling it into Susan's body. It was a tremendous display of power. Susan returned it as though it were a powder puff. That point sizzled for another two minutes of hammering play until Carmen was sabered by Susan's backhand.

She walked back to receive Susan's serve. As if by instinct, she looked up at Harriet. She covered her eyes for an instant, as though she'd gotten a bug in her eye or the sun had given her spots. She collected herself. Susan hit the ball so hard they saw it go by in Brisbane. Carmen was lucky to stop it. The ball flew back across the net. Susan pressed. She flung herself into the ball, twisting her body, and hit a withering forehand down the line. Carmen returned it, but it wasn't that deep. Susan moved in and drove the ball back. Carmen lobbed. Susan hit a pulverizing overhead right at Carmen's body. The ball hit Carmen. Susan had just won the Australian Open.

The crowd, emotionally exhausted by the match, broke free. They hollered and yelled; a few even tried to climb onto the courts. Susan, the victor of the Australian Open, waited at the net. Carmen had sunk to her knees, her head almost down on her knees. She was right on the service line. The crowd kept screaming. Susan looked at Carmen with contempt, then turned and walked up to the umpire and shook hands. The umpire scurried down from her chair and walked quietly over to Carmen.

"There now, Miss Semana, let's get off the court, shall we?" She put her hand under Carmen's elbow, and Carmen meekly got up. The crowd roared again. The umpire walked her back to a chair and told the announcer to give Carmen time to pull herself together.

The Australian Open was the beginning of Susan Reilly's end and the end of Carmen's beginning. Susan would never have a moment this high again. Since she'd built her personality around athletic victory that meant eventually her sanity would be at stake.

In one searing moment Carmen discovered beginnings are easy, it's continuity that's hard. She couldn't keep up the pace. Susan had wanted this win more than she did. Athletic immortality was within her grasp, and she let it slip. What dashed before her eyes when she saw Harriet up there? A murderous shaft of light? A ragged shadow of guilt? Perhaps nothing.

Carmen sat in her chair, towel over her head, sobbing. Was this loss karma or the law of averages? Was this loss a small pain compared to the relentless future? Carmen dimly perceived that this was her first payment on subsequent maturity.

Harriet, sitting high over Carmen's head, cried along with her. Ricky carefully put his earphones on his legal pad.

"Still love her?"

"I wanted her to win this! There aren't many more chances left in her business."

"No, but how wonderful that she got this far."

Harriet stopped crying and quietly said, "If there is life after death, I'd like to think we'll all find each other again. I'd like to think the wrongs we've done will be forgiven. I'd like to think that God will strengthen the love between us. Is that such a foolish dream? Is there never a time when people are bound by more than scar tissue? Ricky, I don't know but I want so very much to believe such a love can come to pass, if not here on earth, then in heaven."

Ricky embraced her. "Love is never lost, only the people."

ABOUT THE AUTHOR

RITA MAE BROWN is currently retracing Stonewall Jackson's steps during the War Between the States in preparation for her next novel.

Explore the Other World
of Sexuality

☐	23819	**The Front Runner** Patricia Nell Warren	$3.95
☐	23108	**Southern Discomfort** Rita Mae Brown	$3.95
☐	24030	**Sudden Death** Rita Mae Brown	$3.95
☐	23708	**Dancer From The Dance** Andrew Holleran	$3.95
☐	23813	**Rubyfruit Jungle** Rita Mae Brown	$3.95
☐	23768	**Six of One** Rita Mae Brown	$3.95

DON'T MISS
THESE CURRENT
Bantam Bestsellers

SPECIAL MONEY SAVING OFFER

Now you can have an up-to-date listing of Bantam's hundreds of titles plus take advantage of our unique and exciting bonus book offer. A special offer which gives you the opportunity to purchase a Bantam book for only 50¢. Here's how!

By ordering any five books at the regular price per order, you can also choose any other single book listed (up to a $4.95 value) for just 50¢. Some restrictions do apply, but for further details why not send for Bantam's listing of titles today!

Just send us your name and address plus 50¢ to defray the postage and handling costs.

RELAX!

SIT DOWN

and Catch Up On Your Reading!

☐	23981	**THE LITTLE DRUMMER GIRL**	$4.50
		by John Le Carre	
☐	23922	**GIRI** by Marc Olden	$3.50
☐	23987	**THE TAKERS** by Wm. Flanagan	$2.95
☐	23845	**THE DELTA STAR** by Joseph Wambaugh	$3.95
☐	20822	**GLITTER DOME** by Joseph Wambaugh	$3.95
☐	23577	**THE SEEDING** by David Shobin	$2.95
☐	20476	**THE UNBORN** by David Shobin	$3.25
☐	05034	**BALE FIRE** by Ken Goddard (Hardcover)	$14.95
☐	23678	**WOLFSBANE** by Craig Thomas	$3.95
☐	23420	**THE CIRCLE** by Steve Shagan	$3.95
☐	23567	**SAVE THE TIGER** by Steve Shagan	$3.25
☐	23483	**THE CROOKED ROAD** by Morris West	$2.95
☐	22746	**RED DRAGON** by Thomas Harris	$3.95
☐	23838	**SEA LEOPARD** by Craig Thomas	$3.95
☐	20353	**MURDER AT THE RED OCTOBER**	$2.95
		by Anthony Olcott	
☐	20662	**CLOWNS OF GOD** by Morris West	$3.95
☐	20688	**TOWER OF BABEL** by Morris West	$3.50
☐	23149	**SMILEY'S PEOPLE** by John Le Carre	$3.95
☐	13801	**THE FORMULA** by Steve Shagan	$2.75
☐	22787	**STORM WARNING** by Jack Higgins	$3.50
☐	23781	**SNOW FALCON** by Craig Thomas	$3.95
☐	22709	**FIREFOX** by Craig Thomas	$3.50